STRIKER

STRIKER

MICHAEL IRWIN

ANDRE DEUTSCH

First published 1985 by
André Deutsch Limited
105 Great Russell Street London W1

Copyright © 1985 by Michael Irwin

ISBN 0 233 97792 9

Phototypeset by AKM Associates (UK) Ltd
Ajmal House, Hayes Road, Southall, Greater London
Printed in Great Britain by
Ebenezer Baylis Ltd, Worcester

Also by Michael Irwin

WORKING ORDERS

Chapter 1

A cutting from the *Chronicle* reminds me what I was like at the time:

This week's 'Snapshot' features a key player in Saturday's Cup Final, quicksilver England striker Vincent Gilpin. Although Manston are hot favourites, having beaten Albion twice in the League, experts are forecasting a low-scoring game. Former Manston centre-back John Carpenter, who saved Albion from relegation almost single-handed, will be back to stifle the threat of tall Noel Mostyn. Of the Albion attackers only young Barry Onions has the pace to cause problems. Chances are that a single goal could decide the match, and if that is the case there is no likelier scorer than Gilpin, at last returning to something like his old dazzling form. He has the temperament, the aggression, and above all the motivation. If he finds the net he will have achieved the legendary feat of scoring in every round of the Cup. Certain reward would be a recall to the England World Cup squad. He deserves it. When he is fully fit few defenders can cope with his tenacity and concentration. Grogan, his marker, faces an exhausting ninety minutes.

Name: Vincent Gilpin.

Age: Twenty-nine last week.

Height: Five foot seven.

Weight: Ten stone six.

Where born: East London.

School: Mountford Hill Secondary.

Wife's name: Claire.

Any children: Awaiting delivery!

England caps: Nine.

Greatest assets as a player: Sharpness and commitment.

Limitations or weaknesses: Lack of height.

Best performance: Haven't given it yet.

Immediate ambition: To win at Wembley on Saturday and to play for England in the World Cup Finals.

Long-term ambition: To be remembered.

Greatest influences on your soccer career: Cyril Islip and Geoff Cowley.

Toughest defender you've played against: John Carpenter in practice matches. Taking him on is like dribbling round a squid.

Do you ever get bored with football? I wouldn't let myself.

Describe your temperament: Restless.

How long will you go on playing? Till I'm finished.

Will you stay in soccer when you hang up your boots? No. Playing is all I'm good for.

Is a footballer born or made? Both.

What advice would you give a young player? Play hard and stay lucky.

What are your hobbies outside sport? Walking, talking and nosing around. I also collect pocket knives.

What do you spend your money on? Enjoyment.

What would you like to be, if not a footballer? Secret agent or deep-sea diver.

That opening paragraph was well meant — the writer was a mate of mine — but the fact was that no one but myself could realise the importance the Cup Final would have for me. There were things in the background that couldn't have been guessed at, and anyway couldn't have been used. They lay outside a soccer reporter's area of interest. Most of them should come out in the course of this book. All I'll say at the moment is that there was a lot on my mind.

On the great day I was glad of this.

For me, working up to any match, never mind a Cup Final, had always been a strain. Many a player has talents I don't, and most are bigger. To make my mark I have to be in a state of tension, or passion. Sometimes it takes a hard knock to rouse me, just as there are boxers who don't get going till they've swallowed some of their own blood. Lately I'd been finding it harder to get this kick-start, and Manston being clear favourites for the Final didn't help. I was even glad Carpenter was playing, because he was a defender you had to respect — the thought of his big, bony legs gave me a qualm or two which I needed. Before any game I try to work up the tension in myself, the chief device being fear. But I don't make a show of it. In the dressing-room I'm a split personality. Outwardly I'm talking, joking, laughing like my normal self — though I believe my voice speeds up. Inside, the nervousness and the concentration slowly start to bubble. Often they get to my stomach, and I have to dive for the toilet to shit or vomit.

At Wembley I did both, and felt the better for it. All the other pre-match rituals were going ahead amid the clean stink of embrocation. Brine was throwing a ball at Paget to get his reflexes working. Mount was kneading his own big thighs. Little Neil Herrick was dancing everywhere, chattering non-stop. Connaught was getting through his routine of bending and stretching. Altogether the lads looked in good fettle. The boss moved from player to player offering valuable pieces of advice, such as 'Mark up tight' or 'Make them do the chasing'. We're changed and greased and ready, and the time's near.

As we walk down the tunnel I'm so concentrated on the game to come that I'm numbed. If you asked me my own telephone number I couldn't tell you.

The Albion players alongside us look nervy. Several of their younger lads are white-faced. Grogan I've never played against. He's squat and hairy and seems jumpy, as well he might. A few weeks back Noel Mostyn took two headed goals off him. If Noel could do him in the air then I can stuff him on the ground. Onions is a skinny kid already losing some front hair. You can't believe he's only nineteen. I glance back to give John Carpenter a nod, but he's expressionless, the tallest man in the tunnel, staring straight over my head. Mostyn won't get a kick against him, but if he keeps him busy there'll be space for me.

The din when we appear roars on and on but I shut my mind from it. I'm taking in the immediate things. The sky's grey above the stadium and there's a wind shaking the flags. The thick turf has dried well after overnight rain. My ankle's not feeling bad — no worse than uneasy.

I relax a little as we line up for the presentation. Once we kick off I'll be shut into the game like a goldfish in a bowl, but there's time for a last look up and round. Some of these ninety-thousand heads belong to people I know. Mum and Dad are perched somewhere, side by side. So are Alan Ruddock and Pete Harvey and their wives. My pregnant wife is up there with all her relatives. So are half a dozen women I know and she doesn't. Claire will be feeling good, Pat Arnold will be feeling sour, Geoff Cowley will be feeling Christ knows what. Poor old Dooner's cursing his luck. I can see none of them, but they're seeing me, and know me from all that distance by the number ten on my back. Soon I'll make them scream.

'. . . our top scorer, Vince Gilpin.'

There's a royal hand in mine, a polite royal word or two. Seconds later we're all frozen upright by the national anthem, with the yobbos howling it down. It ends in a vast mad cheer and we're racing across the pitch to kick in. Paget likes me to stretch him with a chip or two and then whack in a couple of fair shots to wake him up. He's a solid keeper, but could be taller. So could Charley Mount, who seems to hunch himself shorter when he faces a challenge, so that he looks as broad as he's long. Trevor Rees is having a sprint or two. At thirty-three he's lost a little bit of pace, but his experience usually compensates. Gordon Philp does some fancy juggling. He'd be a great player on a stage, but can't always feed his skills into the game.

The ref's whistling us to change ends. As we cross I again give Carpenter a nod, but he's still not seeing me. It needn't be personal — he's not greeting any of our lads. You'd never think he'd played for us. Grogan's looking fierce, and his chin's bristling with stubble. There could be hard contact soon, but he's avoiding my eye. As the teams take up position

4

the crowd's din throbs louder yet, like a racing-car revving up. Jack Jefford blows his whistle and the cheering explodes as Dunn kicks off.

The teams are:

Manston Town: Paget; Rees, Mount, Brine, Connaught; Selby, Philp, Herrick; Mostyn, Gilpin, Fenn.

Albion: Smith; Searle, Carpenter, Grogan, Innes; Kenny, King, Middleditch; Dunn, Seymour, Onions.

Referee: Jack Jefford (Stourport).

A soccer match can't be described — there are too many things happening at once. You can only give a general impression and pick out a few details.

Inside a minute Onions diddles round Rees and centres high and Seymour jumps above Mount to thud a header into Paget's chest. Paget lofts a big kick and I move for it but Carpenter's up behind me to nod into touch. He's marking me while Grogan takes Mostyn. It makes no sense.

Herrick throws in to me. I hear Mostyn's shout and hook the ball over my shoulder into the middle. Noel's racing on to it, almost through, but Grogan crashes him from behind and the whistle goes. Selby's there to flick an instant free-kick and Fenn has a half-chance — but the whistle goes again. Jefford hadn't been ready.

'For fuck's sake, ref —'

'Watch your mouth, son.'

I shut up, because Jefford's already booked me once this season.

We try a rehearsed kick. Mount shapes to belt the ball but runs over it, Philp chips the wall and I dart round. I'm clear of Carpenter, but his long leg shoots past to stab the ball to the keeper. The crowd's rocking from the action at both ends.

I hate Carpenter being on me. The knobbly bugger doesn't mark you — he surrounds you, he smothers you. But it's more than that. I've known him a long time — there are things between us. I don't feel easy with his breath on me. All the same, if I keep him stretched Mostyn can screw Grogan as he did a month back. But I look at Noel and see he's still shaken from that first tackle. He's got no taste for violence. Grogan's puffing his cheeks and looking grim. He'll be in there again. Next second he is. Philp, like a fool, serves up a fifty-fifty ball: Grogan takes it and Mostyn's right leg with it. There's not even a free-kick. The tactic's clear now. Long John wraps me up while Grogan clogs the heart out of Mostyn. He's half done the business in two fouls without a word from Jefford.

At the other end they're hoisting high crosses for Dunn and Seymour to jump at. It's crude but useful, because the big old strikers have sniffed blood and have the height on our defence. Philp's hassled into a miskick and Onions is away again, this time swinging inside Rees and shoving in a low shot that Paget turns wide. Dunn heads the corner over the bar, but there's been a deflection. Corner again. Connaught just beats Seymour to it. Third corner, and the ball's only scrambled away. It's a mess back there. Brine's yelling at the defence.

Onions again. He dallies, dips right and twitches left, leaving Rees on his bum. Mount bursts across full weight to crash Onions into touch, and then has his name taken, while the crowd whistles and boos. Onions takes the kick himself, not even ruffled, and again Dunn and Seymour get in above our central defenders, only just failing to connect.

The game's taking shape, and it's a bad shape for us. Rees is hypnotised by this kid Onions, so Selby keeps falling back to cover him. Given a bit of space their midfield have gone brave and keep pouring forward, shutting down Philp and hammering at our defence. Practically speaking we only have Herrick in the middle of the park, and even non-stop Neil can't do it on his own. Up front Mostyn's bottling out and Fenn hasn't had a pass. I have to drop back to get any sort of service — so far back I'm no threat. Carpenter just lets me go, and he's right. In half an hour I've hardly wasted a ball, but I've done nothing.

At last a clearance from Connaught puts Fenn away. He goes for the bye-line, tucks the ball back and I swing at it first time — but Carpenter's boot comes out of nowhere to squirt the ball wide. I've seen him do it a hundred times, but it's still uncanny. The gangling bugger has no pace, but with his reach and timing he can take a yard off anyone in the game. He's the one who heads the corner clear — while Grogan clatters Mostyn a third time.

Their young midfielders are still coming at us and coming at us. They're making no clear chances, but all the play is in our back third. The game's opposite to all expectations. The half's almost up when little Herrick battles down the left with Fenn, draws Carpenter and flicks me through. My leg's back to shoot when I'm chopped from behind. A kick in the calf from Grogan — and again no free-kick.

Right on the whistle Onions takes another corner off Rees, and for the first time Long John heads upfield. I scream at Mostyn, who has the height, to go with him, but he doesn't move fast enough, and Carpenter puts a header only inches wide.

Half-time blows, and Christ, we need it! I overtake Grogan to say: 'You've got ten minutes, son — why not take out some insurance on your knackers?' In the changing-room I don't feel that bad. We haven't played, and they've pasted us, but it's still 0—0. They've been living off momentum, but they'll never keep up that pace on this turf. The boss rallies us, Steve Brine and Charley Mount rally us, and I try to talk some heart back into Noel Mostyn. 'Get men forward,' the boss keeps saying. 'Put 'em under pressure.' He's got it right for once.

The second half feels better right away. Noel's back to life, Philp's pushing up, and Fenn's getting into the game. The ball's coming through to me and at last I'm in business, breaking right, doubling left, pulling Carpenter from side to side of the pitch to put some lead in his legs. As hard as he is, I'll weaken him. Grogan's off the boil and Mostyn's starting to do a bit in the air. Any time I could get a flick-on and a half-chance. I can take Carpenter. If anyone can take him it's me. He's gasping as I run him and run him, but he's still not put a foot wrong. Selby and I strand him with a quick one-two, but again he throws that long sliding tackle to jab the ball clear.

Their midfield is tiring now, and Onions is fading. Fade,

cunt, fade. Selby drifts forward and swerves a long centre that Mostyn heads just over the bar, with Grogan flat-footed. My ankle's starting to get nasty, but I don't let it slow me because I'm smelling a goal. We're half-way through the half, and one strike will do the job. I get in my first shot — a snap volley the keeper nearly drops.

Within two minutes we're rocked right back. Connaught drives a diagonal ball, Mostyn jumps for it and Grogan jumps for him, skull into skull. The header flies wide, Grogan staggers and Mostyn drops. We yell for a penalty, but Jefford signals a corner. Noel's flat out and white-faced and the trainer has to work at him. Grogan gets treatment too, but he's not damaged. When Mostyn comes round his left eye is closed, and there's a split above it spilling blood down his cheek. Grogan's seen him off at the price of a bruised head. Noel's led off and Mick Long comes on.

It's a near-post corner. As Grogan goes for it, so do I, cracking in an elbow. He drops to his knees, and the whistle shrieks and the crowd howls. The goalie comes at me, but Carpenter hauls him off as Jack Jefford takes my name for the second time in six weeks.

Grogan continues after treatment, but while he's still winded Selby dummies him, Searle has to concede a free-kick just outside the box. As I shape to take it Herrick nips left, but I pass right, and Mount whops a shot through the wall and against the bar. Herrick dives for the rebound, but the goalie beats him to it. Neil's up quick enough, but he limps away — and I know that limp. He's done a groin muscle. I see him wince as he trots. We've missed a goal by an inch, we're down to ten and a half men, and the sub's already on. If we go to extra time they could do us after all.

At once they're showing more fight. With Herrick hobbling we're squeezed back as we were in the first half. Onions is getting back into the game. Mick Long is drafted into mid-field, and Fenn and I are cut off again. The ankle is stabbing at each step, but I keep moving, shouting for passes that don't come.

For twenty-five minutes or so we'd played with some class,

8

but now we've lost it. We're just hanging on, filling the penalty-box with bodies as the opposition keep surging in and the game slips from us. Steve Brine's still shouting, still organising but we're near desperation level. Herrick can't do much. Rees and Philp are kicking anywhere. Paget's punching at crosses he should catch. Carpenter moves up again, and almost carves himself an opening with a huge body-swerve, but Brine knocks the ball off his toe, and Mount hacks it to me in the centre-circle. Grogan comes in feet first, but I flick the ball round him and sprint for goal. Searle's straining across to force me right, but I swing inside him, burst clear, and look up to make a pass. Nothing. No one's made a run. I swerve a left-foot shot for the far corner — not a bad one, but the goalie claws it out and drops on it as Mick Long at last charges up.

From the bench they're signalling ten minutes to go. My ankle's agony after that run, and we've blown a fair chance. I scream at Mick: 'Push up! For fuck's sake take a chance!'

They drive back at us. Onions crosses again, and the ball bobs from head to head in the six-yard box till Brine hooks it out and Philp lobs first-time to send Fenn away on the left, with Long steaming after him in support.

What happens next is very clear in my mind, if not in my memory, because I've relived it fifty times on video. Fenn beats Searle and dashes for the bye-line, with Grogan chasing and Long inside. Grogan tackles and Fenn clips the ball back for Long to carry it on. We're two against one, so Carpenter has to go for him. Mick passes a split second early. Carpenter checks in mid-stride and lunges out his left leg in a desperate tackle. I nick the ball under his knee, hurdle over it, feint left as the goalie comes out, and then fire at the far post.

Thought moves faster than a football. I've won us the game and the Cup and a place in Europe. I've scored in every round. I've licked the bad luck of the day and the season. I've done big John Carpenter. I've ridden my injuries. I've come back. All this flares in my head before the whistle blows for the goal and the crowd explodes and Mick Long jumps on me for joy.

Chapter 2

As a footballer's life-story doesn't take him much beyond thirty it usually includes a chapter or two on his boyhood, uninteresting though that probably was. Otherwise there'd only be a few hundred matches, an injury or two and his marriage to write about. The second reason is that the early years might give the clue to his success. He could have been coached by his father or discovered by a scoutmaster. Or maybe he was a prodigy who walked at four months and could dribble a tennis ball before he was out of nappies.

There was nothing of that sort with me. For a long time I showed no great prowess at soccer or anything else. It was my elder brother Terry who could play a bit. Therefore no one discovered me, because there was nothing much to discover. As for my Dad, the only thing he taught me was how to swim.

We lived at 17 Beaufort, Yorkland Road, in a part of east London where it's natural to play football at Hackney Marshes and watch it at Upton Park. Beaufort was an eight-storey block of flats, four flats to a storey, so we were on the fourth floor. It wasn't too bad a building, but the inhabitants didn't make the best of it. The walls were scrawled on and the landings were usually pitch dark at night because the lamps had been smashed. We had a lift, but it was frequently out of order, and when working stank because kids used to piss in it.

I pissed in it myself a couple of times. For some reason there can be a pleasure in doing this if the lift is in motion while you're doing it. My Dad, being heavy-built, used to pant and curse when he had to use the stairs, but I probably did my leg muscles a bit of good with the thousands of times I ran up and down.

Indoors we had an uncomfortable life, but that wasn't the fault of the flat. It wasn't spacious, but should have been enough for four, having a sitting-room, a kitchen, a bathroom and three bedrooms. Unfortunately there were five of us, because Mum took in Dad's Uncle Peter when his wife died. If she'd played her cards right we could no doubt have got a bigger flat, especially as he was practically an invalid, but my parents had no idea about things like that. In fact Mum thought she was putting one over on the Council by housing an extra person at no extra charge. A further occupant — definitely illegal, because pets weren't allowed — was a mongrel terrier named Barker, that had followed Mum home from the grocer's one morning and nipped in the front door. She didn't have the heart to drive it out. Keeping it was daft, because no dog is designed to live fifty feet up in the air, and in any case none of us took to it — but there it was. The six of us lived together as best we could. I shared a bedroom with Uncle Peter and Barker kipped on the balcony. The flat was never empty, because the dog, being deeply idle, went out only for toilet purposes, if those, while Uncle Peter was too weak to do more than potter from room to room and make himself cups of cocoa. Even in summer he'd huddle up to an electric fire to keep warm. Coming home from school I always had the sense that the air of the flat had been breathed in and out all day.

The space problem was aggravated by the fact that Dad seemed to take up a lot of room. He was a tall, weighty, slow-blooded man. When he was in his armchair by the fire he seemed to fill a quarter of the room — or at weekends, after putting away a few pints, more like a third of it. Terry became sizeable also, at an early age, and when he and Uncle Peter were watching television along with Dad, with Barker unconscious on the hearth-rug and Mum in and out bringing coal or tea, the sitting-room was like a crowded railway carriage. Being by far the smallest I had to squeeze in where I could, and was rarely comfortable. Consequently I spent most of my time out of doors.

Luckily there were several good places to go to. Behind Beaufort was a fenced-off area of asphalt, like a school playground, where the kids from the estate could play football or cricket. The nearest park — though it wasn't much of one, being small and threadbare — was only five minutes' walk. Best of all, the timber-yard where Dad worked was three or four streets away, and I used to spend a lot of time there, climbing on the stacks of wood, or kicking a ball around by myself.

My parents were direct opposites. Mum was small and quick: Dad was ponderous. For work he wore baggy green overalls that gave him elephant's legs and a huge bum. For wet days he had a long old raincoat that hung below his knees. He moved all of a piece. If you called after him in the street he couldn't just glance back — he had to stop and turn his whole body round. By contrast Mum was nippy and restless. She couldn't even go to the corner shop without looking about all the time like a bird. Indoors or outdoors she could never keep still. If she'd been a clock she'd have gained about an hour a day.

What you could say for my Dad was that he was very thorough. Every evening he'd sit in his armchair and read the *Daily Mirror* through from end to end, taking in every word. He'd keep up with the comic strips, have a go at the crossword, look at the gardening notes, though we didn't have so much as a window-box, and study the little advertisements for saucy knickers, magic bracelets and holidays in Skegness. He was a man of habit, and this was one of the habits. On Sundays he'd do the same with both the *Sunday Mirror* and the *News of the World*. He'd remember most of what he read, so he'd know what was Top of the Pops, or who the Home Secretary was, or who was favourite for the Greyhound Derby. Not that he was likely to communicate any of this information, because he was a man of few words, preferring to keep his thoughts to himself, such as they were. Nor did his face give much away. It was large and dark pink, wore no expression and grew only a thin crop of hair.

The difference between him and Mum showed particularly in their ways of washing up. Mum would go at it top speed, stacking the wet dishes into risky piles, drying plates six at a time, and cramming the crockery into cupboards wherever she could make it fit. You always had to be careful opening them in case things dropped out and smashed. When Dad tackled the job, about once a week, he did it very methodically dish after dish, finally dismantling half the gas stove and cleaning the parts.

He'd worked at his timber-yard for years and years, but Mum went through a whole series of jobs. I remember a time when she served in a florist's and used to bring home some of the left-over flowers. The flat would smell of roses or carnations when you came in at the front door, but somehow you lost the sense of it after the first few sniffs. As Mum was a great talker her conversations with Dad were severely one-sided, but that didn't discourage her. When she was telling him something she'd stop at the places where she expected a comment, and if she didn't get one, as was usually the case, she'd go on as if he *had* spoken. 'You're right,' she'd say, 'it *was* unpleasant,' or 'All right, I'll tell you what happened next.' Sometimes she spoke lines for him, as if he was a ventriloquist's dummy. For instance she'd remark that the tea was a bit weak, then growl, on Dad's behalf, 'Weak? It's like gnat's pee,' and then say in her normal voice: 'We've run out. I'll have to borrow some from Mrs Collier.' It was hard to tell what Dad made of all this. Sometimes his face lightened as though a grin was on the way, but it rarely arrived. I hardly remember him laughing at home, though he did in pubs. On balance Mum's style probably suited him. If he'd married someone like himself he'd have had no conversation at all.

My mother was good-looking in those days — dark hair, bright eyes and this quick smile. She was only about five years younger than Dad, but even to me she seemed to come from a different generation. She also had a number of talents, having been an inter-schools sprinting champion, an outstanding tennis and table-tennis player and some sort of champion at ball-room dancing. Dad showed no such abilities. His life didn't take him much further than the timber-yard, four or five local pubs, and West Ham football ground. The exception was that on Monday nights, winter or summer, he used to go swimming at the local baths. His routine was always the same — a loud dive followed by twenty-five lengths of breast stroke. He taught me to swim there before I was six. I remember he kept saying: 'You got to be able to look after yourself in the water.' But he himself never went near any water other than the pool. Two or three times the family had a seaside holiday, but he didn't risk so much as a paddle. For some years I used to go with him to the baths every Monday, but as I could swim faster than him by the time I was nine I got embarrassed and packed it in. In fact I made a point of keeping clear of the place of a Monday. I didn't fancy being there with any of my mates when he was spluttering up and down like a shagged-out walrus.

Even as a boy I couldn't see what had led Mum to marry him — especially as she let us know there'd been plenty of competition. She implied that he'd just hung around till he'd seen off all his rivals and worn her down. 'He's a very determined character, your Dad.' Trouble was that by the time I came to know him he didn't have anything important to be determined about. But he was a powerful personality. He still had force. If he'd been good at anything he'd have been bloody good at it. We were all quite impressed by him, even when we were giggling at him.

Physically I took after Mum and Terry took after Dad. A basic feature of my life is that I was exceptionally small and skinny until well into my teens. My whole style of behaviour came out of that fact. Terry was tall and heavy-set for his age, and very strong. There was a long period in which he could lift me up with one hand, and quite frequently did so. You couldn't call him a bully, because his aim wasn't really to hurt me — it was more that he treated me like he'd treat the dog. If he came to watch television and I happened to be in the seat he wanted he'd just lift me out of it and dump me on the carpet. If I ducked under his arm, or slithered out of his grasp — which I was good at — he'd grab my ear or hair. Naturally I didn't relish any of this, but I didn't actually detest him. He behaved like that because it was the way he was made.

At primary school I saw little of him, because I missed almost a year through illness. First I broke a collar-bone and cracked some ribs when I was knocked down by a Bedford van in Dalton Street. Then, just when I was getting back to rights, I caught hepatitis and was stuck in hospital for weeks. All through my life any bad luck I've had has come in waves. This was the first wave. By the time I got back to school Terry had only a term to go before moving to Mountford Hill — which was fortunate, because I had enough problems without him leaning on me. The illness had left me weak, and naturally I was well behind with school work. Generally I wasn't thought to be too bright. Nine months is a long time to lose at that age, and I'd lost confidence with it. For another year or so I felt out of things. At that stage I didn't have the size or strength or stamina to shine at soccer. I was clever with the ball, but either in the school playground or at the back of the flats I tended to stay on the edge of the game, just making a mark now and again with three seconds of flair. The personality I gradually built up after the illness had nothing to do with sport. I was a joker, and above all a dodger. Being small and quick I was hard to punch or grab, especially after all my practice with Terry. I'd shrink and twist, drop to the ground, rolled up like a woodlouse, and then dart off. The other thing I was good at was climbing. I could scuttle up anything. If a ball went on a roof or over a fence I was always the one who had to retrieve it.

I took a pride in myself as a climber, practising regularly all over the district. I must have been up three-quarters of the trees in Stafford Park. In time I became quite famous on the estate. Kids used to test me out, because I was too proud or too scared ever to refuse a dare. When I did ease off it was only after an exploit that could have finished me. One Sunday afternoon, when there was hardly anyone around, David Mahon and Barry Drake bet me that I wouldn't climb one of the iron pipes that led all the way up the back of Beaufort to the flat roof. Not being daft I was terrified, but I took off straight away, before fear could take the strength out of me. Climbing was my one speciality, and I had to protect my reputation. It was a good strong pipe, but too thick for me to get a fair grip on. Luckily there were heavy brackets every couple of yards, bolting it to the wall, and when I reached one of them I could get a firm push-off. Till about half-way up I wasn't doing badly, though my arms were beginning to ache, and my knees were taking some punishment. I pushed on, whimpering to myself and watching the bricks go by. Then I heard some shouting and made the mistake of looking down. People had come out of nowhere to stare up and yell at me to stop. All the faces were turned up to me, and the ground looked a mile off. Going down would have been as bad as going on. I dragged myself up a few more feet, really struggling now. A window went up six feet from me and some old man in shirt-sleeves leaned out, grabbing towards me. He just wanted to help me, and he succeeded, because he panicked me, and panic drove me on. I was jamming my hands between the pipe and the wall and hauling myself up in jerks. I didn't look down again, but the distance of the shouts made me feel the huge drop below me. But I was almost there: I was passing the top-storey windows. Then the pipe lurched. It couldn't have been more than a few inches, but I thought I was done. The top bracket had come away from the bricks. I was just near enough the top to stock a hand through the drain-hole in the wall at the top of the pipe and pull myself close. Scrambling like a crab I got the other arm over the parapet, wrenched my chest after it, and then rolled over to drop on the flat roof.

I just lay there, sprawled out, gasping and crying, too shaken even to feel relieved that I'd made it. My knees and knuckles were wet with blood, and I'd ripped open the toe of one gym-shoe. I was just getting myself together when the old bloke in shirt-sleeves opened the door at the top of the stairway and called: 'Come on, son.' I went through, snivelling and not looking at him, and he followed me down to the fourth floor without a word. Mum and Dad were outside our front door, looking frightened.

'Here he is,' said the old man. 'Safe and sound.'

As soon as were in the flat Dad started smacking me round the head like a madman.

'You bloody fool!' he shouted. 'You bloody little fool! You could have killed yourself!'

My mother pushed in between us.

'Leave him alone,' she said. 'He's had enough.'

Dad stared at me a moment, red with rage, and then slammed out of the door. Mum took me into the kitchen, sat me down, and got me a cup of tea and a biscuit, all without speaking. I was jerking with sobs, but the jerks gradually slowed down. When I was quiet she cleaned me up and put some dressings on my knees and knuckles.

'You won't go doing that again, will you?'

'No, Mum.'

'What put it into your head?'

'It was a dare.'

'You're daft making trouble for yourself, Vincent. You must be a bit mad, like me.'

She was smiling, and I could see she was quite proud of me, in a way. But I'd scared myself so badly that I just skulked round the flat the rest of the afternoon, trying to keep out of sight. When I did go out, that evening, I was quickly surrounded.

'Look at his hands!' they said. 'Look at his knees!'

'Were you scared?' asked Barry Drake.

'At the top I was.'

I had two days of fame on the strength of that feat. It was the one little sip of glory in the first eleven years of my life.

Chapter 3

Mountford Hill was a roughish school, good at sport but not much else. The buildings were old, but the teachers mostly new. The turnover was rapid because three out of four were speedily demoralised. Their first day they'd bustle in, eager to talk about decimals or the Duke of Wellington, but in no time their only aim was to keep some sort of control. You'd see their faces change colour with rage or fear. One or two even cried. All told it wasn't a place where you were likely to learn much even if you wanted to, which most of us didn't.

We had some craggy louts in my own year — notably Brewer, Chesterman and Gibb. To teach that lot you'd need a degree in psychiatry and a black belt at Karate. Looking back I can sympathise with the staff, but at the time I had my hands full with my own problems. When I started at Mountford Hill I was the second shortest boy in the class and scrawny with it. Meanwhile my brother Terry, built like a bouncer, was already boxing for the school and playing stopper for the soccer team. In a way his reputation was a protection for me, but I wanted to do something on my own account. My best chance should have been at soccer. I could control a ball better than most, and hit a sharp shot for my size. But even at soccer I was liable to get knocked over or crowded out through sheer lack of weight. I had to maintain my practice of lurking on the fringes of a game and making the most of the odd loose ball.

This came to be my policy with most things. I never went flat out, but looked for a flash in the pan. If I could come up with the occasional smart answer in class and knock in a neat goal or two at soccer, all without fully trying, it left people, myself included, to wonder what I could achieve if I ever got stuck in. I liked to have that little something in hand. The tactics worked in the sense that, small as I was, I didn't get pushed around. I managed to give the impression that if anyone went beyond horsing around I might go berserk and do a bit of damage. Every time I shot up a rope in the gym, or nipped round a full-back twice my weight, I picked up a bit of credit and gave myself a little more space to work in.

My best friend, Pete Harvey, was far from being a leading light of the school. He was notable only for three peculiarities. One was that he was accident-prone. He was always cutting himself or pitching head-first off his bike. Actually his whole face looked as though it has been bashed slightly to the left when he was a baby. He wore glasses held together by sticking plaster or paper clips. Secondly he was absent-minded. Contrary to appearances he had a perfectly service-able brain, but it made only occasional contact with the outside world. He couldn't concentrate more than three minutes in class before starting to draw faces on his fingernails or rolling up a trouser leg to pick a scab off his knee. The other was that he spent half his time laughing. He had this terrible laugh, braying like a donkey, with all his teeth showing and tears trickling down his cheeks.

One day Tomlinson, a tough, sour old teacher, who'd been trying in vain to get an answer out of him, said: 'Harvey, there are certain tribes in Africa, or so I have read, that have a vocabulary of no more than fifty words. You'd be very much at home with those good people.' For some reason that really tickled Harv. The idea of making do with only fifty words got right to him. He brayed away till you thought he might be sick. As usual we all joined in, till the whole class was whooping like a farmyard. Tomlinson grabbed Harvey's hair

19

to haul him out of the room, but he'd only got him halfway to the door, still cackling, when Harv began to wet himself. You could see one trouser leg go black. It's the only time I've known someone literally piss himself laughing.

Harvey was more or less a buffoon, but he wasn't ridiculous. For one thing he was fearless. Although a clumsy mover he'd take on anyone who pushed it and fight till he couldn't see. He was also naturally generous. If he had a bar of chocolate I'd get half of it. His temperament was cheerful. He looked to enjoy life.

He hung in with me because I was the joker, the hit and run man, living off my wits. That was my other way of making a personality for myself. I'd do daft things to raise a laugh — and no one laughed easier than Harvey. Being small I was hard to keep track of in class. I'd slide down under the desk and creep around among the legs till I bobbed up in an empty place. 'Where's Gilpin?' became a familiar cry from the masters. I also had a line in smart-arse answers. 'What are you up to, Gilpin?' 'Page forty-three, sir.' 'Now could we please have a little quiet?' 'A little quiet what, sir?' My other talent was for missiles of all kinds. I was very accurate with small catapults, firing pellets or paper clips or bits of rubber. All told I must have been a pest — but a minor pest rather than a serious trouble-maker.

The difference between me and Harvey was that he didn't seem to have it in him to do anything else but horse around whereas I at least appeared to be capable of something more. Now and then a topic would take my fancy, and I'd say something quite bright — about shipwrecks, for instance, or an eclipse of the sun. One morning when I'd actually made three sensible comments in the space of twenty minutes Mr Tomlinson said: 'The truth is you're by no means a half-wit, Gilpin — though by Christ you often behave like one.'

Although I'd have a laugh with anyone I kept myself pretty private. Outside school I didn't see much even of Harvey, because he lived a fair way off. Nor did I spend much time with the kids round the estate. It wasn't that home life was up to much. Uncle Peter was running out of personality as he

20

grew older, and couldn't find much to talk about. If he saw me changing my trousers he'd say: 'Changing your trousers then, Vin?' He no longer spoke for the sake of the words — it was more like waving. Mum and I had the same sense of humour, and would crack a few jokes together, but we rarely got more than ten minutes at a time. She'd be off to the pictures or a basket-weaving class or some part-time job. Dad was always home of an evening when not at the pub, but he remained silent.

The result was that round the age of twelve I was spending more and more time at the timber-yard. It was in a back street where no one came to bother you outside working hours. On the big gate was a sign: 'Warning: Patrolled by Guard Dog', but that just meant that Dad sometimes took Barker there for a stroll. Once I'd squeezed under the gate I was quite secure, and could get on with my private game. Between two brick sheds was an alley a bit narrower than a soccer goal, and walled up at the far end. Hour after hour I used it for an exercise something between shooting practice and squash. I had a series of routines or sequences, with the far wall, up to a certain height, serving as a goal. I'd fire the ball left-foot into the right-hand corner to bring it back off the right-hand wall, and hit the return right-foot into the left-hand corner to bring it back off the left-hand wall, and so on. I chalked up targets and aimed at them in turn, first with one foot and then with the other. In all the variations the idea was to keep the ball moving, with no more than one touch between shots. Hundreds of hours I played these daft games, often in the pissing rain, always by myself, half hypnotised by the blank walls, the smell of sawn wood, and the smack and smack and smack of the ball against the brickwork. The sound of the bounce drove me on and on, toiling away like a mouse in a wheel. Why I enjoyed this so much I've no idea. In its way it was great practice: my left foot became as good as my right, and I learned to hit the ball first time from any angle. But I didn't invent my routine to develop these skills — I practised them for their own sake. In fact for a long time I preferred my private knockabouts to a real game — God knows why.

In my first three or four years at Mountford I didn't grow much, but my mates did. Even Harvey left me far behind, to say nothing of Gibb or Brewer. By the time I was fourteen I felt like an alien. My body was still skinny and almost hairless. It was so depressing to me to be underdeveloped like this that I had a fantasy that there'd been a mix-up over my date of birth, leading people to believe I was two years older than I actually was. Although I kept up a cheeky front there was a bit of desperation in it. I felt like a loser. This was a dead patch in my life.

We had one teacher named Franklin, a tall, stooping bloke whose chief peculiarity was making savage threats. He'd shout: 'You there! Yes, you, sonny, grinning like a chimpanzee. You'll be losing a couple of front teeth if you're not careful.' Another favourite was: 'Step out of line once more, boy, and I'll kick you all the way to the headmaster's study.' He never went that far, but he did whack kids round the skull when the mood took him. Once when he swung at me I ducked, and he caught Harvey by mistake. Harv raised a great outcry, of course, just to start a diversion, so he hit us both and then kept me back after class to write out two hundred times: 'I must not avoid Mr Franklin's blows.' When I'd nearly finished he came in and started talking to me.

'That was a typical bloody performance this afternoon, Gilpin. When are you going to stop dodging and ducking?'

'What do you mean, sir?'

'There you go again, ducking the question. When are you going to sort yourself out? When are you going to take something seriously?'

'Don't know, sir.'

'Do you want to be a layabout the rest of your days? What are you good at?'

'Nothing,' I said. 'Maybe football.'

'I've seen you play football, Gilpin. It's the same. It's the same story. You do something a bit smart, and then rest on your laurels. Why don't you push yourself? Why don't you find out what you're capable of?'

Basically Franklin was an old wanker, always doling out advice on the off-chance of changing someone's whole life. But this time the needle hit the nerve, partly because my old man had been having a similar go at me only the week before. He came in late on a Friday night, gloomy from the pub, and turned off the television.

'Never mind the bloody TV,' he said. 'It's time you were thinking about the future.' This was an unusual speech for him — he'd obviously had more than a few. His eyes were bloodshot and he was breathing beer. 'Your brother's taken a wrong turning, I'll tell you that.'

He didn't have to. Since leaving Mountford Terry had lost three jobs and settled down to some solid loafing. He was still playing soccer, but he'd put on weight and slowed down.

'What are you going to do with yourself when you leave school?'

'I thought of being a steeplejack.' Which I hadn't, but it was the first thing that came to my mind.

'Steeplejack?' cried Dad, struggling to remember what the word meant. 'Why be a bloody steeplejack?'

'I'd like the climbing.'

'The climbing?' Slowly his brain got the idea under control. 'That isn't the job. The climbing isn't the job. What are you going to do when you're up there?'

'Up where?' I asked, to confuse him.

'Up where? Up the bloody chimney, of course — or the tower. Whatever it is you been climbing. What you going to do up there?'

'I haven't thought about that.'

'Well it's time you bloody did think about it.' His face was swollen with the drink. 'You have to have the skills. A bloody chimpanzee can climb a chimney. You got to learn something. You got to stick at something.' He flopped into his chair and stared at me. 'You want to take a leaf out of my book. I've held my job twenty years. You're like your mother — never finish what you start.'

He was partly right, for all he was pissed. Mum didn't follow through. She bought a knitting machine by post, but

23

only knitted half a sweater. She laid in about a hundred-weight of Seville oranges but made no marmalade and left them to turn green. None of her jobs seemed to last long. On the other hand Dad never even started anything apart from the *Daily Mirror*.

Anyway, when Franklin echoed Dad's unusually lengthy speech I thought things over for a day or two. I realised that though I had some pride I'd been satisfying it on the cheap — a goal here, a dare or a wisecrack there. I was living on crumbs. Franklin was right to say I should have a real go at something, and the best bet seemed to be soccer. As it happened it was June when I had these conversations, so I had some time in hand. I decided to work flat out on the quiet to make myself really sharp for the start of the next season.

Put like that it doesn't look a big step, but for me it was crucial. I was giving up my little bit in hand for the chance of doing something outstanding. The next September would decide it. If I failed no one else would even know it — but I would. I'd have found my limits and boxed myself in.

Starting that weekend my sessions at the timber-yard became serious practice. I worked harder and longer, pushing myself till I ached. It was a hot summer, and day after day I came home soaked in sweat. I knew what I'd have to do to make an impression. I'd have to stop hovering and drive myself into the game, win the ball, call for it, risk making mistakes. If I was still under-sized I could at least make myself fit, quick and fearless.

I went into the first school game in September strung up like a banjo. Although I did a fair amount of useless running I kept in touch with the play right through, scored a goal and hit a post, even though I was playing in midfield. The following week I was put on the wing, spun the full-back giddy, and hit cross after cross. For the first time Cracknell, the sports master, noticed I could kick with both feet. By Christmas I was the regular left-winger for the school second team, averaging a goal a game. My reputation had changed: I was still the joker, but I was reckoned the best footballer in my year, and being so small was the team mascot. Not that I was any sort of prodigy. I've often been asked why none of the London clubs picked me out as a schoolboy. The reason was that I wasn't good enough. I'd do a number of bright things, but could never take charge of a game.

At that time the school had a brilliant first team — probably its best ever. There were two outstanding forwards: a fast, black lad named Perez and a rough-house striker named Dawes. But the real star was Alan Ruddock, a midfield player who'd represented England at schoolboy level, and was known to have half a dozen League clubs after him. I'd seen him when he played at Wembley, and even there he was never troubled or hurried. He could dominate a game without breaking into a run: the ball seemed to seek him out. If an opponent tried to hustle him Ruddock appeared to side-step in slow motion before strolling on. He could hit an accurate pass any distance and in any direction without looking up, as though he had extra eyes all round his head. Dawes and Perez lived off him. He was heavy-muscled, like a decathlete, and packed a brutal shot. The Mountford kids reckoned he could have knocked in a hat-trick every game if he'd been bothered, but he was easy-going. Once his side had gone two or three up he was content to ease off. Though he never talked about it everyone knew that he looked to be in League football within a year or two.

Ruddock's example kept my ambitions in check. Here was a lad only a couple of years older than me, but twice my size and strength, who could command the entire pitch even in a schoolboy international. Down at second-team level I was barely master of a strip of it.

Around this time there were several other changes in my life. Uncle Peter died, aged seventy-nine, and so did Barker, aged twelve. At last I had a bedroom to myself. Dad replaced the dog with a black kitten he named Coleman and fed as fat as a prize marrow.

The following summer I went on a school-trip to Paris. In many ways we made a shambles of it. Kids would get lost, or nick stuff from shops or drink wine and throw up. Brewer and Chesterman nearly had themselves arrested for getting into a fight with some students. It should have been a nightmare for the four teachers looking after us, but they managed all right on a shift system, two sober and two pissed. I did my share of horsing around, but the visit got to me. Everything was different — the language, the wide streets, the cafés, the traffic, the money. We might show off and arse about as a group, but without the teachers to look after us and get us home we'd have been lost, done for, pathetic. I didn't relish feeling that useless.

At the end of the summer term Harvey left the school, being nearly a year older than myself. To the surprise of those who knew him he not only tried to join the army but was accepted. He had a posting up north somewhere, and I lost touch with him.

Now Harvey was away I put all my energies into soccer. With half the old team gone, and Dawes and Ruddock due to leave at Christmas, Cracknell had to do some rebuilding. I soon became the regular first-team winger, playing more or less under orders. All I had to do was lurk wide waiting for a pass, and then race for the goal-line and pull the ball back for our strikers. Playing in front of Ruddock was a luxury. Every ball from him found me in space. I soon gathered confidence enough to vary my game by cutting inside for a snap at goal. By Christmas I'd scored half a dozen times.

Funnily enough one of these goals landed me in the nastiest spot of my school career. To understand the episode you have to remember that I was the youngest and by far the smallest of a hard side, very anxious to keep my end up. In general I'd been doing all right, but there was one character who always got on my tit — namely the big striker, Ollie Dawes. He was a noisy show-off, always pushing to the centre of things, niggling and challenging. He hadn't got much sense of humour, but he liked a laugh. What amused him was flicking mud in someone's eye, or pissing on your leg in the showers. He liked to carry things to the point where his victim had to back down, pretending to grin or else take a poke at him — which few fancied, because he was a reckless, violent yob. Ruddock was pretty well the only bloke he didn't try to

26

needle one time or another. Personally I didn't even care for him as a player: he was ninety per cent physical strength and only ten per cent skill, but he thought he was hot shit. Every time he scored his arm went up like Denis Law's.

The last game before Christmas was also the last game Ruddock and Dawes would play for Mountford. We were away to Langton Cross, a fair side, who were actually holding us to one-all at half-time. Then Ruddock scored, and laid on another for Dawes, and we were coasting. Just before the end I was put away down the right wing and dribbled in along the goal-line. The centre-back threw himself into the tackle, but I hooked the ball inside him, just inside the edge of the six-yard box. 'Leave it!' screamed a voice, and there was Dawes storming through, looking to blast a goal. I thought: 'Sod that.' As his boot came down I nicked the ball back, so that he kicked air and fell flat, while I fired a low shot inside the far post. It felt cool and must have looked it. Our lad cracked up, and even the Langton goalkeeper had a grin.

'What the fuck you playing at?' yelled Dawes, boiling mad. He muttered to himself all the way back to the centre-circle.

After the game he laughed along with the other lads about what had happened, realising he'd look a prick if he didn't. But he came crowding over me in the showers with his big bare body.

'Didn't you hear me shout?'

'I couldn't make out the words,' I said.

'That was my ball.'

'I thought you looked a bit nervous.'

He aimed a cuff at my head, which I ducked. I was tensed to smack my knee into his balls, but he forced a laugh and went off.

On the way back Mr Cracknell left the coach early, because it happened to pass his house, and once he'd gone there was a bit of shouting and skirmishing. Dawes got me in a mock wrestling match, pinned me with an arm and a leg and ripped my pants off, laughing loudly to show it was a joke. I held still, ready to nut him as soon as he let go, even if he was to kill me afterwards. But the delay did for me, because it coincided with one of the few inspirations of Dawes's life. The coach stopped at a traffic light. Dawes stepped out, still carrying me, and dumped me on the back of a lorry that was crossing in front of us. There I was with no pants, perched on some cement sacks, with the whole coach-load cheering. Next minute the lorry was round a corner and heading for Hackney at a fair speed.

Never mind how I got home. What burnt me up was being made a laughing stock in front of the whole team. For months I'd been building myself some sort of position in the school by hard graft, and now this big, ugly, thick berk had thrown me. I had to get him. If it had been Harvey stuck on that lorry he'd have laughed louder than anyone, pleased enough to be in the limelight. Not me. I could be the joker, but it had to be on my own terms. I wasn't going to be made a clown by a slob like Dawes.

I doubt I spoke a dozen words the rest of that weekend. My whole body was charged up, ready for a fight. I was scared shitless, not of getting hurt, but of being made to look still more ridiculous. I didn't mind if I was pulped, as long as I'd done some damage first. On the Sunday I was so restless I cycled half the day to burn up the adrenalin. My mind must have been working, as well as my legs, because I came back with a plan.

Mountford was to break up on the following Wednesday, and I aimed to make my move that morning. There was a perfect chance, because the soccer team was to be photographed at midday outside the gym. I played truant on the Monday and Tuesday to leave myself nothing but the one clean strike. When I went in on the Wednesday morning there were a fair few gags — obviously the word had got right round the school. I grinned and rode the punches. In the gym when we were changing Dawes was in his glory. 'Where you been, then, Vinnie?' he shouted. 'Did they nick you for flashing?' He didn't often see a joke, so he made the most of this one.

I still have a copy of the photo they took that day. I'm at the end of the front row, looking small and pretty tense, which I was. My scheme depended partly on guesswork, and could misfire. But the guesses proved correct. After the photo Mr Cracknell went straight off to lunch. I got changed fast and nipped into the bog to make preparations. As I'd expected, when I returned Dawes was still prowling round with nothing on, airing his balls. He liked nudity, perhaps because his body looked a good bit better than his face. I picked up his clothes unnoticed, and drifted towards the door. Fear made me breathless, but I got out a good shout that silenced everyone.

'Ollie!'

He looked up and I waved his things.

'You owe me some clothes. I'll take these.'

For a moment he hesitated, out of astonishment, then dashed at me. I was through the door like a flash, throwing it back at him, darted into the bog and locked myself into one of the cubicles. Dawes and the others came charging up. I could hear laughing and shouting. Everyone but Dawes was enjoying the scene. He shook the door and yelled: 'Come on out, you little fucker!'

'Wait!' I shouted.

The whole bog fell quiet. Suddenly I felt great — bloody marvellous. Everything was working, and I was in total control.

'You can have your clothes back,' I called. 'But there's one thing. They stink a bit.'

This got a cheer, and Dawes yelled: 'Come on out!'

'I'll just give them a wash. There's some water in this bog.'

'You fucking try!'

'There's not much water. But if I stuff them well down . . .'

He came charging into the door. The poxy little lock broke at once, but I'd wedged Cracknell's office chair between the door and the bog, and it held nicely. I shoved Dawes's clothes well down the pan and pulled the chain. There was a huge cheer, and the door was bent in by a second shoulder-charge. I didn't wait for a third, but wriggled out of the little square window like a cat through a cat-door. As I hit the asphalt the chair broke or the door smashed, and Dawes stuck his crimson face out roaring: 'I'll bloody kill you, Gilpin!'

I gave him a big smile and two fingers, and walked off leaving him still cursing. The smart thing would have been to slip off home, but I wasn't going to creep away from a bully-boy like Dawes. Hit and run wasn't good enough. But I did tend to stay among other people. He couldn't actually kill me in the middle of a crowd. I kept an eye open for him in the final assembly, but there was no sign. My exploit was already famous, and all my mates were on the look-out too, knowing he'd be out to flatten me. To do him justice he managed to take us all by surprise, bursting out from the bicycle shed when we were all going home.

I shot off in panic with Dawes pounding behind. But my second instinct was better. Using a well-tried trick I dropped just as he was grabbing for me, so that he tripped over my body. I was up on my feet in the same movement with a single purpose in mind, namely to mark the fucker somehow before he pulped me. I cracked a knee into his head, and swung a punch. Next moment I was down and he was bashing me — but not for long. Someone hauled him off, pinning his arms from behind. It was Ruddock. He seemed to handle Dawes effortlessly, without losing his good-humour:

'Easy there, Ollie. Knock it off now.'

I got to my feet shaking, and sniffing back blood. Dawes was still in Ruddock's grasp. I was pleased to see that he was wearing a weird assortment of odd clothes and had a fair lump under one eye.

'You little cunt!' he spat.

'Sod off, Vin,' said Ruddock, comfortably, and I did.

That episode confirmed the suspicion that I could be a dangerous little fucker if needled too far. It gave me a reputation that stayed with me through my last eighteen months at Mountford Hill. The time seemed to go by in a dream. I had no close friends, and did no studying to speak of. Soccer used up all the commitment I could muster. I seemed to be hanging about waiting for something — such as a new body. A lot of the time I was depressed, or so bored it was like being half asleep. Just before I left Mountford Franklin took me aside and said: 'Apart from football, Gilpin, your school career's been a bloody fiasco. Let's hope you're a late developer.' I quite liked that idea. It cheered me up more than once when I was low. The only other remedy was the anaesthetic of knocking an old football against a brick wall.

Chapter 4

I left school with no prospects or plans. Dad kept telling me to think about the future, but I wanted it to come as a surprise.

After a couple of false starts I got a job with Ferris Clark, the big engineering company. They put me in Vehicle Maintenance, which pleased my old man because he assumed I'd be learning to grind valves and take gear-boxes to bits. It might have come to that one day, but to start with my work was mostly washing down lorries, plus the odd technical challenge such as changing a number plate or a windscreen-wiper blade. In charge of the section was a fat bloke named Bill Duckworth, who took the piss all the time but never smiled.

'Right, Vincent,' he'd say, 'we're going to make you a mechanic. You see this? It's what we call in the trade a screwdriver. A screwdriver. The thing to remember about it is: Always hold it by the thick end. The thick end.'

I got on well with Bill Duckworth and the lads in Vehicle Maintenance, because I made a lucky start. Ferris Clark were hot on sport of all kinds, and had excellent facilities. Among other things they organised an inter-departmental five-a-side competition, on a knock-out basis. Normally V.M. had done nothing in this, but in my first year Martin Leeds, who played for the Company's second eleven, got us organised, training twice a week. We had a stubby little goal-keeper named Bob Amos, too short for the full-scale game, but a marvel at five-a-side. Some reasonable play and the luck of the draw took us through to the final against the holders, Central Supply. For half the game they pasted us. They scored two and might have had six if it hadn't been for Amos. Then Leeds scored with a long shot, and I tucked home a loose ball, both inside a minute. Supply were amazed and the little crowd was raising the gym roof. I could hear Duckworth bellowing: 'Take them, my sons, take them!' In the last few seconds I twisted between two defenders and stabbed in the winner. Vehicle Maintenance had won its first trophy of any kind.

That performance took me straight into the Company's first-team squad. Ferris Clark had a strong soccer tradition. Every Thursday we had a coaching session with John Stanton, the former Millwall player. He singled me out early on, saying I could be a bit useful if I put on a pound or two. I was phased into the team as a winger, and soon became a regular.

Ferris Clark played on Saturdays. On Sundays I turned out for a little ramshackle local side, that played on the Marshes. With them I developed a new approach, because I came to realise that I had the reflexes and the close control to take a yard off anyone marking me. I'd drift along at half pace, doing the simple things, till I sniffed an opening, and then I'd be through like a shot. I felt like a veteran boxer who loafs and watches till he lets go his knock-out punch. The goals I scored gave me confidence that helped my game with Ferris Clark.

My Dad often watched me play on the Marshes. I'd look up and see him standing there in his long raincoat, parked on the touchline like a dead tree. He didn't move, even if it pissed with rain, and didn't raise a shout. I never spoke to him, and he never spoke to me. When the last whistle blew he turned away at once. None of my mates knew he was my old man, and I didn't tell them. Neither of us mentioned the game at home.

This was all in keeping with my way of life at the time. I had close contact with nobody. The lads in V.M. were a good bunch, but I felt about them what you feel about people you meet on holiday: no point getting in too far, because you won't be seeing them long. Not that I had any plans — I just couldn't imagine a lifetime in Vehicle Maintenance. I had no interest in the workings of a motor.

When I met old mates round the flats I'd stop for a wisecrack but then move on. I always gave the idea that I was on my way somewhere else. Sometimes when I was nattering on a street corner I'd break off to jump on a passing bus, not even knowing where it was going. Around this time I got into a habit I've never lost of drifting in and out of places through idle curiosity. I'd wander through department stores, or libraries, or museums, with nothing in mind. I walked or cycled for miles, looking at the streets and parks, stopping for a cup of tea in some old café, waiting for some diversion.

In the last part of that opening season with Ferris Clark a time-switch clicked and my body at last began to change. About nine tenths of my growth from boy to man took place in a few months of that spring and summer. I was like someone who'd drunk a potion in a horror-movie. My muscles swelled, my voice broke, my face and prick grew longer. Hair was sprouting out of my legs and crotch and chin. When the soccer season ended I more or less sat back and watched myself go. There was no telling where I might finish, especially as I had a tall father. I could see myself six foot ten, with a dong down to my knees. In fact by the autumn my body had settled down, and I looked pretty much as I've looked since. When the soccer season started I was five foot six and I've never passed five seven. My face was now triangular instead of round, and on the narrow side. It's been modified since by a scar or two and a couple of nose-breaks, but it was, as it still is, a very ordinary face. At the height of my career I could usually pass unrecognised in a crowd.

There was no doubting the effect on my game. My legs seemed to have doubled in thickness. I was like a kid with a new bike. Every aspect of my play was transformed: I was quicker off the mark and stronger in the tackle. I could hit the ball harder. The extra power gave me extra confidence, and I was trying things I'd never dared before. 'You took my advice,' said John Stanton.

I enjoyed that season. Stanton was a good coach in the sense that he gave us a style of our own — and it was an attacking style. We'd win or lose by daft scores like 5—4. The defence took horrible risks and paid the price, but up front with so much attacking support, life was easy. We'd pour men forward, and I had the knack of being the one left over — the man in space. I was making or scoring goals in every game.

In April Stanton asked me how I'd fancy a stab at part-time professional football. He'd put in a word about me at Coombe Forest, the Athenian League club where he'd ended his career. Within a week I was playing in a trial game. The Forest manager, Eric Bourne, asked me to come along to pre-season training in three months' time. If I showed the same form he'd sign me. It was all so simple I could hardly take it in.

The weeks that followed were like a long holiday. Working on the lorries at Ferris Clark had become just a source of pocket-money. Real life was football, and I was taking a breather from it. In August I'd be a paid player, looking to start a career. I said nothing at home, in case it all fell through, but in my head I had no doubts.

It was a hot summer that dried the park yellow and melted the tar in the roads. I started going out with a girl named Karen Sadler, who served in the canteen at Ferris Clark. She had a small white face and long black hair. Normally she looked tense, but if you could get her to smile she was a different person: her eyes shone and she got a faint flush in her cheeks. I got friendly with her in the first place through cracking jokes, insulting the food and so on. She was very shy, but I pieced her story together when I'd walked her home a few times. Her father had walked out some years before, and not been heard of since. Since then she'd lived alone with her mother, who suffered from depression and rarely left the house. Karen was in her first job, and glad to get a chance of meeting new people, but being timid she'd made no friends as yet. I'd come along at the right time.

So far in this life-story I haven't mentioned sex. Through growing up late I'd been at a disadvantage with girls and had kept myself out of their way apart from a bit of clowning. Now it was different. By the time Karen joined the canteen I was two inches taller than she was, and feeling confident because of my soccer prospects. Since I was also a quick talker she assumed I knew my way around. In fact I knew comparatively little about sex, though expert in everything you can do on your own. When I at length put a hand on her breast — the left one — she reacted so violently, jerking and moaning, that I thought I must have hooked a nymphomaniac first time. Actually she was a virgin, but very lonely. We were screwing by the end of the month.

I can't explain the pattern my life took without saying what this did for me. I'd never known such pleasure. Once when my ribs had been cracked I'd nearly fainted from the pain of a sudden cough. Instant agony, straight to the brain. My first fuck with Karen jarred me just as violently, but with joy — an electric shock of joy. We were in Blunstone Park behind some rhododendrons, late on a sunny May evening. I hardly knew what was happening to me — the flowers flashed colour and the new leaves on the trees were exploding like fireworks. I came to with Karen clutching me and crying, and a gentle breeze cool on my bare bum.

After that I couldn't get enough of screwing her. It was more like a drug-addiction than a relationship. She was as desperate as I was, and the pressure was increased by the fact that we had nowhere to go. Her mother couldn't bear the idea of her going out with someone, never mind bringing him home. We could never depend on my place being empty for the evening. Everything had to be out of doors. We tried all the local parks. We tried the timber-yard, which Karen found too uncomfortable, though I felt at home in the familiar smell of the wood. At weekends we'd take the underground — really the overground — out into the

36

country and get off where we saw a fair clustering of trees. The fine weather made this all fairly easy, though the journey home could be a sticky experience.

Karen was good-looking, and also a nice girl, but she didn't have much variety or much to say for herself. Living with her depressed mother seemed to have put her out of the habit of talking. She was always looking to me to give a lead. I could keep her interested and make her laugh, but I began to have to work at it. Gradually we had less and less to talk about, and would walk twenty minutes at a time without a word. When we moved on to physical communication we were like a couple of ballroom dancers starting up a well-tried routine. It didn't seem to have much to do with normal life. But these doubts really came later. Through the summer we never flagged, and I was in the best spirits I'd ever known. Everything seemed to hang together. I'd got a new body as a reward for my commitment to soccer, and a girl-friend as a reward for my new body.

Pre-season training with the Foresters was harder than any I'd previously known, but I was fit and agile and basically enjoyed it. After one more practice game I was signed on. When I broke the news at home Mum said: 'I always knew you'd surprise us.' So appropriately she didn't seem surprised. The old man turned the announcement over in his mind and growled out: 'Well, don't let it go to your head. You're not a star yet, you know.' Like old Franklin he wanted to say something wise. But he was excited, for all that. He had the news round the local pubs inside the hour.

My first full game was in September, a mid-week match with only a couple of hundred spectators at the Foresters' scrubby old ground. As we came down the roped-off path to the pitch I heard voices calling: 'That number eleven looks sharp, Bob.' — 'He *does* look sharp.' It was Bill Duckworth and Bob Amos, there to cheer me on and take the piss. Off and on through the game I'd hear them yell: 'Give it to Gilpin!' I had a quiet match, but half-volleyed a good goal in the second-half that gave them something to cheer.

For the next few weeks I was on the fringes of the team.

Although I managed some sharp runs and passes I could be pulled off for not making enough general impact on the game. 'Get stuck in,' Eric Bourne would tell me. 'Put yourself about.' I was perfectly willing to try, but it simply wasn't my style. I'd end up chasing shadows.

Quite possibly my soccer career could have dried up there, almost before it had started, if there hadn't come a sudden change in circumstances. I came in for training one December evening and found Eric introducing a newcomer to the rest of the lads. It was Alan Ruddock. He gave me a wink, but only had the chance of a few words while we were changing.

'Hallo Vince. You've filled out, my son. Ollie Dawes wouldn't fancy his chances now.'

'What happened at Villa? I thought you'd be in their League side by now.'

Alan gave a little sleepy grin. 'A few knee problems. A few personality problems.'

I noticed a neat scar on his leg — and also that he'd filled out a bit himself, being several pounds overweight. He showed the old strength and skill, but was slow and a shade cautious, favouring the leg that had been repaired. By the end of the session he was pretty blown, yet seemed satisfied.

'That's the first step,' he said.

I never found out exactly how he came to leave Villa. Possibly he made things hard for himself, because placid as he was he could be a hard man to budge when he'd made his mind up on something. He'd come home partly for family reasons but chiefly because he thought Coombe Forest was the right setting for a carefully staged comeback following the knee operation. Although he never let out more than a hint of what was in his mind I could read him. He still had faith in himself, and with good reason, but he'd lost a couple of years and knew that this could be his last chance to get back to big-time soccer. Over the winter and spring he'd recover his fitness and get back confidence in the injured knee. He was well enough known inside the game to attract the scouts if he showed anything like his old form.

He worked hard. By January he was running the midfield,

and was already the outstanding player in the side. By February we were channelling everything through him, and he'd changed our whole style of play with his long passing, opening up both flanks. Nobody profited more than I did. Again and again he gave me a clear run at the opposing defence with a cross-field ball. No longer was I straining to get into the game. He himself was playing with peculiar concentration, as though he'd bet himself that he wouldn't waste a ball all season. If you'd charted out his play, as in one of those diagrams showing where a batsman scores his runs, you'd have demonstrated that he used the entire pitch, dropping the ball down the centre or swinging it out to either wing. Thanks to him the whole team was prospering.

Eric Bourne, the manager, could hardly take it in. He'd had an undistinguished career himself — a few years of third-division football, a few years of non-League football, and some assorted coaching experience — and suddenly here he was with a success on his hands. We'd shot up the table and gates had doubled. Although Eric must have known how much of the transformation was due to Ruddock you could see him getting new confidence in his own ideas. It was natural enough. He'd come up with some tactical plan, we'd go out and win, so it came easy to believe that it was the plan that had paid off. All that spring Eric was happy as a sparrow.

I once said to Ruddock: 'You can't take him seriously. He'd be just as happy working in a factory and running a Boy Scout team.'

'That's right,' said Alan. 'That's what I like about him.'

'But he'd never make it in League football.'

'Why should he want to? He's contented here.'

Years later I realised that Alan had been right, and that I'd been looking at Eric in the light of my own ambitions. You can keep a cat without wishing you were a lion-tamer. Most League managers are a bit mad, which isn't surprising because they're in an unnatural atmosphere. Each week they're perched on a bench, hoping and praying and screaming for victory in a ninety-minute match. If they get it they've had a week of triumph, if they don't it's been a disaster. A manager who can't take the tension goes under. A manager who likes it too much comes to live for it. Once you're committed to the challenge it must be hard to find a middle way. Eric Bourne would be happier as a big minnow in a small pond.

I saw quite a lot of Ruddock at this time. He and I used to come in for extra training with Colin Finch the centre-back, who was a fitness fanatic. After the session we'd sit about over a lager — a drink I was just taking to — and chat about this or that. Alan had only a limited interest in talking about football. He preferred to latch on to some unexpected topic such as rabbit warrens, or the workings of the sewage system. Often he'd sit silent for a bit, grinning to himself, with the subject still going round in his head. He'd come up with some further remark about it long after I'd moved on to something else. Unlike myself he had a number of recognisable hobbies, including photography and draughts. He worked part-time with his father in a small building firm, chiefly on the electrical side.

Dad had joined the Foresters' growing band of regular spectators. Over supper one night in a rare burst of speech he said: 'That Ruddock — he's a player. He can do it all, can't he?'

'Pretty well.'

'That's a first-division player. They could bloody use him at Upton Park.'

Dad wasn't a bad judge of a player, and I wouldn't have disagreed with his verdict. If Alan did have a weakness it was that he couldn't *quicken* his game to speak of. He gave the impression that he was playing at three-quarter pace and could pull out something extra if he had to. But once or twice when the team was up against it I saw him go flat out, only to lose some of his timing and accuracy. This was the one advantage I had over him: I did my best work at speed. Another of my developing gifts he didn't much need to show. I was tricky at close-quarters. I could sense any movement beside or behind me, and my reflexes were trigger-quick. Realising this I was cutting in more frequently and looking useful where most players don't — in a crowded penalty box. But you couldn't have said much more for me then. If Ruddock was a first-division player then I might make the third or fourth.

By April the talent scouts were there in numbers. We knew they were after Ruddock, but we all raised our game. Coombe were having their best season for years. Approaches must have been made behind the scenes, but Ruddock and Bourne both kept quiet about them. Eric was obviously anxious to play his cards right. He didn't want to lose his star player, but a fat fee could do the club's finances a power of good.

At a midweek match near the end of the month it was being whispered that Arsenal, Spurs and West Ham all had senior representatives in the stand. Apart from that it was a nothing game on a breezy night, and by half-time we were strolling about with a three-goal lead, two of them made by Ruddock. Just after the break our goalie took a back pass and tossed a long ball out towards Alan. At the last second the throw died in a gust of wind, and Ruddock had to stretch for it just as one of the opposing strikers came powering up to crack it on. Alan went down with a short scream, and I knew his knee had gone before they signalled for a stretcher.

When I got to see him in hospital they'd already done an exploratory operation and told him he could forget about League football. I couldn't think what to say to him. I'd had no practice in serious conversations. All I managed was: 'Fuck me, Alan, there's no justice.'

His manner was as easy as usual. He said: 'Oh well, it was bound to happen. I had a weak knee waiting to get done.'

'It could have waited ten years.'

'We've all got to go some time. I'm getting out before I'm over the hill.' He seemed quite cheery, considering. 'The way I look at it, I've got to just reverse my way of life. Instead of playing soccer for a living and doing a spot of decorating on the side, I'll be a full-time builder and keep sport for a hobby.'

'What sport will you be allowed?'

'The doc says anything that doesn't throw too much

weight on the knee — cricket, table-tennis, snooker, marbles . . .'

I noticed his knuckles were swollen.

'What have you done to your hand?'

'I was punching the wall.' He saw I was embarrassed, and added: 'But that was yesterday. Anyway, it isn't my wanking hand.'

I was doubly sorry for him because in a way his whole personality was based on football. If he was relaxed and casual it was on the foundation of being a star performer, a man with his picture in the papers and a famous future ahead. It had suited his personality to have something to be modest about. It didn't surprise me that shortly after leaving hospital he also left town.

For me the summer that followed was like the previous one, but without the excitement. I'd hit a flat patch. I was a bit of a hero at Ferris Clark, because of the football, but in another way I wasn't taken seriously — I wasn't a real trainee. Karen and I were still vigorously going through the motions, and I was still enjoying them — but rather in the way my Dad enjoyed the pub: habit as much as pleasure. And if I'm honest, which I wasn't at the time, I was getting uneasy with her because I could see she wanted something I wasn't going to give. The signs were most obvious in her attitude to sex. She was more passionate than ever before, because it was her way of getting closest to me, but after we'd finished she was sad, because the fucking hadn't secured what she wanted to go with it — such as intimate conversation or a hint that soon she must leave her mother and move in with me. Everywhere we walked she held my hand. Sometimes I felt as though I was handcuffed to her. She'd sit silently with me on a park bench, gazing at me with big dark eyes, her face very pale against her hair, and I'd be fidgeting to get away.

Apart from any doubts I had about Karen personally I didn't feel like thinking about the future. Many a star footballer writes that he always knew he could make it to the top. My ambition had become simply to make it to the bottom. I thought I might just make a decent little career in the lower divisions — but I wasn't even confident of that. Alan's injury took some of the heart out of me. If he couldn't succeed, what chance had I? But in another mood I thought that if luck played such a big part in life I might just happen to land among the fortunate ones. To keep my chance alive I carried on the weight-training all summer with Colin Finch, who was an expert at it. Colin was actually another example of effort losing out to bad luck. He'd worked at his body all his adult life, and it looked great, but all that fine tuning had done very little for his soccer ability, which was the thing he most cared about. Colin's training schedules did me more good than they ever did him. He was like a great violin-maker who couldn't play the instrument.

The following season, minus Ruddock, the Foresters went back down the hill. Their gates dwindled, though Dad still came, once or twice bringing Terry, who by this time resembled him pretty closely in size and gloominess. Mum had never once watched me, and somehow I'd never expected her to. Without Alan's passes to run on to I wasn't the player I'd been the previous season, but I was physically that bit harder, and won enough possession and made or scored enough goals to keep my ambitions warm.

Just a year after Alan's knee went I had my big chance. Or if not big, small. Anyway, a chance. I'd scored a couple in a home match and was feeling good. In the club bar Eric Bourne came over to me with a smoothly dressed character in tow.

'Vincent, here's a gentleman would like a few words with you. Mr John Judd, manager of Stanborough Town.'

'Well done, Vincent,' said Judd. 'You had a very fair game.'

Before he'd even let go of my hand I knew that this was it. I was into League football for better or worse. But I could hardly keep from laughing. Judd was coming on like Matt Busby, Eric was shitting pins in his efforts to live up to the moment, and I was trying to shake hands with the air of a promising striker. We couldn't have tried harder if Stanborough had been high in the First Division instead of low in the Fourth. Judd chatted me up for ten minutes, darting little glances all over me, as though he was guessing my weight or counting my balls. Then he took me off for what he called a serious talk.

Over a meal at a steak house he sketched out a future for me. I tried to ask shrewd questions as we talked terms, but it was all sham. I'd have signed for nothing. I didn't care what sort of dump Stanborough might be; this was the new life I'd been hanging about for.

Judd came round to the flat afterwards, though I tried to fob him off. What with the surprise and the importance of the occasion Mum and Dad were in poor form. Judd put on another instalment of his act: 'We think we can do something for your Vincent, Mrs Gilpin, and we hope he might do something for us.' Mum let out a squawl or two of nervous laughter. Dad nodded a lot, saying repeatedly: 'Fair enough, Mr Judd. Fair enough.' In a business situation like this the three of us knew about as much as the babes in the fucking wood. Judd didn't know much more, but at least he had a performance to put on.

Within twenty-four hours Bourne and Judd had worked out a gentleman's agreement. I was to join Stanborough in the close season, and Coombe Forest would receive a modest fee.

Chapter 5

As I'd never lived alone and never been further north than Luton the idea of heading towards the Humber was quite intimidating. But when the time came to leave, what chiefly made me nervous was the possibility that I'd make nothing of myself, but come creeping home in a year or so like Ruddock from Villa. My life could be more or less decided in the next few months.

When I was signed Stanborough Town F.C. were going through a mediocre phase that had lasted about sixty years — in fact ever since they joined the Football League. They'd won nothing, and it had come to be reckoned a fair season for them if they avoided having to apply for re-election. By reading around in football magazines and annuals I found out more about their squad. The defence had played together for some years and weren't too bad, but the rest of the team came and went like the teachers at Mountford Hill — old players who were past it, and youngsters who never made it. They had one notable forward, Nick Hawthorne, who'd won a couple of Under-Twenty-One caps years before when he was with Sunderland. He'd only joined Stanborough when he was on his way down in the world through injury — having lost a cartilage or two — but had still cost them a fair sum. Buying him was one of the few daring gestures the club had ever made, and it had failed. It was like buying an old sports car: you might get a zippy performance out of him when he was in working order, but most of the time he was off the road.

Judd had been managing the club only since January, since when they'd risen from twenty-first place in the table to finish sixteenth. It wasn't a miracle, but it looked like progress. Stanborough was his first chance in League management after several years with non-League clubs. It was a stepping-stone in his career: he'd move on from it or lose his footing. What was certain was that he wouldn't stay. People didn't stay at Stanborough.

I swiftly made my mind up that I would be no exception to that rule. Before I saw the place I'd imagined carving out a steady little career in Stanborough, and helping to build something up. One look at the ground told me that you'd never build anything here. I'd never seen such a poor stadium. The outside was a patchwork of dirty bricks, warped planking and rusty corrugated iron — it was literally made of junk. Seen from the inside the one stand could have looked half respectable if the paint wasn't flaking off like dead skin. Even the terracing had weeds sprouting out of it. At the north end there was a great diagonal crack across it, and you could sense the grass roots and dandelion roots working underneath to lift off a quarter of the standing-room like a great concrete scab. The whole stadium had the look of an old station on a branch line soon to be closed down.

A town tends to get the football club it deserves, or can afford. Stanborough is a textile centre, down on its luck. It depressed me on my first visit before ever I'd seen the stadium. The buildings were blackened, and many a house or shop was boarded up. The air was thick with bad breath from the chemical factories. I remember walking the streets thinking that Stanborough was like the worst of home. If I'd knocked on any front door my Dad could have opened it in his shirt-sleeves. What could keep anyone in the place other than bad luck? As it turned out I was to spend two years with the club, but I never came to see the town as anything but a place to go through on my way to the ground. When I wanted a break I'd go to the coast, or drive south as far as Lincoln or Nottingham. But though the town depressed me it also gave me a new incentive: I had to succeed as a footballer if only to move on.

I have to mention, though I'm not proud of it, my last action in London, which was to ditch Karen. Once she heard I was going north her anxiety obviously increased, but she didn't like to push any direct questions about her future with me in case she got a negative answer. She just clutched my hand, stared at me like a faithful dog, made love with great passion and then silently cried. I wasn't up to it. For weeks I put off any explanations by saying we'd sort things out nearer the time, and finally I diddled her by pretending I was going a week later than I actually was. I made a special date with her for sorting things out on the evening of the day I was to leave. While she was waiting for me in Blunstone Park I was already in Stanborough. It felt bad to think of this, but luckily there were new experiences to distract my mind. I know all this sounds ugly, but there was nothing I could have said or done that would have made things easier for her. I couldn't do anything to help because I was off on a fresh start. If I'd still been tied up with Karen it wouldn't have *been* a fresh start.

In my first few weeks with the club I lay low, anxious not to make a prat of myself. I settled in fast. Thanks to my sessions with Colin Finch I was tough and fast, and could take the training in my stride. For sharpness and ball-control I was the equal of anyone there. If this was League football — even though it was the rough end of League football — I had the raw materials to make a career. By the end of September I was the outstanding player in the reserve side, obviously a prospect. Altogether I'd have thought things were going well, if I hadn't had Cyril Islip on my back.

Bringing Cyril in as trainer-coach had been Judd's one major move since taking over. It had been Cyril who had first watched me with Coombe Forest before Judd himself came down, so he obviously had an interest in me. His own career as a mid-field ball-winner had shown he was a hard little bugger. He'd been famous for shutting out class forwards by snappy tackling and yapping his defenders into position like a sheep-dog. Even though I'd watched him play several times as a kid his appearance took me by surprise. In his track-suit he looked no bigger than me, and with his turned-up nose, his mouth an inch open half the time and his little chin sloping back into his throat he was like a mouse in a cartoon film. In the changing-room he'd sit quiet, blinking about, but once out on the field he was a different man, so charged up with excitement he couldn't stay still for a second. Even his voice changed, getting higher and shriller. But the most extra-ordinary thing was his language. It wasn't that he swore — most footballers do. He used the dirty words of a little kid.

'Move yourselves!' he'd keep screaming. 'This is a training session, not a fartabout. You're piddling round like a pig's dick.'

I quickly became his chief target. At every step his shriek was in my ears. 'Make space, Vin! Come off him! Pull him wide! Make space, make space, make space!' Gradually his nagging got on my nerves. 'Go, Vin, Go! What a piss-pot! Move!' If I said anything back he'd yelp: 'No lip, Gilpin! You're here to work and learn, work and learn.' I'd have thought he had it in for me, but then coming off the training field he'd calm down fast, like a kettle coming off the boil, and be quite complimentary. 'Not bad this morning, Vin. Looking sharp.'

All this was fair enough, but later he got into a nasty groove of working me against Ed Freeman, one on one. Ed had been signed that summer, a meaty big defender, confident because he was so strong. Cyril repeatedly matched the two of us in a series of exercises. In particular he'd chip ball after ball to me in a marked space, where I had just Ed and the goalie to beat. He'd scream us on alternately: 'Take him, Ed! Flatten him! Quicker, Vin! Fight the fucker! Use your arms!' He was like the cheer-leader at a cock-fight.

After one of these sessions I said to Ed in the shower: 'This is bloody ridiculous. We're kicking each other to bits.'

Ed was smug: 'That's the game, Vin. You have to learn to take it.'

'But it's only practice. That mad little fucker's going to do for one of us.'

'It won't be me, Vince,' says Ed, wearing a silly grin, as though he'd put me down. I realised I'd have to start looking after myself.

Next day Islip was screeching us on again through the same routine. I went flat out not only to beat Freeman but to hurt him more than he hurt me. Twice I left him on his backside with a quick turn, but then he knocked the wind out of me, going for a header. I came back quick enough to win the next ball and crack Ed on the shin. Cyril was as happy as a kid with a lollie: 'That's it — piss on him!'

We had work-out after work-out along these lines, with Ed and I on the brink of maiming one another. Off the field we never spoke about it again, but I did at last have a word with Cyril himself. I must have caught him too soon after training, because he was on the boil again straight away.

'What? Are you a winger or a wanker? What d'you think you're getting paid for?'

'Am I being paid to get kicked?'

'You're being paid to learn not to get kicked.'

'I've got ways of my own —'

'Look, son, I don't give a dog's bollock for your ways. You're here to learn *my* ways.'

'But you were a midfield player — you had to go looking for the ball. I can lose a marker —'

'You'll lose him a fucking sight easier if he thinks you might whack him in the nuts.'

We'd reached the changing-room by then, and he began to simmer down.

'Soccer's about space. You find it or you make it. In the box you'll find bugger-all, so you *have* to make it. You got to be a battler, Vin, a ball of barbed wire. You got to use your knees and your nut and your elbows and your backside to grab half a yard. The defender uses his to stop you. You and Ed can sharpen each other like two scissor-blades.'

'But he's a central defender. I'm a winger.'

'We could be changing that.'

He went off, leaving me to think about this hint.

Cyril was unusual in that football was his only interest. He wasn't married and showed no awareness of women. He spent a fair bit of time sinking pints and talking soccer, but it was the talk that mattered to him, not the lager. He'd have been just as happy with Tizer. What he did with himself of an evening it was hard to imagine. For sheer lack of versatility he was in my dad's class.

It was simple to take the piss out of Cyril off the field, and no one did so more persistently than Nick Hawthorne. Nick kept several running gags going against Cyril, one of them being a rumour that he was illiterate. If the lads were talking about a newspaper article or a notice on the board he'd read it aloud for Cyril's benefit as though he was being tactful. Other times he'd talk tactics with him very seriously, getting more and more complicated till poor old Islip was lost. What was funny in these cases wasn't the joke itself, but the fact that Cyril could smell a joke in the air, like a fart, but didn't know what it was or who it was aimed at. He'd lick his lips and blink about, very unsure. You'd never think that here was a man who'd chopped some of the finest footballers of his day. If he ever did get suspicious he showed another of his peculiarities: rage somehow tightened his throat, so that he'd go to shout and actually let out a weaker sound that his normal speaking voice.

But when we were working the laugh wasn't usually on Cyril. For one thing he'd pushed the first team up to the middle of their division. For another, he was a tough, stringy little sod for his age. In training he still tackled like a rat-trap. Thinking things over I decided that he wasn't the tit he appeared. He sounded stupid because he only had childish words at his disposal to express his powerful feelings about the game. His advice could still be worth taking. By Christmas I had a clear edge on Freeman, being not only quicker but nastier.

John Judd spent little time with the reserve players, but he did call me in halfway through the season to say: 'I thought I'd have a word with you, Vincent. You've made some progress, and it hasn't passed unnoticed. All right, Vincent? It hasn't passed unnoticed.' As usual he spoke his lines carefully, as though we might be secretly televised.

With the move to Stanborough I'd had a chance to carve out a new kind of social life, but I didn't seem to have taken it. I joined in the chat, the jokes, the practical jokes at the club, but more out of politeness than enthusiasm. Away from the ground I'd see a bit of Vic Lowden or Roller Fagg, but that was about it. I wasn't being stand-offish: I just liked to have some life to myself. It was my London style all over again. But if I had no close friends I had numerous acquaintances. I liked to be on chatting terms with shop-keepers, waitresses, newspaper-sellers or the landlords of distant pubs. All my spare time I kept moving. I'd dip into a book, watch half a TV programme, have a swim at a local sports centre or drive out to the coast. I'd learned to drive and bought myself a banger.

There were a fair number of women in the general vicinity of the first-team squad, some getting passed on or passed round. One girl, in particular, had been servicing the whole back four. She should have been on the training staff. Not fancying this merry-go-round I could have been hard pressed for a bit of ecstasy, but the problem was solved, or brought under reasonable control, by a stroke of luck. I had digs in the northern suburbs, and happened to meet a woman of thirty-three, living in the same street, who shared my interests in this area. She was married to an up-market greengrocer whose work kept him out all day. I won't reveal her name, but I will mention her weight, which was nine stone twelve, only four pounds less than mine. We'd have made a great see-saw team. When I made her acquaintance I was like a drowning man clutching at a lilo. The strange thing about our relationship was that it was strictly confined to her house, which I approached by way of the back garden. We never once went out together. After Karen she seemed very easy-going. She laughed a lot, and served us big meals in bed.

As the season wore on I came to have the odd chat with Nick Hawthorne, who was something of a loner because the lads were put off him by his peculiar sense of humour, which didn't make anyone laugh and wasn't intended to. I joked back at him, and got on quite well on a sort of table-tennis basis.

'You have to be patient,' he told me. 'I don't start thinking I've lost my form just because I've had five or six poor seasons. I could play another ten years at Stanborough, and still only be forty-two.'

'Look at Stanley Matthews,' I said.

'Right. Almost as good at fifty as he'd been at forty-nine. Mind you, he wasn't playing for Stanborough.'

'What made you come here?'

'I thought I'd come bouncing back, following my first cartilage op. But I rolled sideways. Now I'm bunkered.'.

'But the team's going up in the world.'

'We'll be back. We've got a tradition to keep up.'

In the odd game Nick still showed flashes of brilliance, but even apart from his injuries and his inconsistency he was no real asset to the club. His attitude took the heart out of the lads. They came to believe that they weren't much good — which on the whole they weren't. I think it was Nick's way of protecting himself. He carried on as though nothing mattered much — not his own form, nor the team's results, nor even the game itself — the reason being that if nothing mattered then his own failure didn't matter, and he certainly thought of his own career as a failure. I quite liked him, but his attitude sickened me. It was a warning. I made my mind up that whatever happened I'd never cop out in that particular way — I'd have a go.

In the new year I was played as a striker for the first time, and led the reserves to six victories in nine games, scoring eight goals and laying on half a dozen others. Those were the bald facts, but for me those two months were a revelation, like the time when my body started growing in earnest. I wasn't just an improved player, I was a new player — a born-again striker. My great weakness, which was a tendency to die out of the game for long spells, was cured in one. With the ball regularly pumped at me I never had time to freeze, or even to think. It was play and run, play and run. Whenever we came forward I was in the action. Through this I made a great discovery about myself — I could play and play and never tire. It wasn't simply a matter of stamina or persistence: my speed and reflexes held up. I never lost concentration. My whole view of myself changed now I knew I had this extra gift. I suddenly realised that if I was given the service I could take any marker — wear him down, gut him and finally get through him. I went into every game confident. A bad first half wouldn't faze me. Sooner or later my man would start to falter. If I'd been a boxer I'd have been looking for the knock-out in the twelfth or thirteenth round.

A first-team chance had to come, and the immediate cause of it was one of Nick Hawthorne's many injuries. John Judd called me in to break the good news, and went on breaking it for twenty minutes. '. . . it's a big responsibility, but it's a big chance. I'll be frank with you, Vincent, this won't be a one-off. That wouldn't be fair on you and it wouldn't be fair on us. You'll have several first-team games before the season's out. You'll have a full chance to show us what you can do, and it's up to you to make the most of it.'

In fact I started the game on the bench. What I chiefly remember is seeing Cyril Islip's reactions at close quarters. He squealed at every turn of the play, quivering all over. When Ed Blackburn belted a free-kick against the cross-bar he leaped up yelping: 'Bum on it! Bum on it!' During a bad patch he sat back whimpering: 'Snot! Sheer snot!' As we went a goal down he slumped as though he'd been shot. They put me on for the second half, out on the left wing. It felt strange to be playing wide again, but I had a few good spasms. An equaliser came from the penalty-spot after I'd been tripped.

By the end of the season I'd played ten games, or parts of games, for the League side, every one of them on the wing. I scored a couple of goals and in general felt I wasn't doing too badly, but after my golden spell in the reserves I had some sense of losing ground. My anxieties were put to rest after the last match of the season, when Cyril Islip came to sit with me on the coach. He said: 'All right there, Vin, you've done a job in the first team, but we've not seen the best of you yet. You're not a winger. You're never a winger. Because why? Because you just play your own patch. You don't use the width. You don't look up. When you play your best is when you're boxed in. You don't mind a marker up your bum because you can tell which foot he's on without looking. You belong in the penalty-box. Next season we'll have you a striker — a full-time striker.'

Those few first-team games were enough to bring in a fan letter or two, mostly just requests for autographs. But one morning I found myself looking at a pageful of familiar writing:

'Dear Vincent,

I saw in the paper that you scored a goal on Saturday. You must be doing well. I expect you'll be surprised to hear from me after all this time. You must have thought you'd finished with me after you left me like that without a word. That was mean of you after all our time together, and I was very upset, but it isn't why I'm writing to you now.

Although I didn't know it then I was expecting a baby when you left, and on February 16th I gave birth to a son, Jonathan. He is a fine boy and doing well. I am bringing him up myself. Mum has been amazingly good about him.

At first I did not mean to tell you as you left me to face it all on my own, but now I think you should see him. A boy ought to know his own father. The football season must be nearly over. Can't you come to London and see us?

Write back soon,

With love from Karen'

The letter had an immediate effect on me: I had to go to the toilet. I knew the sort of feelings I ought to be having, but what I did feel was trapped. Here I was, after years of effort, out on my own and just beginning to make it, when Karen's letter comes like a tentacle, two hundred miles long, to clutch me by the balls.

She had to get an answer of some sort, or in a week or two

she could be knocking on the changing-room door. After a lot of walking and thinking I sent her a letter full of conscientious horse-shit. The news had come as a shock (that bit was true) and I was very sorry to find out that I'd left her in the lurch like that. Naturally I'd had no idea. But the truth was that I was now going out with a girl I was planning to marry. I was into a different life. It wouldn't be fair to any of us if I was to come to London now. I'd look forward to meeting my son one day, when he was older, but now I was living so far away it wouldn't be good for him to get too attached to me. If she was short of money, though, I'd certainly make a regular contribution. Meanwhile I wished her all the luck in the world, and hoped that one day she could make a fresh start with someone who deserved her. I can't recall the letter in full detail, because embarrassment fogs it out.

Karen's answer came pretty quick and pretty cold. If I had so little interest in my son then yes, I could at least contribute to his upkeep. The sum she asked for was about a quarter of what I earned, but I made arrangements with the bank immediately, glad to buy my way out of trouble.

By winning the last game of the season Stanborough were able to leap-frog over three other teams into tenth position. Judd told the local paper that we were going from strength to strength, which was pushing it, but at least there seemed to be a fair chance that we'd be in the promotion race the following year. With that prospect, and the knowledge that I was now recognised as a striker, I finished the season in good heart.

My problem was that I hardly knew how to pass the summer. I had two or three days at Beaufort, but didn't care for more, partly because it wasn't too frisky there, and partly because I kept thinking of Karen and the kid. For the rest of the holiday I retreated to the north-east, where I divided my time between sessions with the greengrocer's wife, exploring the coastal area and swimming in the North Sea.

After my high hopes for the club and for myself the following season proved frustrating. From the start I was a first team regular, playing as a striker alongside Ed Blackburn. The usual side was: Loveridge; Kellogg, Anstey, Reid, Brown; Lowden, Dunmore, Harrison; Hawthorne, Blackburn, Gilpin.

Thanks to Cyril Islip the back four were tough and well-organised, but we had no mid-field to speak of. Under any sort of pressure they disintegrated, leaving Nick, Ed and me to fend for ourselves. When we got some service the three of us managed some bright moments, but this happened all too rarely. There I was, sharp, aggressive, eager to learn, eager to play, but having no ball to play with. Most of the season we were just outside the promotion battle, because we were drawing too many of the matches that we should have won. I stuck in a few goals, and was winning some praise, but I felt that I was playing at about fifty per cent of my true capacity — never mind improving as I'd hoped.

But my career always moved in sudden jerks, and one of the biggest of these was to come at the very end of that season. The turning point was an away match at Hartford. The week before we'd blown our last real chance of promotion by losing at home. Three of the four top places were already booked; the fourth was between Hartford and Stanborough. But our chance looked purely theoretical. This was in the old days of two points for a win and one for a draw, and Hartford were already six points ahead of us, with both clubs having six games left to play. The statistics that mattered were:

	Played	Won	Drawn	Lost	Points
Hartford	40	19	11	10	49
Stanborough	40	14	15	11	43

Their goal average was way ahead of ours, so if they beat us they'd only need two points from their last five games — even if we won all ours. Earlier in the season they'd stuffed us 3—1 on our own ground, and they'd improved since then. Islip and Judd were naturally doing their best to gee us up, but they weren't getting through. Personally I was still glum as a slug from our defeat the week before.

Hartford kicked off like runaway horses. Within five minutes I knew we'd be pasted. Loveridge had made three wild saves, and Reid had kicked off the line. Blackburn and even Hawthorne were already back helping the defence, leaving me nothing to do but chase clearances. In the first forty minutes I'd run five miles and scarcely had a kick. But just before half-time Nick Hawthorne broke away on a throw-in, tricked the full-back, drew the centre-back, and flicked the ball inside for me to score from close in. We'd gone a goal up with our only shot of the half, and the crowd went suddenly quiet.

In the changing-room Cyril was dancing with excitement.

'You got 'em, lads. You got 'em by the pisser. Now swing on it.'

At the whistle they stampeded us again, forcing half a dozen corners. Our game was to hit them on the break — and after five minutes one came. Kellogg whammed the ball downfield, Blackburn got in a skewed back-header, and Nick Hawthorne was away again. He shook off his marker, side-stepped the centre-back and stabbed in a shot off the post. I couldn't believe it, and nor could the crowd. Two minutes later we were mounting another attack and Nick was chopped down. He took the kick himself, curling a high ball right across the area, and Gil Morris came out of nowhere to get in a header. The goalie pushed it out, but I ran it back over the line. The loudest noise was the Hartford defenders cursing each other. The game was over. We scored two more before the end, and I got both of them.

Afterwards the lads were more excited than I'd ever seen them — half pissed with success. John Judd kept saying: 'We can still go up. Well done Vince Gilpin. Well played Nicky Hawthorne. The door's still open.' It was — but only just. If Hartford could squeeze six points out of their remaining five games they'd wipe us out whatever we did. 'They won't make it,' Islip told everyone who'd listen. 'We've done them. Here's their next result: nought-nought. It'll be a nought-nought draw. They'll give away nothing but they'll get nothing. If we win Tuesday night we'll have 'em by the curlies.'

But the Tuesday game looked a tough one. We were

playing at Millwood, where Geoff Cowley had recently come in as player-manager and was dragging the club off the floor of the League by brute force. After looking stone dead at Christmas they were set to claw their way out of the re-election places. Cowley had done an Islip job on them, driving, cursing, organising. The difference was that, unlike Cyril, he was still in there kicking, at the heart of the defence. Few goals were being scored at Millwood, and few teams were winning points there. The consolation was that Hartford were due there two weeks after ourselves. If it was rough for us it would be rough for them.

On the Tuesday it pissed with rain. The windscreen wipers clicked double speed all the way to Millwood and we all sat quiet, wondering if the game would be called off. But the cloud thinned before the kick-off, and we squelched out on to a pitch like a marsh.

Cowley was famous as a good pro and a hard man. He'd broken a few bones in his time, including a couple of his own. But fresh from the Hartford match I fancied my chances, and was even hoping he'd take me rather than Ed Blackburn. He did. First goal-kick from our end and he was behind me saying: 'No hat-tricks tonight, son.' I had a good look at him. He wasn't that big, but he was a knotty, leathery, beat-up bugger, who'd taken knocks and stitches and would be hard to hurt. But what you first noticed about him was his thick black eyebrows — or rather, eyebrow, because it was one big one right across his forehead like a moustache. It helped to make him look dangerous. I gave him a grin, and said: 'Wait and see, Dad.' Next moment the ball was dropping our way, and his knee went into my back as we both went up. No free-kick. A little later I went past him on the left, but his follow-through took my rear leg. When Hawthorne got away Cowley slid him into touch so hard that he cracked into the fencing. Only ten minutes gone, but we were all plastered with mud. Cowley was using the conditions well. If his tackle missed the ball he slithered straight through his man as though he couldn't check his skid. The rest of his side showed the same spirit, clipping at Nick Hawthorne's shins till they sickened him. He soon stopped wanting the ball. Stanborough were starting to wilt in the heavy going. It was becoming a game like the previous one — our defence against the opposing attack. But after Hartford I couldn't get it out of my head that we could win all the same — that we could make our own luck. Near half-time I turned Cowley and almost got Ed Blackburn through. Next minute I turned him again and he cut me down, but I was up before the pain hit me to lift the free-kick just over the cross-bar. I fell as I struck the ball, and Cowley fell too, banging the wind out of me. I got up slowly and moved shakily for a minute or so to put him off his guard. Next high ball I reared back at him in the best Islip style, and lifted my head into his jaw. He went down limp, and I was half scared at what I'd done, but the ref said nothing. Cowley had to have treatment before he staggered up with his face white under his big black eyebrow, and blood trickling out of his mouth. Just as the half-time whistle went he got his studs into my thigh, so that I came off bleeding myself. But the score in goals was still 0—0.

In the second half the rain came gusting down again, and great puddles shone under the flood-lights. The ball wouldn't run or bounce. Ground passes stuck in the mud and high kicks died where they dropped. To make any headway you had to fight and chase and hack the ball to the wings where the grass was thicker. We were soon back on the ropes again. The lads were trying hard, but they hadn't the drive and bite of the other lot. Cowley had his side under the whip, shouting the moves, waving and cursing them on. Our defence held, but conceded corner after corner. From one of these, about a quarter of an hour from the end the ball squirted clear and their left-back hit a long shot that skidded through everyone into the far corner. That was that. As we went back for the re-start you could see we were done. Our lads were weary and drenched and muddy and knew their season was finished. But Cowley had a grin on him as wide as his black eyebrow, and that made my guts burn. I'd get at that fucker. Col Reid, our skipper, had gone quiet, so I yelled us on. I'd thought I was sold myself, but I got some new charge of force, running for everything, calling for everything. Cowley and I tangled again, chasing a long ball, and I took a thick lip — but I was back on my feet before he was. I thought: 'I can do him. I can do this cunt. I can do this team.' Lowden came forward after winning a tackle, and I screamed for a pass, pelting through at inside-right. Cowley was at me as it came, but I burst clear of his tackle and was away. As the keeper dashed out I squared the ball hard into the six-yard sludge, and Ed Blackburn slogged it home.

There were only six or seven minutes left to go, but the goal had given us the lift we needed, and we had our best spell of the game. At last our midfield got forward, hacking some passes through the wet mud. I could sense Cowley's legs going and never stopped moving, churning right, checking, wheeling left, sniffing back water like a channel-swimmer. But my brain was clear and I still had a bit in hand. As Cyril Islip was on his feet, shrieking that there was a minute to go, I took a pass from Dunmore, somewhere near the penalty-spot, sent Cowley left, switched right and dug the wet white ball high into the top corner.

At the whistle Cowley shook hands and said: 'Well played, son,' and I couldn't speak. I was so shattered I could hardly struggle off the pitch. Cyril greeted us with the news that his forecast had come true: Hartford had drawn 0—0. The other lads started shouting and laughing, but I never raised a squeak. Those last ten minutes had emptied me. In the coach Islip came to me and said: 'You did it on your own, son. Fantastic. You did it on your own.'

He was right. This wasn't just the best performance I'd ever given, it was a new dimension, a new gear. I felt like a 1,500 metre runner who'd just knocked ten seconds off his best time. I sat in the coach half numb with exhaustion, but thinking: 'If I play like that I can go anywhere.'

We won our last four matches comfortably. Hartford lost at Millwood, but would have just held us off if they'd won their last game, away from home. Since they managed only a draw we were promoted by a single point, and they stayed down.

Our late burst had shocked the whole town to life. The last game of the season, that clinched us promotion, attracted the club's biggest gate for six years. When the Hartford result came through the crowd poured on to the pitch singing and cheering and grinning. The whole team had to come out in the stand to give them a wave, and there were speeches from the Manager and the Chairman. It was amazing to me, the happiness we'd caused. John Judd and I had become local heroes overnight. I had mixed feelings myself, but Juddy loved it — loved seeing his picture everywhere and being asked to explain his methods. He had a favourite line for the media: 'When I came to Stanborough I promised to put the club on the map inside three years. I think I can say I've kept my promise.' He and Cyril were given new contracts, and all the first-team players were offered improved terms — especially myself. There were plans to repair and re-decorate the stadium in keeping with the club's new status. But I couldn't forget that all the changes looked back to ten fierce minutes in the mud at Millwood. What a lottery the game was! The best you could do was fight for a hopeful ticket.

For the first time in my career the newspapers were pouring it on:

'The boy has improved out of sight. He could make it all the way to the England team.' That's the verdict of coach Cyril Islip on 22-year-old Vin Gilpin, whose goal-scoring feats took Stanborough past Hartford and into the Third Division in an amazing sprint finish to the season. What's the secret of this pint-sized striker, who has set the whole town alight in his first full season in the first team? Wily old campaigner Islip thinks it's mostly in the mind. 'Vince is quick and hard and has two good feet. But the great thing is his mental attitude. He's always willing to work and learn and improve his game, and out on the park he never gives up. With Vince up front you're always in with a shout.'

Gilpin himself takes a cautious view of his success. 'I've worked hard for it, but it could still be a flash in the pan. The real test will be whether I keep knocking them in next season.'

If he does, then the striker who tucked away nine goals in his last six games could be on his way to a scoring record. But will it be for Stanborough? Already there are signs that the big clubs could be jostling for the services of this wiry, tireless striker, currently the hottest property in the Fourth Division. But his services won't come cheap. 'I'll fight every inch of the way to keep Vincent at Stanborough,' says Manager John Judd. 'He's central to my plans for next season.'

The truth was that for all my ambitions I wouldn't have minded hanging on for a bit. My success had been too short and sudden. I wanted time to get familiar with it. Another half-season or so at Stanborough would have suited me. But the matter seemed to be out of my hands. I had to read the papers each day to find out what might be happening to me. Seven or eight clubs were supposed to be chasing me if the journalists were to be believed, including Derby, Coventry and Sheffield Wednesday. 'Wednesday?' I thought. 'A Second Division club? Fucking nerve!' It was hard not to be taken in by all the praise slopping about. My reputation was rising day by day without my kicking a ball.

To clear my head I took a week in London, arriving on a Monday afternoon. It was a surprise visit, but I didn't doubt I'd be welcome. Since I still had a front-door key I went straight in, not really expecting to find anyone at home. The flat smelt the same as ever: floor polish, fried bacon and a faint whiff of cat. I was on my way to the kitchen to make some tea when I heard some sounds from the main bedroom.

'Anyone at home?' I called, thinking Dad might be off sick.

'Is that you, Vincent?' came my mum's voice, a bit breathless. 'I'll be out in a minute. I was having a lie down.'

'Right,' I said, and banged the kitchen door, but nipped softly into Terry's room, which was next to hers. Squinting out along the connecting balcony at the back of the flats I soon saw some middle-aged bloke scramble out of her window and scoot off down the stairs. By the time Mum came through I was back in the kitchen with the kettle on the gas.

'I was having a lie-down,' she said. 'I've had a nasty head-ache. Well, Vin, what a surprise!'

'Sorry to wake you,' I said, laughing inside my head.

She was watching me to see whether I'd guessed anything,

but I'm good at hiding my thoughts. I got her some tea, she gradually relaxed as I nattered on about soccer. When the old man came in, around six, he was so pleased to see me that he half smiled. I felt sorry for the poor old bugger, with his bed being used while he was working. Coleman the cat had grown even stouter, and walked heavily. If you'd fitted a bleeper to its ear to track its movements you'd have found that it lived its whole life in a very restricted area, just as Dad did. Its balls had gone, of course, so it had only a few quiet pleasures left — a meal, a crap and a stroll.

I kept wondering who it was that had been shafting Mum, but could pick up no clues. From one point of view it was a giggle, but from another I was taken aback. Here she was at forty-four still putting herself about and finding takers. Was my dad getting any, or had he given up like the cat? The whole business of sex seemed a bit of a farce. Did it muck you around and tickle you up all the way to the Darby and Joan club?

It was a quiet week. The flat was empty all day because Mum was working full-time and Terry had moved out to live in Canning Town. I sat around a lot of the time remembering what it had been like to stay home from school. There was nothing much I wanted to do. I chatted with some of the lads I knew from the estate, and paid a visit to the timber-yard, which looked and smelt the same as ever. More than once I was tempted to visit Karen, or spy on her, but I didn't risk it. Most evenings Terry came over, and he and Dad showed me off at the pub. It never felt right. Dad couldn't think of enough to say, and Terry said too much, carrying on as though we'd been great mates and shared many a laugh. By now he looked ten years older than me, but he was happier than he had been, with a job in a furniture factory and a regular girl-friend. Mum was as chirpy as ever, but her mind often seemed to be elsewhere — probably with the bloke who was humping her. I thought I should clear out and leave the flat empty for her.

One way and another that visit depressed me. What a narrow life! All the time I'd been away this had been going on day after day, unchanged. What kept them all going? Even when Mum stole a little treat for herself there was someone to barge in and interrupt it. This was the time when my ideas of money and pleasure first began to catch up with my soccer ambitions. I didn't want to live like this and now I didn't have to. I remember lying in the bath and stroking my thighs, glad they were strong enough to get me out of Beaufort.

Back at Stanborough things looked little better, especially as the greengrocer had had the nerve to take his wife off on holiday. There was no place for me in the town in the close season. Plenty of people were stuck there and had reason to be stuck there. They were working in factories or shops. They had homes there, and relatives in nearby houses. I had no such ties. Why should I hang about the place when I had it in me to get out, and to be well paid for doing so?

Judd had been away, but one day in June he called me to his office. I hadn't been in the stadium for some time, and was amazed at the changes. The front entrance had been repainted and they were working inside on the fencing and the stands. I scarcely knew the place. All this out of six winning games. Because of my mood at the time all the changes said one thing: goals mean money.

When Judd told me that City were making inquiries I knew I was on my way before he'd finished the sentence. To be fair to him he tried to be fair to me, pointing out the disadvantages of the move. City might have been League champions twice in five years, but that meant there was hot competition for places. They had four good strikers already. It could be a long time before I got a chance. The likelihood was that I'd spend the first year in the Central League side. They were famous for bringing on young players, but they also discarded a fair few.

None of this touched me. I knew that of the four strikers Byers was old and on the blink, Sheard was just a promising teen-ager with only half a dozen first-team appearances to his credit. As against the other two, Orr and Gorman, I'd take my chance. In a way I was hardly even bothering to think that clearly. In the words of the old saying: I needed a new challenge. If I could get the Stanborough ground re-painted I could break into the City first team — and the big money and the women and the continental holidays. I saw Ken Carlton, the City manager, the next morning, and had signed by the end of the week at a fee about fifteen times my dad's annual pay.

I was excited, of course, but the whole thing seemed unreal. People like me didn't sign for City. Now that I was leaving Stanborough it seemed no time since I'd first arrived. The lads being all on holiday I had few goodbyes to say. I did have a word with Cyril Islip, who told me: 'Keep your nose in front, Vin. Always get in first.' As regards the greengrocer's wife I had half a mind to slip away on the quiet, as I'd done from London, but it wasn't really on, what with the transfer news all over the papers. In any case I reckoned she'd be more philosophical than Karen, and so it turned out.

'Oh, I'll miss you, Vincent,' she said. 'We've got used to each other's ways, and you've given me many a laugh.'

That wasn't what I'd hoped to be remembered by. Funnily enough she'd had no interest in football, and had never seen me play. She liked to be comfortable, and knew how to look after herself. I reckoned she'd soon find another bed-mate. We both took it for granted that we wouldn't meet again. Stanborough wasn't the sort of place you'd go back to if you'd once got clear of it.

Chapter 6

In dreams you can perform strange feats with no fear, no effort, no explanation. Often in my sleep I've found myself flying, riding a thousand feet of air like a glider, with open fields stretching for miles below me. Once I hovered over the Stanborough stadium, calm and motionless, hearing the shouts of the crowd, and watching twenty-two tiny players, including myself, scuttle and collide on the little green rectangle of the pitch.

In memory my first season with City was as simple as such a dream. I never struggled, never questioned. New opportunities of all kinds came and came, like passes dropped into my stride. It wasn't that I could do no wrong — I had some poor games and did some daft things — but I felt no anxiety. If a chance was lost there'd soon be another.

Keith Gorman being injured, I got my first-team chance in the opening game of the season, up front alongside Bill Byers. With a career to play for, and a forty-thousand crowd to face, I should have been petrified, but I felt no more than my normal pre-match fears. Partly I was thinking that at worst I'd look better than Byers. Bill was thirty-three and bulky with it, and had been out for months with ankle problems. Pre-season he'd laboured and bluffed his way through training, moaning all the time. When I was in sprints with him he gasped: 'Take it easy, boy — there's no prizes.' On a long run he'd dodge behind a tree and take the shortest way home. At the end of each session he slumped back groaning: 'It's not worth it. It can't be worth it.' I was amazed he'd made the team ahead of Ian Orr. Before the match I watched him strap up each ankle in turn, taking so much time and care he could have been fitting on artificial feet.

I knew he'd be useless, and I was wrong. The whole game was uncanny because everything went so easily. I felt like a replacement part in a smooth-running machine. City were a quality side, of course — all internationals bar me and Gary Pargeter — and most of them had been playing together several seasons. But still more important was method and commitment. They never stopped working, never stopped calling the moves. It was pass and run, pass and run. There was always support for the man on the ball — always something on. Bill Byers was amazing. He couldn't sprint, but that hardly mattered, because his anticipation and his timing were so good. Now he was in a real match there was no pissing about. He was always in where it hurt, laying off the ball with head, boot or chest, so well balanced that defenders seemed to bounce off him. With this service I couldn't go far wrong. I did nothing that spectacular — it was mostly one-touch stuff and short dashes — but I was always useful, always contributing. Bill and I seemed to read each other by instinct, and were always half a yard ahead. Their central defenders were tackling shadows. Gary Pargeter gave us an early lead, breaking through from mid-field, and later I laid on a goal for Byers and he made one for me, to give us a 3—0 win. I came off the field not elated, but confident, knowing I could think fast enough, move fast enough and fight hard enough to hold my place. I was a First Division striker.

Over the next few weeks I was to need that confidence, because although the team was winning and my form held I wasn't getting much encouragement. It was a tradition at City that the club came first: there were no stars. No young player was going to be allowed to fancy he was hot shit because he'd stubbed in a goal or two. It was an oldish side.

Chandler, Byers and Arnold were all over thirty, and most of the others were twenty-eight, twenty-nine, married men who'd been settled in the team and the town for a fair time, and seen players come and go. They'd accept me as long as I did a job on the park, but they weren't going to fly any flags. The media might have made more fuss if they hadn't been taken up with Gary Pargeter, who was in freak form, or with Bill Byers's come-back. When I got written up at all, it was for my uncanny understanding with Bill, and words like 'chemistry' and 'telepathy' were used. In proportion to the goals I was scoring I got very little star treatment. But the situation suited me. If the papers had raved I might have started to think too hard about my game, and wonder what I was doing right. Instead I went smoothly on, week after week, like a player in a dream, passing and moving, passing and moving, always near the centre of a pattern.

What might have woken me was the moment when I dived at a centre from Hickmott and a West Brom defender volleyed my head. A broken nose and a line of stitches kept me out for a couple of weeks, and let Keith Gorman in, but somehow I wasn't too perturbed. Sure enough City were promptly shunted out of the League Cup and lost a home League match. Gorman hadn't even played that badly, but he and Pat Arnold were dropped, Bryant and I came in, and the next result was a 2—0 away win. What I remember most from that fortnight was the sight in a mirror of my busted nose wobbling free in the middle of my face. Half concussed, I still had to laugh. The doc could have given me a new personality by welding it into a new position, but he stuck it back where it had always been, and I picked up where I'd left off. The other lads seemed friendlier now I'd had my face kicked open for the good of the side. I only missed two more games all season.

Even now I was scoring every other week I was able to strike a balance between being famous and being unknown. Naturally I had to surface quite often. The club arranged a fair few charity activities, visiting hospitals and orphanages and so forth which I enjoyed. I'll chat to anyone for ten minutes when there's no commitment. Near the stadium I'd be buzzed by autograph hunters. To keep my end up I'd developed a sharp signature, with the capital V and G meeting in a great hooked point, like a vulture's beak. Away from the ground I was rarely recognised, my face being so ordinary that it's as good as a mask. With my small eyes and mouth, and colourless hair, I can pass for invisible. I recall that I once got inside a moderate bird by telling her I was Vince Gilpin, and then got shot of her by saying I wasn't. But that was a couple of years later.

As against the year before I was better off, better dressed and driving a faster car. But despite these changes, and the fact that the town was so much bigger, I pretty soon found I was putting together the same sort of life I'd led at Stanborough. It was strange to see it take shape, just as before, as though it was a finger-print. I thought: 'Sod me, this must be what I'm like!' Again I had no close friends at the club. As the youngest member of the first-team squad I found it easy to stay on the edge of things. Provided I held my place I didn't give a fart about being one of the boys. Away from football I was back to my old ways of poking round in odd districts of the town, or in the villages round about, making a scattering of acquaintances over a wide area. It came to be that wherever I walked or drove there was someone I could drop in on or have a word with. There'd be an old lady who was knitting me a sweater to order, or a bloke who was fitting a sun-roof on the car. Partly this prowling was just for sociability, but in a way it was connected with the great quest for cunt. I was in a dilemma at this time about getting my end away, having found no worthy successor to the greengrocer's wife. In any case, I was after something less cosy and more thrilling — more like the early days with Karen. But after what had happened with Karen I was a bit wary, especially as the club took a hard line on bad publicity. It wouldn't do to hit the wrong headline: ' "City star raped me," claims pregnant teenager.' On the other hand I wasn't the night-club type, and bought sex didn't seem appetising. In general City liked their players to be married and settled, and most of them were, but what I'd seen and heard of these relationships hadn't greatly appealed to me. Perhaps I just didn't fancy being married to a footballer's wife.

Luckily some temporary relief became available. I was lodging with the Kitchener family, out in the Oakwood district, and through Mrs Kitchener's son Graham, an ardent City supporter a year or two older than myself, met one or two female fans with a warm concern for the physical well-being of a promising player. Involvement was limited on both sides. For me it was like signing an autograph with my dick.

It was through one of these contacts, a girl I'll call Maureen, that I had an unexpected encounter. We were battering away in her flat one evening, and between rounds she nipped out to get us a take-away meal. When I heard a key in the front door I thought she must be back, and came out in the passage to meet her, bollock naked. The person who stood gaping at me, however, was not Maureen but Pat Arnold, our Scottish international mid-field player.

'Hallo Pat,' I said, speaking cheerily but feeling cautious. Here was Arnold with his own key, for Christ's sake. Perhaps he always came round on odd-numbered dates and had got out of sequence. Perhaps he really fancied Maureen, and would take a poke at me. On the other hand Maureen wasn't the type of girl anyone really fancied, and besides, Pat was married.

He was pretty taken aback himself. Normally he was a lively talker, but all he managed now was 'Focken' hell!'

As he spoke Maureen appeared with a bag of hot food, and stopped in the doorway, amazed. Dead silence. Maureen's face had changed colour. Pat looked at her and looked back at me, totally disconcerted. Then the joke of it got to me, and I started laughing. Maureen glared, which made me laugh more, and then Pat started up. Suddenly it was like the two of us against Maureen. It isn't often you laugh naked in mixed company: I was so tickled that I cackled all my strength away, and had to hang on to the door-post to stay on my feet.

Maureen threw down the bag and shouted at Pat: 'Get out! Get out of here!'

70

'I'm away,' he said weakly, still trying to get hold of himself. 'I'll leave you the key.'

He chucked it to me and edged his way out past Maureen. When the door had closed I could still hear his laughter echoing back up the stairs.

'You can get out too!' said Maureen to me, looking savage. But I was able to talk her round, and we had a fair evening, considering. I even got her to see the funny side of Pat's visit, but she didn't see it for long, because she shook me off over the next week or so, and took up with a medical student.

What came out of the episode as far as I was concerned had to do with Pat Arnold. Pat was just past his best as a player, and had been squeezed out of the League side by Pargeter, but he was a class performer with a dozen Scottish caps to his credit, and was still in the first-team squad. He was handsome as a film-star — black hair, blue eyes, white teeth and a straight nose. The game had left no scars on him. He'd have looked perfect for a gigolo, except that he had this little jaunty grin on him, as though he couldn't take anything seriously, including himself.

The morning after the encounter he gave me a sharp glance or two in training, but said nothing. I wasn't the type to make a story out of what had happened, but he couldn't have known that. Afterwards he asked me to join him for a drink, and drove me in his BMW to a pub on the edge of town, where we were the only two customers in the bar.

'I'm sorry about last night,' he said. 'It was a surprise for all concerned.'

'Maureen said you were an old friend.'

'Right. But it was a few months since I last paid my respects. I'd no right to charge in.'

'No harm done. She's not too sensitive.'

'Parts of her are. Or so I recollect.'

'Ohmygod! Ohmygod!' I gabbled, to show I knew what he meant.

'Does she still stay that? And claw the cheeks of your bum?'

We sat grinning over the lager like two blokes who'd found out by chance that they'd climbed the same mountain.

Maureen was no Everest, but it was still interesting to meet a fellow-enthusiast.

'You can be a quick talker,' said Pat, 'but I've noticed that you give focken' little away.'

He was right. I'd always been one to keep quiet about myself, and since coming to City as the youngest member of the first-team squad I'd been extra cautious, to avoid being made a prat of. It obviously suited Pat that I could keep my trap shut. Suddenly I was sorry for him: poor married fucker goes out for a frisk, doesn't get it, and finds himself at the mercy of the young jock who's taken his place. Many of the lads talked cunt by the hour, but Pat wasn't one of them. He was thought of as a family man.

'I'll keep you out of the papers,' I said. 'Even a married man needs to break out once in a while.'

'Once in a while?' said Pat, looking as if he'd bitten a lemon. 'Once in a while?'

'All right, twice in a while.' I was puzzled by his reaction.

'You're talking as though I'm focken' de*crepit*.' He seemed seriously offended. 'I'm thirty-two years old. Carlton tells me I've lost half a yard, and the focker could be right. But what I've lost on the park I've sure as hell gained in the bedroom. And when I say "bedroom" I include parked car, railway carriage, garden shed, alleyway, shop doorway, field, wood and 'phone box.'

'Tuck it away,' I said, unimpressed. 'You sound like Colin Cox or Barry Warner.'

'Cox and Warner? I can't have made myself *clear*. They're novices. Boasters. For them it's no more than sta*tistics*. When did you ever hear me talk in that strain?' He pushed his glass aside and leaned closer. 'I'll tell you something I've told no one else, and I'm telling you because you can keep quiet. I am the most promiscuous bastard in the Club. I am the most promiscuous bastard you ever *saw*. I screw all the time, but I don't talk about it. And I don't talk about it because I take it seriously.'

He *was* serious, too. He could have been talking about his religion — a devout fornicator.

'You didn't look so serious last night.'

'Last night?' He allowed a little grin. 'Last night was daft. But you can have a laugh about sex and it's still serious. There's nothing like it. There is nothing *like* it.'

'I'd agree with that,' I said, serious myself. 'But how do you manage when you've got a family?'

He was pleased — as though I'd asked a good question. 'That's the extra challenge. Like beating the off-side trap. You've to work to small margins. That's half the point of it, working to small margins.' He was fired up, like a stamp-collector, talking about stamps. 'For me that's the essence of it. Judgment and risk. Last night was piss-poor judgment and a focken' stupid risk. For me a good, keen risk — a well-*chosen* risk — sharpens up the whole fuck.'

He proceeded to tell me about his sex life in considerable detail. All I had to do was put in the occasional word, like a TV interviewer nudging along a willing talker. But true to his word he wasn't giving me a body count. The emphasis was on the trouble he went to and the chances he took. He'd screwed his mother-in-law in her own garden shed during a week-end visit. The night City lost the Cup Final he had the Chairman's niece in the club's London hotel. About once a quarter he made it with Ken Carlton's secretary.

'Bugger me!' I said. 'She's old enough to be your mother.'

'Nothing like. She's old enough to be *your* mother, maybe. But that's not the point. It's the unexpectedness. Who'd think that tweed skirt had a cunt inside it? She's a rare specimen.'

I still couldn't get over it. 'Is she the oldest you've had?'

'No.' Handsome grin. 'Not by a few years. But I prefer not to go further on that one.'

'Do you fancy old women?'

'Only if they've a leg missing. No, you're not with me. Look, the sexual act is located in your prick, right? At least, that's where it finishes. But if it starts there, too, you may as well settle for a wank. You have to involve your *mind*. You need an *interest* — a special *interest*. It could be almost anything — your first Chinese girl, the first time you've done it in a cemetery. The little engine can pull a different train each time.'

I listened to all he said with considerable interest, partly because it's natural to be interested in sexual matters, and partly because he was really relishing his own story. It was already in words in his mind, and his blue eyes lit up as he spoke it. I was his chosen audience, and he gave me a performance.

In the weeks that followed, Pat never returned to the subject again, or even talked to me any more than to the other lads. But the conversation stayed in my mind, fretting a little. Pat's sex-life was barmy, but he had some passion in it. I was reminded how I'd felt in the early days with Karen. I'd lost that excitement. As it happened my various outlets, including Maureen, were all cut off for one reason or another by about January, and I was reduced to wrist-work to keep the wolf from the door. Around this time I won my first England Under-23 cap, to add to the indignity. It didn't seem right, an England striker wanking.

Still, I hoped that Pat was getting the women he needed, because the team was doing well and he wasn't even making substitute. By Christmas we were three points clear at the top of the table. We faltered in the New Year, losing a couple of League games, and skidding out of the F.A. Cup on a frozen pitch at Deepdale. But we rallied again, and were back in the lead by the end of February.

That same February I met Claire. It was at a beauty contest — not a serious one, but a local affair for some charity. There was a lot of chance about our meeting: Claire only entered at the last minute, for a joke, and I came on the panel of judges as a substitute for Bill Byers, who had flu. My vote helped Claire into third place. I managed a chat and a drink after the contest, but only just twisted a date out of her. She was only nineteen and had never heard of me before, obviously knowing no more about football than I did about ballet-dancing.

But she must have made some inquiries, because by the time I took her out she realised I was reasonably famous. As a result she was altogether heartier and chatted freely. I pieced her situation together over a meal. Her family had not long moved in from the country, so she didn't yet have many friends. Her father was a Post Office engineer, and she was working in the fabrics department of a big store. She'd had a boy-friend in the country, but was now shaking him off.

Across a table, with a Babycham pepping her bloodstream, Claire looked even better than she had in the competition. Her eyes shone and she laughed often. There was something daring in her manner, as though she'd made up her mind to try and take me on. She flicked out several cheeky little questions. Didn't I get bored, kicking a ball about every day? Wasn't it like being a professional schoolboy, but without the lessons? I joked back, but touched her up with a hint or two about the kind of money that had been paid for me and the kind of money I was earning. She dressed well and moved well, but pretty as she was her appearance was slightly comical — chiefly because her neat face seemed too small for her mass of brown hair. There was only a year between her and Maureen, but Maureen could have been thirty whereas Claire was like a school-girl. She hadn't yet fixed on a particular grown-up style, for her hair or anything else. But she would, she soon would. She had spark and energy; she was out to make something of herself. I liked that. The recklessness in her manner was a sort of compliment. She was thinking that I just might be her great chance, and that if so she wasn't going to bottle out. Already that first night out I was thinking I could be on to something. We were both ambitious, both late developers. Maybe we could carve out a way of life that was a little bit unusual. So I wasn't dismayed that I failed to get to close quarters that night — and for several weeks to come. She wasn't going to be just a quick lay, and I was interested enough to take a bit of time and trouble. Between football and Claire the winter passed nicely.

One Saturday evening I was getting away after a match when a voice called my name and I looked up to see Harvey, one and a quarter times his former build, grinning with delight.

'Hallo, Harv. I thought you were in the army?'

'I am.'

'Then why aren't you off killing someone?'

'It's Saturday, isn't it?'

He let out his old hee-haw laugh, showing twenty-six of his teeth, and obviously pleased as hell to see me. If we'd been a couple of dogs he'd have been wagging his tail and sniffing my bum. And I'd probably have had a sniff at his. The sight of him made me feel that I hadn't had a close friend in a long time.

I took him off for a drink. It was strange talking to him after a seven or eight year gap, with him a soldier and me a footballer. The army must have suited him, against all the odds, because he looked better and had more force to him; but his basic personality hadn't changed. He was full of good humour, and kept laughing, as though he had thoughts he couldn't get into words. It was amazing to me how many old school-mates he had news of — Chesterman, Powney, Perez, Gibb. Once or twice he'd actually revisited the school itself, an idea that would never have occurred to me. I was so concerned with pushing forward I never had time to look over my shoulder.

'It's unbelievable,' he kept saying. 'You used to be just a quick little tich. Where did you find those thighs?'

He was now a sergeant, or something of the sort, and had been newly posted to a camp about seventy miles away. Though it was hardly credible to me — because in the old days you could hardly have trusted him in a dodgem car — he'd been trained as a driver of heavy vehicles, and consequently got around a bit. Down in Dorset he'd run across Alan Ruddock, who was living in a village with a wife and two kids, and working with a building firm. 'Christ!' I thought, 'the time's going by.'

I was glad to meet Harv, and looked to meet him again — but he left me uneasy. For years we'd sat together, eaten together, horsed around together, peed together, and now here I was laps ahead of him in money and prospects, all because I was handy with a football. There was no sense in it.

At Easter I met Claire's parents. A week later, the night City clinched the First Division championship, I turned the occasion to advantage by screwing her for the first time. She proved a bit shy, but made the right sort of noises, if in a slightly uncertain way, and told me how much better at it I was than her country boy-friend, the only other character she'd tried it with. Luckily she asked few questions about my own past, so Karen's name was never mentioned, still less Jonathan's. Incidentally, I'd upped the allowance I sent them in proportion to my higher pay at City, but had had no word of acknowledgement.

Most changes in life came about gradually, but you can notice them quite suddenly. Near the end of the season I was in Stockholm with the England Under-23 side, playing well and scoring a goal. The whole season had gone so smoothly for me as to be ridiculous, but to a surprising extent I'd taken my good luck for granted. Up to a point I thought I'd earned it. For years I'd pedalled away uphill, sweating and straining. It seemed only fair that I'd reached a down-gradient and could free-wheel for a spell. But that night in Sweden I thought over what had been happening and what might come next. I couldn't sleep, so sat staring out of the hotel window at the lighted Stockholm street. It was the only time I'd been abroad since the school trip to Paris. I said to myself: 'You can do it. Ten years at the top — travel, fame, money. You can build yourself a good life. But here you are still living like an apprentice. What about a house? What about a wife and family?' Which meant, of course: 'What about Claire?' By the time I got on the plane next day I'd pretty well made up my mind to marry her in the summer.

Back home, though, I didn't feel so keen — anyway, not keen enough to say the word. It gradually came to me that I wasn't feeling anything much about anything. The game in Stockholm had been my last high-point of the season. Now the title was won a lot of the spring had gone out of the City side and out of my own game. In May we went on a little tour in the Middle East, playing a few friendlies in fierce heat against mediocre opposition. Despite the conditions the lads enjoyed themselves, larking around, knocking the ball about, and still doing enough to win. I stood out from the rest by being useless. Somehow I couldn't get into the spirit of the tour at all. On and off the pitch I was like a zombie.

Back home Ken Carlton called me into his office.

'You were rubbish on tour,' he said.

'I know.'

'Well, don't worry about it. You're the sort who can only play for real. Anyway, you've had a good season.'

I had. I'd scored twenty-one goals. Byers had got twenty-three, but I'd been carrying him for the last quarter of the season when he'd run out of steam. Carlton wasn't lavish with his praise, but that was his style. He liked to come on tough.

'You'll be wanting to see me about money,' he said. 'Let's keep it short. We can work out the details later, but I'll double what you've been getting.'

I pretended to think about it, but had no thoughts. 'That'll do me,' I said.

'You know what's wrong with you?' asked Carlton. 'You're knackered. Burnt up. You've done your share of running, but that's not it. It's the concentration. You concentrate so hard on your game that you've drained yourself. You need a break. Go off for a few weeks and forget about the game. Have a few drinks and a few birds. Unwind yourself. I'll wind you up again in July.'

As it turned out that was the best conversation I ever had with Carlton. I knew he was right: from every point of view I could do with a breather. Within a week I was off on a package tour to Majorca. I'd told Claire I was following the manager's orders, and she accepted that explanation, which seemed a good sign.

Actually that trip showed how abnormal I'd become. There was nowhere I particularly wanted to go and no one I particularly wanted to go with, given that I was still trying to sort out my views on Claire. Lots of footballers take holidays in Majorca, so I thought it would sound all right for me to go there. That was all. I got on the plane in some fear, wondering who I'd meet, how I'd get on, how I'd cope with the language.

I need never have worried. Someone recognised me the first night, and after that I could do no wrong. It was simple. People are pleased as hell if someone whose name is in the papers buys them a beer. I'd always liked acquaintances, and here I was picking up twenty or thirty at cut rates.

As a bonus I found myself a new hobby that almost became an obsession. I bought a mask, a snorkel and frog feet, and spent hours swimming round the bay below the hotel, staring down into the under-water world. I loved that. There were fishes of all colours and sizes — swarms of tiny ones, all pointed in the same direction, wicked big loners, lurking near the sea-bed, and strange ugly ones, with little arms as well as fins. Some looked luminous, as though they had a filament shining inside. A few fat, slow ones lingered by the rocks, seeming to graze off the fur of them like cattle. In places there were forests of weed, swaying in the current so that you might catch the gleam of a fish nosing through the greenery. I gazed and gazed on these peaceful scenes, sucking in air from above through my little plastic pipe. I didn't know what any of the fish were called, and I didn't want to know. It was enough for me to watch them go their rounds, drifting or darting. Sometimes one would hang so near that I was sure I could grab him. But as I reached out a great magnified hand, off he'd flick, never bothered, always in space. On the sea-floor I'd see the odd shell, gleaming with mother of pearl, and often I dived deep down with bursting ear-drums to bring one up. They didn't look anything great when you got them out, but that wasn't the point.

Almost without effort on my part I found myself humping away with a woman in her thirties. She was in wonderful shape and very brown, but her skin felt dry as paper from the sun. Night after night she worked over my body with a good deal of relish, but she expected a similar return from me. We performed well together without much conversation. In a way it was more like tennis than sex.

I arrived home much refreshed. Pre-season training came

easy. Claire seemed to sense that I might be moving closer. She was too smart to say anything direct, but tried the odd testing hint, like a judo wrestler shifting his grip as he manoeuvres for a throw. The decisive move, when it came, was a needless slip on my part. I was being inverviewed on local TV, and along the way the following exchange occurred:

INTERVIEWER: How about girl-friends?

GILPIN: How about them?

INTERVIEWER: Any special one?

GILPIN: (*off-balance*) Yes. You could say there is.

INTERVIEWER: Could we soon be reading about Vince Gilpin's wedding?

GILPIN: (*buggered*): Well, you never know . . .

There was no excuse. I could have said: 'It's early days' or 'Mind your own fucking business', but I didn't. Claire and her parents had all heard the interview, and now my balls were in the mincer they began to turn the handle. The wedding took place in September. My parents came up with Terry, both very pleased, though Dad had to be towed through the ceremony and the party like a broken-down lorry. I'd half feared that Karen might show up to denounce me, but there was no word from her, even after the wedding photographs had appeared in the papers. Bill Byers was best man, more through public expectation than because I knew him well. I didn't know anybody that well, including Claire.

Chapter 7

My downfall at City took me completely by surprise. One moment I'd lost my footing, the next I'd dropped clean through the floor.

At the time I got married the team was playing only moderately well, because we'd had a crop of injuries. Port, Warner, Bryant and Hickmott had all been out at different times, forcing Ken Carlton to do a lot of re-shuffling between midfield and defence. He'd even had to put Pat Arnold at left-back for a couple of games. But we were still lying seventh or eighth, and looking to push for the top again when we had a settled side. Although I wasn't scoring often I was playing pretty well, and felt confident that the goals would soon start coming. When a knock on the ankle put me out for a match or two I was honestly more bothered for the team than for myself, never dreaming that my place could be at risk.

I might have read the signals sooner if my attention hadn't been distracted by domestic affairs. Marriage had given me a second part to play. Claire and I had moved into a house we'd bought on the Coombe Road estate: three bedrooms, gas central heating, garage, gardens front and rear laid to lawn. Personally I'd always thought of a house as simply a brick box for living in — you needed certain basic facilities, such as water, heat and light, and the rest was just make-up. But that wasn't how Claire saw it. The move filled her with excitement. She took everything as a challenge. There were walls to paint or paper, so you had to teach yourself interior decoration. There were windows to shut off, so you had to make curtains. Didn't we have a patch of land the size of a tennis-court? That meant gardening. Claire had given up her job at the department store, so she had plenty of time for these activities. Moreover she was pretty good at them, knowing a lot about curtains and carpets and how to match colours. Since she worked so hard on the house I thought I ought to help her, though I had no talent for decoration and we could easily have afforded to pay skilled men to do the work. Under her orders I painted doors and window-frames, cork-tiled the bathroom floor and dug out some flower-beds, all with reasonable success. Married life was taking up all the time left over from football. I began to think I must be settling down.

The day I was passed fit Carlton called me in.

'Gary Pargeter's down with mumps,' he said. 'I'll be playing you in midfield on Saturday.'

I wasn't keen, but I didn't object. Keith Gorman hadn't done badly in my place, and the squad was still plagued with injuries. We all had to pitch in. Against Everton on the Saturday I only half knew what I was up to, but I worked like an ant. Carlton said: 'OK, Vince. You never stopped trying.'

After that piss-poor compliment I was surprised to find myself in midfield again the week after. Again I ran my legs off, but this time played a bit as well, making one of the goals in our 2—0 win. I wasn't a natural tackler or marker, but I could chase and harry and pass. As I walked off the pitch I felt pretty pleased with my performance even before Carlton gave me a big thumbs up sign. But the good cheer washed away with the mud, and I saw how neatly I was knackered. Gorman and Byers had done well up front. If I played badly in midfield I could be dropped, and if I played all right I could be stuck there. It was no use looking for sympathy. Several players had been shifted around since the start of the season, and in any case City had a strong tradition of putting the squad before the individual. Gorman and Arnold hadn't moaned when they'd lost their places the previous season. So it wasn't for me to come the wanker after a couple of games out of position.

Two or three weeks later Gary Pargeter was fit again, and it looked as though Carlton would have to choose between me and Gorman as partner to Byers. But coincidentally Hickmott broke a toe, so Chris Cox was pulled back to take his place and I was switched to the left of midfield to do Chris's usual job. I was still expected to do my share of chasing, but I had to be ready to run wide, make ground down the wing and get over a few crosses. In fact I was more or less back where I'd started at Stanborough. For a week or two I did reasonably, but always felt frustrated. My best skills just weren't being used. Meanwhile Gorman and Byers were both getting on the score-sheet. I could read the writing on the shit-house wall: when Hickmott was fit Chris Cox would move back to midfield and Gilpin's bum would hit the bench.

By the end of November it happened. Ken Carlton had a word with me to soften the blow:

'You'll likely be sub for a match or two. You've shown me what you can do, Vince. I know I can slot you in up front or in midfield, depending what we need.'

'Great!' I thought. 'Now I'm a fucking utility man.' But all I said was 'OK Boss.'

Over the next six weeks I never got more than a fragment of a game. Carlton slapped me in like Polyfilla wherever there was a hole. Only once, when Byers had concussed himself, did I have a chance of half an hour up front, and then I played like a turd through over-trying. It was hard not to be anxious. What chiefly kept me going was the thought that sooner or later Byers or Gorman would take a knock and I'd have a fair chance to win back my rightful place.

It happened in the third week of December, like a Christmas present: Gorman did a groin muscle in training. That was on a Tuesday. An article in the local paper two days later set things up nicely. As it happened it was by Larry Hellman, a mate of mine:

Keith Gorman's injury casts a cloud over City's championship prospects but it could be a cloud with a silver lining. The stage is set for a renewal of the Byers-Gilpin partnership that did so much to clinch last year's title. Given their cruel luck with injuries this season City have done well to cling to sixth place. Gorman has done a more than useful job alongside Bill Byers, but it may be that a touch of the old Gilpin magic in the six-yard box is what City now need to lift them back to the top of the table.

When the side was posted on the Friday morning I was again down as sub. Playing at number 10 was Robin Sheard, a nineteen-year old who'd been scoring a goal or two for the reserves. I couldn't believe it. My first thought was to go straight to Carlton. My second thought was to wait till after the game. Next day City won 3—1. As Sheard capped a fair game with a good goal, and I didn't even get on the pitch, the delay had done me no favours. I spent a bad Sunday thinking things over.

By nature I'd never been a moaner: I'd worked for my chances in the past, and I'd do so again. I knew Sheard must have been picked because Carlton wanted a versatile sub. But then I thought 'Yes: I'm so fucking versatile I've lost my identity.' I looked again at the Sunday papers:

There were murmurings when manager Carlton replaced the injured Keith Gorman with the inexperienced Robin Sheard. The obvious choice had been Vince Gilpin, last season's goal-scoring hero. But the doubters were silenced by Sheard's performance in City's 3—1 over Forest. The nineteen-year-old showed the poise of a future international as he set up a goal for Pargeter and cracked in a brilliant half-volley on his own account. No wonder Ken Carlton was willing to part with Ian Orr in the close season. On this form Sheard could become a first-team fixture — and City would still have Gilpin and Gorman in reserve . . .

There was plenty more like that. What it all meant was that I was now City's fourth-choice striker. After years of climbing the ladder I was slipping back down a snake. Sod being a utility player. I knew Cyril Islip had been right: as a serious footballer I was a striker or nothing. I'd have to talk to Carlton and make that clear.

But by the time I went to see him on the Monday I was a bit cooler. Things change fast in soccer: I could bounce back as quick as I'd dropped out. Even Bill Byers couldn't last forever. Perhaps in a month's time I'd be playing alongside Sheard. What I'd be saying to Carlton I wasn't sure, but I certainly didn't mean to whine or make threats. Basically it was a matter of getting my worries off my chest. I could have put a little soothing speech in his mouth that would have kept me quiet for weeks. But our conversation went as follows:

'OK, son, what can I do for you?'

'I've been wondering about my prospects here . . .'

'No need to wonder. You're on a three-year contract.'

'I came here as a striker —'

'You came here as a footballer, son. And you'll play where I put you.'

He sat sticking out his black jaw like some tough-guy sergeant in a war film. His image, which he worked at, had always been 'hard but fair': this was the hard bit. I just had to piss in his eye. I said: 'Even if it's playing with myself on the bench?'

That reddened him. He snapped: 'Watch your lip, lad. And just remember you play where you're bloody put. If you don't like it you can find another club.'

'I don't like it.'

'What?'

'I said I don't like it.'

I spoke very casually, and it was that needled him, more than the actual words.

'Are you asking for a transfer?'

'Yes.'

He jumped up in a fury, shouting: 'Right, my lad, you go on the list. You go on the bloody list. At the club's pleasure and the club's good time you can sod off.'

'Make it quick,' I said, and walked out.

The other side of the door I couldn't believe what had happened. I'd gone in with a worry and come out three minutes later on the transfer list. The conversation had accelerated like a Porsche and shot straight into a brick wall.

That was Christmas week, and it was an eerie time. I said nothing to anyone about what had happened, and waited for the next move — but there wasn't one. No word at the club, nothing in the papers. I began to think the whole incident had been forgotten — but I couldn't count on it, and wasn't sure I wanted it forgotten. All right, I didn't want a transfer. But I also didn't fancy the idea that Carlton was just humouring me, like a kid with a tantrum. I wasn't going to let things lie. If he didn't break the silence pretty soon, then I would. Funnily enough I wasn't too depressed now there was a row brewing. In fact I was larking around as I'd used to at school, full of daft wisecracks. On Christmas Day, when Claire's family came round, I was positively uproarious.

On the Saturday, to my own surprise, I was down as sub for the match at Portman Road. I came on for the last half hour, when Bryant turned an ankle, and gave my best-ever performance in midfield, flicking on pass after pass and making Gorman's goal to nick us a draw we didn't deserve. Carlton said 'Good game, Vince,' without much expression in his voice. On the journey home I felt pretty good but also reckless. As I played cards I was thinking: 'Pretty fair, Vin. You can do it for this lot or any other. If Carlton can't see it, get on your bike.'

More than once Claire had done something noticeable to the house while I was playing away, in order to surprise me when I got back. Not that she ever did surprise me much, because I wasn't that interested, but I went through the motions. When I got back from Ipswich I found she'd had new carpets and curtains fitted in the bedroom, and hung a pair of pictures on the wall. I praised what she'd done, and went to sleep in fair spirits.

But I woke early in quite a different mood, as though my brain had caught a chill in the night. Yes, I'd played all right at Portman Road, but it had been in midfield. Carlton would want to keep me, but he'd want to keep me as a utility man. And I wasn't a utility man: I was a striker. I'd have a second chat with Carlton, but unless he'd changed his views I really would have to go. I lay in the pink light from the new curtains and looked round the room. We'd redecorated it completely, every surface, wood or plaster. And in a week or two the house could be back on the market because I'd be off to Newcastle or Southampton. The thought made me gloomy, but then made me laugh. I laughed so hard I woke up Claire.

'What's funny?' she asked, still half asleep.

'Nothing. I'm just having a morning laugh.'

Since our marriage Claire had come to a number of City's home matches, but she still knew nothing about the game. To her I was successful because I was a City player; she hardly registered whether I was in the team or on the bench, and I said little about the matter. Now I wondered whether to make a long speech beginning: 'I've always seen myself as a striker, but Carlton . . .'. But I knew it was hopeless. We didn't talk like that. Our relationship was based on me being famous and cracking jokes. Anyway, she wouldn't know what I was talking about. For her soccer was twenty-two men chasing and kicking a ball. She cared nothing about tactics and positions. Then I thought that in a day or two I might *have* to try and explain — and tell her we'd have to flog her beloved house. That set me laughing again. In the end I fucked her without a word, and got up to make some tea.

The Sunday papers cheered me a bit: they all had a few kind words about my part in the Ipswich game. Carlton was quoted as saying: 'If Vince Gilpin hadn't made something out of nothing we'd have come away empty-handed.' I liked him saying that. Making something out of nothing was my speciality. But how often could I do it from midfield?

When I went in to see Carlton next morning he looked friendlier. His first words were: 'I thought you might be back.'

'You thought right then.'

'Been having some second thoughts?'

'Not about being a striker.'

'Look, son,' he said. 'I'm not keen to lose you. Why should I be? I brought you here in the first place. And you've done a job for us.'

I said nothing, waiting to see how far he'd go.

'I should have had a word with you when I picked Robin Sheard. I had reasons for picking him which were none of your business — but I should have had a word with you.'

'To say what?'

'To say you're still a valued member of the squad. Have you got that clear?'

He was offering me a little craggy smile, and it pissed me off. I knew his type — I knew the drill. Rough-house, bully-boy stuff, and then a little glint of a heart of gold. I've never bought that kind of con.

'What I haven't got clear,' I said, 'is whether you see me as a striker or a dogsbody?'

'Both,' he said, hard again.

'I knocked in a fair few goals last season.'

'You should have done, the service you were getting.'

'Are you saying anyone could have done it?'

'I'm saying you'd find it a bloody sight harder with another club.'

'Another club might play me up front.'

'They might, son. And you might not get a kick.' He let this one sink in, and then took a very reasonable tone. 'You think about it, Vince, like you did last week. You've got a wife and a house to worry about now. You're playing for the League champions — the most successful side in the country. You're in the first-team squad and you're making good money. Take my word, son: when you've been in the game a year or two longer you'll learn not to bugger about with good luck. Many a footballer's lost his bread and butter because he was looking for jam on it. Don't be one of those, Vince. Don't be a mug.'

I knew he was making sense, but I hated his manner. I'm always likely to do something daft rather than knuckle under to a know-all. Carlton was a smug bugger whose advice I didn't want. But I was still calm enough to hesitate. I came back to my main point.

'I'm a striker.'

Carlton must have thought from my voice that he had me going, because he immediately came on strong:

'Right, son. But come the crunch, which would you rather be: a utility player with City or a striker with Crapheap United?'

As that was a question I'd already been asking myself I was able to give an immediate answer, and a cocky grin along with it.

'A striker with Crapheap United.'

Ken hated me grinning — he always had. He snapped: 'Then that's it, son. If that's how you feel you can put in a written transfer request. So get out and think it over.'

He was angry all right, but his expression told me that he was sure he'd called my bluff. I bought a pad at a newsagent's near the ground and wrote out the transfer request over a glass of lager, signing it with a good vicious hook where the V met the G. Carlton was out when I went back, so I left the letter with his secretary and went straight off to give Larry Hellman an exclusive.

As it happened Claire was out that night, visiting her mother. Alone in the fresh-painted house we'd soon have to quit I worked up a strange, nervy mood. Any move from City looked like a move downwards. My best soccer season could be behind me. I sank a couple of scotches — rare for me, because I'm no drinker — and kept wandering from room to room. There was nothing on the television that could hold my attention. I had a long bath and ate three oranges in it, and afterwards stood on my head for a spell, with my bollocks dangling upside-down.

Next morning at breakfast I passed Claire the paper with the back page uppermost:

GILPIN SET TO GO

City's hopes of retaining their First Division title took a jolt yesterday when Under-23 international Vince Gilpin asked for a transfer. Gilpin, a bargain-buy from Stanborough and a goal-scoring sensation last season has been operating in a midfield role lately, and spending a lot of time on the subs' bench. The change in his fortunes dates from last September when he was side-lined with an ankle injury. Keith Gorman took advantage of the opportunity to renew his old partnership with Bill Byers, doing enough to hold his place when Gilpin was fit again. There were no complaints from Vince, who filled in energetically in midfield as City struggled with a spate of minor injuries. But when Gorman himself took a knock it was young Robin Sheard who got the call to play up front — and the teenager has responded with a couple of sparkling performances. Small wonder that Gilpin has doubts about his future when he sees Sheard and Byers in possession and Gorman waiting in the wings. Like Ian Orr, who found himself in a similar situation last season, he has opted to look for goal-scoring opportunities elsewhere.

But he took his decision more in sorrow than in anger. 'Ken Carlton has to do what he thinks best for the club,' Vince told me. 'I accept that. I didn't mind being switched around midfield when City had problems. But if I'm not even the second-choice striker then it's time I was on my way. In the long run I have to see myself as a goal-scorer.'

Manager Carlton was not available for comment last night. The likelihood is that he will want to hold Gilpin to his three-year contract which still has eighteen months to run. But if Vince does go on the list there will be no lack of offers for this quick, hard, elusive striker.

'What does it mean?' said Claire, looking at the first sentence or two in amazement. 'What does it *mean*?'

She gradually began to find out as she read the rest of the article. All the life went out of her face. It suddenly struck me that nothing very disagreeable had ever happened to her before.

'Why didn't you tell me?' she asked. 'Why didn't you ever talk about it?'

It was a good question that I couldn't find much of an answer for.

'We'll have to move,' she said. 'We'll have to sell the house. After all that work.' She was crying already.

'It's rough,' I said, not really bothered.

The pennies were dropping one by one. 'We might go hundreds of miles . . .'

90

'Anywhere in the First Division.'

'Then what about Mum and Dad?'

'They'll stay here, won't they? We can still visit them. What about *my* Mum and Dad?'

Before a row could get going the phone rang for the first of many times that day.

It signalled the beginning of a long, bad spell — longer and worse than I'd ever imagined. When you read about a soccer transfer it seems simple: 'Bertie Bloggs yesterday signed for Arsenal at a fee of £300,000.' But behind the announcement can be hours of talking and quarrelling with wives, in-laws, managers and accountants, none of them fully clear what's going on. I never knew the full story of my own transfer, and I don't think anyone else did. As far as I can guess Ken Carlton wanted to keep me, but on his own terms. He thought I might give in if he delayed long enough. On the other hand if I was really set on going he could get a tidy fee for me and strengthen the side at the back, where it was beginning to look slow. To keep the options open he gave nothing away as to which clubs, if any, were showing interest. Once again I was reduced to reading the papers to keep up with my own life-story. If I was to believe all I read half the clubs in the First Division had made inquiries — but there was little sign of follow–through.

The weeks went by, and as a footballer I was only firing on two cylinders. Carlton used me as sub a few times, and I had a couple of matches in the Central League, but the life had gone out of my play. You can't keep your edge as a striker without competitive practice. Just as a boxer can get ring-rusty I was six-yard-box-rusty. At home we hadn't the heart to do anything more in the decorating line, so sat round without much to say.

It was March before I signed for Oldfield in exchange for a six-figure fee and a teenage full-back. If I hadn't been desperate to get away by then I'd have had mixed feelings about the move. Oldfield was a good example of a club that always finished fifteenth in the First Division. After fighting their way up through the League they'd got so high, but couldn't seem to get higher. They had a good stadium, a good youth policy, a good Board of Directors — but the fans were still waiting for the pay-off. If you wanted to criticise the club you'd ask: 'What have they ever won?' If you were praising it you'd say it was the club of the future — but without mentioning a particular year. It had always been a well-managed club, which meant, among other things, that very little had been spent on new signings. I was the nearest approach to a star that they'd ever invested in, and as such I was supposed to lead the way to the silverware. It was a great chance or a great responsibility, depending how you looked at it.

At the time I left City were out of the F.A. Cup and down to eighth in the League. I'd have felt worse if they were doing better. Carlton shook hands without much zest, but managed a 'Good luck, son'. Other good-byes were also pretty brief — I'd been drifting out of touch with lads in the first-team squad. The one exception came when Pat Arnold drove me out to the pub where we'd talked before. I was surprised at the invitation, because we'd not had more than the odd casual chat since our previous visit.

'So you're on your way,' he said, as we drove. 'I'm moving myself — to the Third Division.'

I was amazed, because I'd heard nothing and Pat had been having a good run in the first team.

'It'll be official in a day or two. Player-coach at Belstone. A new chapter in my career.'

'Are you pleased about it?'

'Focken' delirious.'

In the pub he talked of this and that, but grinned to himself as though his mind was elsewhere. Funny how your thoughts can show in your mouth.

'Why are you moving?' I asked — and knew at once that I'd hit the wavelength.

'Fear.' He had a quick glance round, but the bar was almost empty. 'The truth is that I've fucked myself into a corner.'

'What's that supposed to mean?'

Pat leaned forward, fixing me with his blue eyes. 'I get up in the morning and open the bedroom curtains. I'm greeted with a wave from the next-door garden — a friendly *wave*. It's Chrissie Holland, a good friend of my wife. I've been knocking her off these past three months. I take the dog for a walk and there's her husband off to the station. 'Morning, Pat.' 'Morning, Tom.' I go to the training-ground and in the showers I'm standing dick to dick with Reg Simmons —'

'Reggie Simmons?'

'I poked his good lady a fortnight ago.'

'Sod me!'

'Three afternoons a week I pick up my daughter from school. Kerry Arnold, aged eight. I've fucked her form teacher, Miss Walters.'

He took a drink, looking over his glass to see what I was thinking. But my face rarely shows much expression. If anything I felt envious, but I said: 'You've been living like a madman.'

'I don't disagree. That's why I'm getting out.'

'Why Sheila Simmons? Did you have it in for Reg?'

'Not at *all*. Reg is a mate of mine. You have to remember what I told you: a man needs an *interest* to sharpen his prick. I could fancy screwing a nun, but it wouldn't be to spite the focken' *Pope*.'

'Maybe not. But would Reggie Simmons buy that argument? If everyone carried on like you we'd have chaos.'

'But they don't. That's the whole focken' *point*. They don't. The reason being that they don't find the *pleasure* in sexual intercourse that I do. People vary in their physical feelings. Take Doug Chandler. He regularly has his teeth fixed — he has them *filled* — with no focken' injection. And that's not courage. It happens to be the fact that he has highly insensitive teeth. It's the way he's *made*. Now my prick is the opposite of Doug Chandler's teeth. It needs special treatment.'

'Fucking getting it, too, by the sound of things. You'll need to ease off now you're a coach.'

'You're right. I'm going to start being mature. Or maybe just more cautious.'

'Why did you tell me all this?'

'Ach, you're leaving, like myself. Anyway —' He stopped to chew on an idea. 'Anyway, take a spy. A secret agent. There he is in Moscow working his balls off nicking top secret files. He's got everyone fooled. Naturally he's hells pleased with himself. He looks at his face in the shaving mirror and thinks 'I'm a focken' *marvel*. No bugger suspects me.' But just the same he'd love a spectator — just one spectator to prove what was happening. You're my spectator. After all, we were thrown together. Have you seen much of Maureen lately?'

'Married man,' I said. 'Under house arrest.'

'How are you finding marriage?'

I played the safe ball: 'It's all right.'

He thought this over, watching me and smiling. The grin always took your eye because it seemed to be produced by his own thoughts rather than aimed at someone else.

'It *is* all right. That's what's focken' *wrong* with it. You want a bit extra. You want a sur*prise* now and then. That's human nature.'

'Then why isn't everyone at it all the time?'

'Because they also want a quiet life — a secure life. It's easier to make do with *Playboy* and one off the wrist. People settle down. It's the first stage of dying.'

'That's my old man,' I said. 'But not my old woman,' I thought.

Pat drank some lager very slowly, as if it was turning his thoughts like a water-wheel.

'You need some *colour* in life. Take Miss Walters, the school-teacher. Thirty-four, divorced, living with her mother. Then one winter her body is regularly penetrated by a veteran international footballer. That's an interesting thing to happen. Even if she hates me in the end it's something to remember. She's had a colourful *experience*.'

'Can't you have a colourful marriage?'

'To start with, maybe. They tend to turn black and white. The trouble with women — *one* of the troubles with women —

94

is that they get sex mixed in their minds with other activities, such as having children.'

'Or setting up house,' I thought.

By the end of the week Pat and I had both left the town. But again the conversation with him lingered in my mind like a kitchen smell. Without fully knowing it he must have confided in me because he sensed that I had the temperament, or was in the mood, to pay attention. I'd been noticing over the six months of marriage that what really turned Claire on — turned her full on — wasn't me, or anything I did, but talking about the house, or the garden, or clothes, or cars. In a basic way I'd misjudged her. One of the things I'd really liked about her was her freshness and liveliness. Compared with the players' wives I'd met she seemed so much more eager. But since then I'd come to realise what she was eager *for* — it was to be more like the women I found boring. She'd changed her style of clothes and had half her hair cut off, so that she looked pretty much like any footballer's wife. And she'd put most of her energy and emotion into tarting up the house and buying gear to put in it. I'd sometimes thought that a real kick for her would be having it off with the dish-washer.

Claire's discontent at leaving the beloved house had been softened by the excitement of the transfer. She'd been the centre of attention to family and friends, and Verney, the Oldfield manager, had chatted her up a streak. Before I'd kicked a ball for the new club she was leafing through stuff from the Oldfield estate agents, choosing how she'd spend fifty or sixty thousand quid. At her age I'd been washing down lorries for Ferris Clark.

Chapter 8

With the new season less than a week away hopes are running high at Piper Road. Improved form last spring took the Swallows to tenth spot — their highest ever League placing. After years of patient team-building Oldfield could at last emerge as a force to be reckoned with in the championship struggle.

Manager Sam Verney has taken some stick in the past for the club's failure to hit the headlines. But at the start of what could be a make-or-break season for him he is cautiously optimistic. 'It's taken a bit of time,' he told me, 'but we're nearly there. This could be Oldfield's year. Our youngsters came on a ton last season. If we can find a little more consistency and just knock in that extra goal or two, we can challenge the best.'

Key figure in that vital goal-scoring department will be Vincent Gilpin, signed in March for a club record fee, but yet to show his true form. Three goals in twelve games last season wasn't much to crow about, as Gilpin himself is quick to acknowledge. Why the poor start? Vince is reluctant to make excuses, but his first few weeks at Oldfield can't have come easy. 'It was months since I'd played up front,' he recalls, 'so I wasn't as sharp as I should have been. And it took me a bit of time to adjust to a different style of play.' Vince also had his problems off the field, living out of a suitcase in a local hotel and snatching the odd day whenever he could to visit his wife Claire, still 150 miles away in their former home.

Now all this is behind him. He and Claire are comfortably

installed in their newly-bought house on the edge of town. The pre-season signs are that Vince has regained his old sharpness and come to terms with his new team-mates. A promising tour of Portugal brought the Swallows three wins out of three, with a Gilpin goal in every game. There could hardly be better news for Sam Verney and the Piper Road faithful. It is five years now since Oldfield clambered out of the Second Division. The fans are hungry for success, hungry for goals, hungry for star quality. Vince Gilpin could provide all three.

The *Chronicle* report was accurate rather than true. Oldfield had squeaked tenth place on goal average by winning their last game of the season. If we'd lost it we'd have dropped to sixteenth. Our victories in Portugal had been against sides I'd never heard of — they could have been scratch teams of grape-traders or mule-drivers. We'd played well enough, but hadn't been tested. On the personal level it wasn't the separation from Claire that had bothered me in the spring, but having to spend so much time visiting her when I could have been staking out new territory and making a few acquaintances. I still didn't feel I belonged to the town.

The compliments in the article may have been well meant, but to me they just spelt more responsibility. It was right that the team was nearly there — but I didn't relish being the clever bugger who was supposed to take them the rest of the way. Sam Verney wanted to keep all of us under pressure — especially himself and me — because that summer he felt the squad was ripe. It was a mixture of youngsters who'd come up through the youth scheme and veterans bought on the cheap. The right-back was eleven years older than his partner, and the goalkeeper's deputy was young enough to be his son. But most of the young lads had had at least a couple of sessions of First Division experience by then. The senior players weren't looking bad, but in the nature of things one or two of them would soon be on the blink. We all knew that if the team was to come good it would have to be soon. But we had it in us. There was ability in the side. Dave Alley, who played alongside me, Mick Smith and Andy Weaver all had pace and courage and fair close control. Roy Wheel, in midfield, looked better still. Put together the best fragments of his game and you'd have a better player than Gary Pargeter, who played in the same position for England. The trick was to find out what was holding the fragments apart. Something in his mind? Something in his temperament? It seemed just a matter of pressing the right switch. You'd have said the same about the team as a whole. In practice, or on tour, we could hit a fast, clever rhythm for fifteen minutes at a stretch, backing up and switching the play by instinct, always a pass ahead of the opposition. But then we'd somehow get out of step and lose the momentum. Usually what threw us was frustration. If we scored when we were on song we'd likely stay on song. Goals would whip us forward — and I was supposed to be scorer-in-chief.

As such, I was Sam Verney's gamble — his one gamble ever. Without attracting much publicity he'd won himself a reputation in the game as a youth coach, a team builder, a good man with a shoe-string budget. But he wanted more. He wanted a top-six team — a trophy-winning team. Having put together a useful squad that could fight and run and read one another's game he'd found himself still a piece short, because the ball wasn't hitting the net. I was the missing piece — and he'd broken the bank to get me.

That August I was nervier than I'd ever been. After my performances of the previous spring I hadn't many excuses left. Physically I shouldn't have needed any — I was as quick and hard as I'd ever been. But the responsibility was getting to me. With City I'd in a way been playing for myself. If I'd lost form then Gorman or someone would have taken my place and the team could have chuntered on without me. Oldfield didn't have those resources. I had to come good so that the team would come good and so that the world would see that Sam Verney hadn't wasted the club's money.

I'd have felt better if Sam himself hadn't seemed so tense. From what I heard at the club he'd been a comfortable character in the past, hard to upset. But now he'd set himself a challenge: at forty-five he was going for broke. The strain showed in his flesh. He had the pouchy, small-eyed face of a man with a hangover, and easily took on a look of misery or defeat. I liked Sam, but I didn't care for his appearance. As his one great gamble I needed to believe that I'd been backed by a winner, and most of the time he didn't look like one.

A good start could have done wonders for both of us — and we nearly got one. Oldfield drew their first match away, 1—1, and I made the goal. Mid-week we drew 0—0 at home, but on the Saturday we won 2—0, and I scored a beauty. Three days later we snatched another away draw, to be unbeaten after four matches. Then we did lose — but it was at Old Trafford, and only by a doubtful penalty.

Altogether the players weren't feeling too bad. We'd had at least one fair spell in every match, and never lost our concentration. I wasn't on form yet myself, but I was only just off it, making chances but snatching at them. One more goal would set me up nicely. The only person who seemed edgy was Sam himself, whose cheeks sagged a bit more for each point we dropped. After we'd drawn two more games, without my scoring, the local press was still trotting out Sam's cliché: 'This could be Oldfield's year.' At our best we looked poised to shoot up the table.

Between games, incidentally, I was being kept busy in the new home, where Claire had quickly set about replacing every wall-paper and carpet. We were back where we'd been the previous autumn, bollock-deep in fabric samples and colour charts. Claire went at the redecoration with some animal instinct, like a bird lining its nest with mud, or a badger stuffing its burrow with straw (if that's what a badger does). This being her second go she had more experience and more daring. I did a bit of painting, under strict instructions, but couldn't work up much motivation.

Home to Leeds we played our best football of the season, and I had my best-ever game for the club. Dave Alley gave us the lead in the first half, after I'd carved the opening, and early in the second I headed home Roy Wheel's centre. But my goal was disallowed for some daft reason, and in the last twenty minutes Leeds got back into the game because Roderick was injured. The equaliser came two minutes from the end, and our lads trudged off feeling pretty bad. Verney was almost too choked to talk to us.

A week later we lost at West Brom, the consolation for me being my second goal of the season. With three changes all we could manage the following Saturday was yet another draw — our sixth in nine matches. By this time my morale was low. I'd begun to think that it wasn't an accident that I'd not been scoring. Instead of using me as a spearhead the team had somehow absorbed me into its general style. Sam Verney should have seen what was going wrong and done something about it, but by this time he wasn't thinking straight. He was treating a home draw as a defeat and an away draw as a victory we'd let slip. Although he didn't rant and rave his anxiety was infecting the whole squad like flu. Through the media he kept apologising to the fans as though we were in the relegation zone instead of the middle of the table. Later we learned that the club Chairman, Ted Hardiman, had been getting on his back, but my guess is that Sam would have cracked even without Ted's assistance.

Obviously the lack of a win was making us all itchy. After tying 1—1 at Ayresome Park — 'Draw specialists Oldfield do it again' — we had our great chance of the season so far: home to Manston Town, who hadn't managed a point, or even a goal, in five previous away matches. Having been promoted pretty well by accident the previous season — just happening to be in third place when the music stopped — they were plopping straight back. 'If we blow this one,' Verney told the papers, 'there's something badly wrong.' It was like handing them a loaded gun.

But he'd have been up against it anyway, because Oldfield versus Manston proved to be *Match of the Day*. Sam could never be himself when the spotlight was on him.

'Remember, lads,' he told us before the game, 'you've got an audience of millions. Go out there and show the whole country what Oldfield can do.'

That would have come all right from some managers: from Verney it was just embarrassing. In any case we were already tight wound and needed no words. We knew Manston had a fair defence but no midfield and only one forward — a youngish striker named Louis Peck. If we shut him out and kept the pressure on, then sooner or later Manston would go.

From the opening whistle our midfield took over and squeezed the game back into Manston's half of the pitch. We attacked down the right and forced three corners, and then down the left to force a couple more. Their goalie saved from me, then from Alley, then from Smith. Peck hardly had a touch of the ball, and their defence was continually off balance. We were doing everything right, by Verney's standards — it was just that we were doing it too fast, and wrong-footing ourselves. Manston hung on, but we could sense them going. At half-time there was still no score, but even Sam wasn't too grieved.

'Just keep it up,' he said. 'Keep it there. When you've scored one you'll score five.'

The second half followed the pattern of the first for twenty minutes till Roy Wheel broke through the middle to crack in a shot the goalie couldn't hold, and Dave Alley thrust in the rebound. We'd scored our one, and straight from the re-start we were back for more. I almost put Alley in again, but the keeper took the ball off his toe; then Hedges threaded the defence with a centre, but I headed over from six feet out. Within a minute Town got in their first attack of the half. Peck chased a long ball, shook off the centre-back and hit a cross-shot in off the far post. The stadium went dead. We had it all to do again. Christ knows we gave it everything we had, chasing, shouting, steaming, but they pulled ten men back and somehow choked us out. When the whistle blew on another draw the half of the crowd that was still left broke out booing like a dairy herd. We stumbled off punch-drunk and burning-headed after our eighth game without a win. Poor old Sam was yellow in the face and could hardly speak. For the last twenty minutes the yobbos had been singing loud and clear for the TV microphones: 'All we are saying is "Verney must go!"'

For me that match was the lowest point I'd reached all season. There were still excuses I could make to myself, but what was the point? Two goals in eleven games was piss. Even if I had been swallowed into the pattern of the side it was my own fault. It had been up to me to stamp my personality on the attack. Verney had bought me as an international-class player who could lift a promising squad. I hadn't lifted them — in fact they'd sunk me — so I couldn't be international class. Perhaps cunt Carlton had been right and I'd only been a top First Division scorer because I'd had the City machine behind me. Now game after game I was being held by defences I'd screwed eighteen months before. To make things worse I was getting caught more often by the hard men, because my timing was a fraction out. I did some damage in return, of course, but I half felt I deserved to get whacked for not scoring. I'd been going home on match days with hacked legs and a bruised mind.

At least the fans hadn't yet got after me. There'd been no chants of 'What a waste of money!' or 'Gilpin's a fairy!' — at least, none that I'd heard. Then again, I couldn't imagine a chorus of 'There's only one Vinnie Gilpin!' if I hit the net. The fans didn't seem to notice me much, on the field or off it. I felt as though I was disappearing.

Arriving home after the Manston game I found Claire in the kitchen. She'd heard a match-report on the radio, and unfortunately tried to strike a cheery note.

'So you did it again! When are you going to start winning?'

'When we play the Girl Guides.'

Although my left calf was throbbing, where I'd taken some studs, and there was a lump over my left ear, I wasn't in an evil mood — just a bit surly. But as I moved to the sink for a glass of water the blood suddenly boiled in my head. I slung the tumbler hard across the room, and Claire screamed as it exploded against the wall.

'Sorry,' I said. 'I'll clear it up.'

I was cool again, but scared to find that rage could take me like an epileptic fit. Claire was crying as I swept away the fragments of glass into a newspaper and stuffed it into the bin. The new paintwork was scarred. I managed a kiss, and said: 'Let's spend the evening in. I'll get us a Chinese take-away.'

Claire brightened up at this friendliness. She trimmed herself up as nicely as though we'd been going out, and then had us watching one of those TV quizzes where the audience clap the prizes. In the excitement of it she forgot the Oldfield result and my bad temper. Later we saw an old Richard Burton film while eating sweet and sour pork. All told, it was pretty well an evening you could have had in hospital.

The cherry on the cake was Match of the sodding Day. How would you fancy seeing a replay of *your* day's work? But I had to watch — I had to face it. Besides, I might have learnt something. It was a miserable forty minutes. There was Gilpin dashing into the screen and dashing out of it, knocking passes this way and that, helping with everything and creating nothing. Poor little useless fucker. I could see myself for what I'd become — just another chaser. By contrast that Lou Peck did sod-all for eighty-nine of the ninety minutes, but when his one half-chance came he grabbed it like a true striker. He'd had the courage to be selfish because he knew he could pay off his debts with a single kick.

Verney was questioned, looking like a survivor from an air-crash. Avoiding the interviewer's eye he got out the usual stuff. The side had lost a little bit of confidence . . . trying too hard . . . not getting the breaks. It was all true, but it was boring. Was he disappointed with his big buy, Vince Gilpin? Well, Vince had suffered from the general over-anxiety . . . not for want of trying . . . always looking for the ball . . . just needed a goal or two. The poor old bugger was doing his best on my behalf, but it all sounded hopeless. Never mind the words Sam was struggling for, the interviewer had recognised the tune and didn't hesitate to call for the chorus. He quoted the pre-match comment to the press. *Was* something 'badly wrong?' The crowd had been hostile: did Verney feel his job was on the line? That was Sam's chance. That was when he should have put the studs in. He'd dragged a pissy club into the First Division and kept it there. Against all the odds he'd balanced the books. His team had lost only two League matches all season. So what was this cheeky crap about his job being at risk? But that wasn't Sam's way. He just covered up. It was down to the Chairman . . . always had good relations . . . still had two years of his contract to run . . . but at the end of the day yes, the manager must carry the can.

Next minute the Chairman himself, Ted Hardiman, was being interviewed.

'Obviously I'm concerned. I'd be failing in my duty as Chairman if I *wasn't* concerned. Sam Verney's done a lot for Oldfield, and that must never be forgotten. He's always given of his best. But I have to take a broad view. I have to consider what the fans are feeling, and I have to think about the future. No decisions have been taken yet, but today's game has given me a lot to think about.'

Each word eased the knife a little further in: I knew Sam was doomed. But as several more days passed with him not yet fired I got a little spirit back, and began to think we might still fuck Fate. The following Saturday at the Dell we went frantic, running like greyhounds but getting shot of the ball as though it was a time-bomb. When we'd gone two down I snatched a goal back and we staged a five-minute rally — but the Saints scored a third and we were dead. Sam Verney was fired on the Monday, and told the press he went with no hard feelings. I doubt if he had any feelings left. Within a fortnight Billy Kershaw was appointed in his place.

Hardiman was tickled silly to have got him. My guess is that he'd had feelers out for some time. On TV he told the town: 'I think we've struck lucky. Billy Kershaw's an experienced manager and he's a flamboyant manager. He may have had a spot of trouble here and there, but he's won trophies. He's the man to bring a bit of colour to Piper Road.'

Personally I went off Kershaw in the space of his opening chat to the players. He came on like a school-teacher, making long pauses and looking round to make sure we seemed impressed.

'I'm your new manager. You'll have heard a bit about me, but you can forget what you've heard. Judge by what you see — because that's what I intend to do.

'One thing I'll be bringing to this job is experience. The majority of you have belonged to this one League club. I've belonged to a dozen as player or manager. Oldfield is the twelfth. It hasn't always been a success story, but I've left some sort of mark at every club I've been with. Oldfield won't be an exception.

'Mr. Verney left me a young squad. I like that. A Kershaw team has a certain style, and a young squad learns it quicker. So we should be well suited. I hope we are, because if not there could be a few good-byes. You won't be wanting that. But I've seen most of you play, and I know the ability that's in the squad. We've got the makings of a team . . .'

So he wanked on. Afterwards Del McBain, our right back, who was thirty, said to me:

'It's what I thought. He wants a boys' team. I won't be here much longer.'

'But he likes a veteran or two in his squad. He always has.'

'Yeh, but he brings in his old favourites. By Christmas he'll have Barry Reid here or Ken Dainton. If you're over twenty-four you can get on your bike.'

'I'm twenty five.'

'Yeh. You might just make it.'

As Kershaw made himself known to the players over the next day or two I didn't get more than a word or two. I could tell I was on probation. Against Spurs on the Saturday we played as we'd played for Verney — good running, fair passing but no poise. We managed another draw, but hardly deserved it. Kershaw was reasonably cheerful afterwards, as I suppose I should have expected — a surgeon can't start chopping up a healthy patient. Doing the rounds in the dressing-room he had words of praise for several of the younger lads, but to me he said nothing. In fact he looked past me: the old invisible thumbs down.

Claire and I were due to go out that night, but I was too despondent to care. While she was up in the bathroom I lay back in an arm-chair, staring at the ceiling with my eyes half closed and my mouth half open, trying not to think. After a time I found myself singing with no tune:

'I played like a shit-heap. A stinking shit-heap. Whatever I had, I've bleeding lost it . . .'

105

Claire had come in with wet hair, and was staring at me.

'What are you singing about?'

'About the future,' I said. I was in a daft mood. Next minute I was singing again: 'I can tell which way the wind is blowing. And fucking cold it is too. So pack your bags — pack your bags, Mrs Gilpin. We'll soon be on the move again.'

'What are you on about?' she asked, going anxious. 'Are you just joking?'

'I don't know.'

'Did that Kershaw say something to you?'

'No. That's the trouble.'

'Why? What's the harm in it?'

'It means I'm not part of his plans. Sorry, Claire — we're going to be looking for another new house.'

'We can't! Not again! We've only just got here!'

There were tears in her eyes, but I couldn't be too sorry. She was just crying for the house.

'Easy come, easy go.' Then I was singing again, if you can call it singing: 'Good-bye house. Good-bye fitted carpets. Good-bye double glazing —'

Claire rushed out of the room and I lay back staring at the ceiling again with a sour little grin. My hard-won career was unravelling like an old sweater. For a year now, nothing had gone right, and Christ knew what the next year would bring. I felt as though I was on my own. So did Claire, probably.

During the training the following week Kershaw made no contact with me. He wasn't hostile: it was more as though I'd been brought in from Yugoslavia and couldn't speak the language. All the same, he picked me for the next game, against Coventry. I lasted fifty-eight minutes, being pulled off by Kershaw after a shit-for-shat foul on the centre-back — an offence which brought my bookings for the season level with my goals at three-all. When Mel Stoneman, who took my place, laid on the only goal of the game for Dave Alley I knew I was kippered.

Kershaw called me in on the Monday.

'I'll get straight to the point, Vince,' he said. 'I've been here a week or two now, and I can see my way to shaping a

106

fair side. What I have to tell you is, there's no place in it for you.'

He stopped for me to say something, but I didn't.

'We need a big, seasoned striker up front — a target man, who can do a bit in the air. Dave Alley could play off a man like that.'

'So could I. So I did, with Billy Byers.'

He shook his head. 'You've had your chance at Piper Road, Vince. Try your luck elsewhere.'

Claire was out when I got back home. My mind was numb, but I had a fidgety energy I didn't know what to do with. My mood took me back to the day I'd put in the transfer request at City. That had been nearly a year ago — a year in which I'd done nothing. Unable to sit down I prowled the house, taking deep breaths. For no reason at all I had a huge hard on. My whole system was at sixes and sevens. I had a wank and a beer, and then fell asleep in an arm-chair. The phone woke me: it was Del McBain. He and Steve Farrar and Gordon Miles were all on the list as well.

For a week Claire and I hadn't mentioned the possibility of a transfer: it was like an illness too serious for daily conversation. But she must have thought over what I'd said (or sung) to her, because when I broke the news she had her questions ready.

'Couldn't you refuse to go?'

'Technically. But it would do me no good.'

'Oldfield haven't had much of a season, have they?'

'Not too brilliant.'

Embarrassment didn't cost her more than a split-second pause: 'Well, if they want to sell you, who's going to buy you?'

I should have been relieved that she'd finally got the point, but I didn't like her jabbing it in my face.

'I could go back to Stanborough.'

'But they're in the Fourth Division! You're better than that. You *must* be better than that!'

I didn't answer.

'Well, how good *are* you?'

'How do I know?' I was suddenly savage. 'How the fuck do

I know? If I was a runner I could tell you. Or if I was a boxer. I'd run faster than some other fucker, or break his jaw. Soccer's a team game. I'm good at one bit of a team game. Or I used to be. Maybe I've lost it.'

Claire should have said: 'Of course not. You're as good as ever.' She knew sod-all about the matter, and I'd have brushed her answer aside, but that's what she should have said. Instead she asked: 'Can a player just lose his skills like that?'

'Why not?'

'But why should you? You're still the same person. You've got the same body.'

'You need confidence. You need a bit of luck. You need support.'

'You can get all that with another team.'

'Sure. A team like Stanborough.'

'Don't keep saying that! Stanborough's impossible!'

Her expression showed she was just beginning to think it *was* possible. She was horrified, which gave me pleasure. I'd been suffering for bloody months while she never felt a pang. In all her life she'd never tried to do anything difficult, so she didn't know the taste of failure. Now she was getting her first mouthful.

Her paleness showed up the mark of a spot on one cheek, reminding me how young she was. I spent half a minute trying to see her point of view. Here was the ground suddenly cut from under her feet, for reasons she didn't understand and through no fault of her own. She had her own self-chosen job, looking after the house and her appearance and my clothes, and she did it well. The trouble was that beyond a certain point I didn't care if it was done well or badly. She might have felt the same about my football of course — but thousands didn't. And in any case she needed me so that I could lay on the money for her house and interests. Besides, I'd sweated and bled for years over my work, while hers cost nothing. If she wasn't sorry for me I sure as hell wasn't going to feel sorry for her.

Next day the papers had the obvious headlines: 'Kershaw

Clear-out', 'Autumn Sales at Piper Road'. One report said: 'Managers are unlikely to be trampled underfoot in the rush for Gilpin's services. His meagre goal-scoring record for Oldfield has made nonsense of the fee Sam Verney paid for him.'

On the Saturday I was a member of the reserve side, playing at Filbert Street in the eerie silence familiar to footballers who don't quite make it. I played hard, but didn't score. As the teams came off I heard a familiar voice call 'Hey, Vin!' — and there was Harvey in the little knot of pensioners and small boys round the tunnel. We had a drink after I'd changed.

'Why come today?' I asked him.

'Thought I'd get a chance to speak to you.'

'You could give me a call any time.'

'Don't know your number. Besides, you must always have people on at you.'

I gave him the number. 'You daft prat,' I said. 'I can always get you a ticket. At least, I can till I'm transferred.'

Harv's sideways face went all serious: 'What's gone wrong, Vin?'

'Fuck knows.' Being with Harvey made me feel ten years younger — in other words, childish. It was a relief from taking my problems seriously. 'I can't seem to get it right these days. I had it, and I lost it.'

'Never! You'll be back. They've just wasted you at Oldfield.'

He looked really upset. It came to my mind that I was probably the only celebrity he knew. He didn't want me disappearing from the papers. I went to change the conversation, but what came out took me by surprise.

'Can you do something for me when you're in London?'

'Sure.'

'It's a bit personal. I had this girl-friend in London a few years back. When I went to Stanborough I lost touch with her. Months later she wrote and said she'd had this kid by me. Well, I was the only bloke she'd ever gone out with. But I've never seen the kid, and I never hear a word from her any more. I just send her money. Could you poke your head around on the quiet and find out what's happening to them?'

Pete was all fascinated. 'Do you want me to talk to her?'

'No. Well, only if you can do it without mentioning me. Use your judgment.'

I gave him the details and told him there was no particular hurry. He promised to scout around when he was in London on leave, though he didn't get there that often. Afterwards it struck me I must be barmy to think of risking Harvey as a private detective. Use his judgment? He'd never had any. At least, he hadn't had any when he was fifteen: maybe his army training had given him some. Karen had recently been in my mind because Claire had taken over the handling of our financial matters, and I'd had a job explaining away the standing order. Why I'd come out with her to Harvey I had no idea — perhaps it was just the East London connection.

On the Tuesday it was announced that Oldfield had signed veteran County striker Ken Dainton for a five figure fee. He'd played for Kershaw at three of his other clubs.

'Ken's a big man,' Kershaw told the press, 'big in every sense. He's a powerful lad with a lot of character and a lot of heart. He'll give us something up front that we've been missing.'

'Thanks,' I thought.

I went to Kershaw's office on an impulse, and said that my dad had been taken to hospital with heart trouble, so could I have a couple of days in London. Whether he believed me or not he said 'Back Thursday morning.' At home I told Claire that Kershaw had advised me to take off on my own for a couple of days to clear my head. She never questioned this daft story. I reckon both she and Kershaw were glad to get shot of me for a space.

Having no reason to go anywhere in particular, I headed for Stanborough. It wasn't much of a place, but it was the best I could do in the way of nostalgia: things had gone well for me there. Actually I by-passed the town and spent the night at a boarding-house on the coast. Visiting a shop or two and a pub where I'd been known I had a fair welcome. It cheered me up to see a few old acquaintances.

'Don't tell me about that Kershaw,' said Frankie at the Lion. 'He's a screaming nut-case. That's why no club keeps him more than a couple of years. You'll be knocking in the goals when he's in Broadmoor.'

Between drinks I gave a buzz to my old companion, the greengrocer's wife. She sounded more surprised than delighted to hear my voice, but agreed to entertain me the following afternoon. I had the sense to bring her bottles of scent and wine and that warmed her up. In fact, for all she'd put on a pound or two, it was a good little visit, if a bit respectable — like going to the zoo with your auntie.

Afterwards, by way of contrast, I went to watch Stanborough, who had an evening game. I stood at the back of the half-empty terracing, with a whole barrier to myself. It was strange being back there as a spectator, turning my past life inside-out. No one in the crowd recognised me. Of the squad I'd known only Kellogg, Brown and Lowden were playing. Islip and Judd were long gone, of course, and the club had been relegated the previous spring by a handsome margin. The bad old days were back. I could see by the Woolworth's flood-lights how the stadium was rotting again. The paint I'd seen put on was half peeled away. There were fresh weeds sneaking up through the concrete. All the improvements we'd won through promotion seemed to be wiped out. Trying to lift a club like that in a town like that was climbing the greasy pole.

It was a freezing cold night and the match was terrible. I watched in silence and left before the end, more depressed than I'd felt in Oldfield.

Having reached home after midnight I slept late, and Claire had to wake me to take a phone-call. It was from Kershaw.

'How's your dad?'

'He's on the mend.'

'Good. You may or may not have heard that Manston Town have got a new manager. He'd like a chat with you this afternoon.'

I hesitated. 'Who is he?'

'Geoff Cowley.'

'I'll hear what he's got to say.'

I thought over this development at breakfast, while I was lying to Claire about the previous day. At least it was a First Division club after me — but only just. Since their draw at Piper Road Manston had lost every game, and were way adrift at the foot of the table. Moreover the squad was known to be falling apart: half of them were already on the transfer-list. Manston was a Second Division outfit at best. It hadn't got the money or the crowd or the tradition to be more. Surely I could look for something better than Manston? All the same I was a bit flattered that Cowley had thought of me: I'd won the respect of a hard man. And he'd done enough as a manager in the lower divisions to show he was no bloody fool. I'd listen to his offer. But I didn't tell Claire I was seeing him: she'd have had opinions I didn't want to think about.

When I first met Cowley that afternoon I almost laughed, because his appearance was so different. I could hardly believe that this was the clogger who'd tried to kick me off the park at Millwood. He was wearing a dark suit. His formerly black hair and his one thick black eye-brow had silvered to the colour of wire-wool, as though he'd been made up. His face still carried a scar or two, but it looked serious and middle-aged. You could have thought he was a boxer who'd hung up his gloves to become a priest.

His manner had changed, too. I'd been expecting the hard sell, and even a bit of bullying, but he couldn't have been more mild.

'Let's drive somewhere quiet,' he said. 'We can talk as we go.'

It was just starting to rain as we left the car park. Heading out of town in his Volvo Cowley started up a bit of a chat, but very relaxed, as though we were just kicking in.

'You played against Manston — what did you think?'

'What can I say? Poor side.'

'They took a point off you.'

'Yeh. And our manager was fired.'

'So was Manston's.' He enjoyed a little grin. 'What's wrong with my lot, then?'

'You just don't have the players . . .'

'Paget? Steve Brine? Trevor Rees?'

'All right, I'll give you those three. And that Lou Peck can do a bit up front. That's about your lot.'

'Ian Farthing?'

'He can pass a ball if you let him. But he's on the list.'

'Not now. First thing I did was take him off it.'

'So you've got yourself a five-a-side squad.'

In a way I was deliberately niggling him, because I couldn't believe in his new appearance. I was sure he'd froth up under pressure. But he just drove in silence for a minute or two, with the windscreen wipers swishing away.

'I wasn't doing badly at Brent Park,' he said. 'They'll make the Second Division next season.'

'So will Manston.'

'You don't think we could stay up?'

'Not a prayer.'

He gave me a glance. 'Then why do you reckon I moved?'

'More money?'

'A bit more. I wasn't bothered.'

'More independence?'

'I had a free hand at Brent Park.'

'OK — why *did* you move?'

Cowley frowned, as though this was a totally unexpected question instead of one he had forced on me. By now we were clear of Oldfield, and the rain was pissing down.

'Where are we?'

'On the Ring Road.'

For a good mile he drove without a word. Cars went by us, tossing up spray. When he did speak it was very carefully, like a man trying hard to be accurate. I came to know that style well over the next few years — a quiet style, but with a lot of force behind it. He seemed to be holding himself back, talking in low gear to slow down his thoughts and feelings. You always had a suspicion he might suddenly let rip — especially if you'd played against him — but he never did.

'In my time,' he said, 'I was a useful player. Nothing too special, but a useful First Division player. Later I did a fair job as a player-manager. I could pull a side together, and make the most of whatever it did. I steered a couple of weak clubs out of trouble. But for me, being a player-manager was firstly being a player — getting in the thick of things, making the young lads keep fighting. Very physical.'

'I remember.'

'So when I packed up playing I thought I might lose control, and the team would suffer. And it did. For a year it did. But all the time I was gradually sorting myself. Doing a turn-around. I'd been thinking like a player, and I wasn't a player any more. I had to learn to think like a manager, and suddenly it came easy — it came very easy. I stopped feeling I was a player forced to do a bit of managing: I was a manager who'd once been a player. It took me a year to realise it, but I'm a better manager than I ever was a player. Far better. That's what I'm really good at.'

He went silent again. He hadn't been speaking in a boastful way, but as if he had something to explain. I was waiting to see how he'd get to the subject of Gilpin.

'Three things I can do — three things in particular. I can spot a player. I can spot a talent most managers would miss. I find bargains. Second, I can get the best out of a player — make him give a performance he never knew he had in him. Third, I can put together a team. Give me a mixed bunch of middling players and I can fit them together like a jig-saw.'

'All right,' I said, 'I give up. Why *are* you moving to Manston?'

'I was coming to that. Haven't we passed that pub before?'

'Yeh. We're on our second lap of the Ring Road.'

'Never mind — it's too wet to get out. Look: you get a really good new manager in the game only about every five years. By that I mean a manager who can make a club — make a trophy-winning club out of nothing. I'm one of those. But no one really builds from nothing: you have to use materials other people can't see. That's why I'm moving now, and that's why I chose Manston.'

114

'So where's your materials?'

'I know who I've got, and I think I know who I can get.'

'And I'm one of them?'

'Look, Vince, you're the first. I haven't had this job two days, and I'm here hustling for you.'

'How do you know I can still do it?'

'Seen you play. Saw you on the box against Manston. Saw you at Filbert Street last week-end. You can still do it all — take a pass under pressure, make space, turn a defender. You've been used all wrong at Oldfield. You've been wasted.'

He suddenly turned the car into a lay-by and switched off the engine. We sat side by side in our warm tin box in the pouring rain, while I tried to get my thoughts together.

'You'd play me alongside Louis Peck?'

'No. He's leaving.'

'But he's your only goal-scorer. He's the one the crowd sings about. Why sell him?'

'To make the money to get you.'

Cowley was watching me from under his grey eye-brow, knowing he'd scored a point because I'd be flattered.

'Who else are you after?'

'Can't give names. A midfield player who never stops running, and the best centre-back in the League.' He paused. 'Both from the Third Division.'

'You're crazy,' I said. 'You haven't got a chance. It'll be all over in six weeks.'

'Like to bet on it?' Cowley gave a little smile, very calm. 'Do you think I'd stake my career on a certain loser?'

I sat there pretty blank, trying to think of something to think, and he suddenly turned round to me in a quiet passion.

'It's a gamble,' he said. 'Of course it's a fucking gamble. But the odds are good — take my word. Or they will be if I get you. If I get you I'm away. I remember you at Millwood. You played out of your skin because there was a chance in a thousand of promotion. And you brought it off. You were the only one out there believing in miracles. That's what I need at Manston, because I'm going to bring off another one. You've been frigging around this past year. You've done nothing. I'll see you get the best service you've ever had. You owe yourself some goals. If you can get a dozen by the end of the season, we're there. If Manston so much as stay up, it's a triumph. You'll be back in the England reckoning, and we'll both have the freedom of the town. Come on: you're like me. You want to do something big. Take a chance.'

He'd stirred me, but I still thought he was probably barmy. I didn't know what to say. After a minute Cowley sat back, apparently calm again.

'You won't get a better offer,' he said. 'You could go to a bigger club at a bigger wage, but you won't get a better offer.'

I opened my mouth without knowing what was going to come out and said: 'If the terms are right, you're on.'

When I told Claire what had happened, it froze her. She could only get out little questions, a word at a time: 'Where?' 'Why?' 'When?' Although she knew nothing about soccer she knew Manston Town was doomed — I'd told her so. By the time we got to bed she'd cried her face out of shape. I was sorry for her, but couldn't think of much to say.

Chapter 9

Two thirds of what Cowley was to do for Manston Town he did in his first fortnight. He had to move fast, because even apart from results the club was in terrible shape. Two players had recently gone, and four more were on the list, including Louis Peck and Challock, the team captain. Another lad, Howard Bush, was out for the season with a broken leg. The reserve side were bottom of the Central League. Luckily for Town Cowley had seen his way past all these problems in advance. Of the available players there were two he prized: Steve Brine as a defender and organiser, and Ian Farthing as a provider. He moved Steve from left-back to centre-back, in place of Challock, and made him the new club skipper. He talked Ian off the transfer-list, telling him he'd be starting a whole new career with Manston. The other three on the list were sold in a matter of days. Of the regular first-teamers who remained Cowley reckoned Paget was a solid keeper, if lacking in height, Rees a handy defender — he'd won a couple of Welsh caps with a previous club — and Dooner a half useful muscle-man up front. To this chosen five he counted on adding myself, John Carpenter from Belstone, and Neil Herrick from Bristol. The rest of the squad would have to be patchwork, at least to the end of the season, because he'd have no more money. But he already had in mind a formation and a style of play for his new side. More than that, he knew all the players he'd gone for, with the exception of Farthing, were proud men and fighters.

The rest of the football world, not having his judgment, at first thought he was crazy. He'd sold the two best-known players at the club, and brought in Vince Gilpin, a washed out case, and John Carpenter, a twenty-six-year-old who'd had seven seasons in the Third Division, as replacements. In that first fortnight Cowley was bringing off, behind the scenes, everything he'd planned; but the only visible stroke of luck he had was that his opening game as manager was rained off. It was to have been at home, and the fans were ready to scalp him for selling Lou Peck. I signed on the Monday, and was glad enough to be making my first appearance away from home. Though I'd been talked round by Cowley I wasn't that optimistic myself. All I had to go on was a hunch or a hope that he was a winner.

Some footballers seem to have total recall: they can describe in detail all the goals they've scored. My memory doesn't work like that, for football or anything else. More than once, in a romantic mood, I've thought: 'I'll remember this fuck all of my life,' and all that's stayed with me afterwards has been the colour of the curtains. But I do have some clear recollections from that first match I played for Manston. I'd taken the big leap, and now I was to find out if the parachute worked.

We were playing Manchester City, who were fourth or fifth in the League at the time. The team was: Paget; Rees, Carpenter, Brine, Mallison; Farthing, Barrett, Henshaw, Long; Dooner, Gilpin.

It was an experimental side, to say the least. Four players had been switched to new positions, including Steve Brine and Mick Long, who was normally a reserve winger. Ian Farthing hadn't kicked a ball for six weeks. John Carpenter had only signed the day before. On paper wc were a 4-4-2 formation, with Mick Long pulled back into mid-field, but the idea was that Ian Farthing should operate just in front of the back four, so we were really 4-1-3-2.

What with all these changes and the team's pathetic record the lads would have been apprehensive in any case, but we had an additional worry in the peculiar shape of John Carpenter. What little I'd seen of him had made me fear that after all Geoff Cowley was a nutter. Off the pitch you'd never have taken him for a footballer. Though he was tall he was skinny, and carried himself badly. He had a head as small as mine, without much hair on it, and wore a pair of horn-rimmed glasses. I'd have guessed his age as nearer forty-six than twenty-six. On the field, admittedly in a single shortish training session, he'd looked out of his depth. He was narrow-built, all arms and legs, but he had no pace, and seemingly no co-ordination. Nothing he did was crisp or clean. He'd pass the ball with his ankle, or head it with his ear. The best you could say was that he wasn't over-awed. He'd hardly spoken a word all day, but there was no tension in him.

In the dressing-room at Maine Road before his First Division début he sat leaning back into a corner, so relaxed he could have been half asleep. I remember how the lads kept glancing at him, wondering what they'd been lumbered with. In a way he'd become the main focus of attention, because it was by his performance we'd judge whether Cowley knew what he was doing. Cowley himself was calm, but very intent. He'd given us clear instructions and he went over them before the kick-off, but there was no blood-and-tears pep talk: he relied on us catching his own mood. His last words were: 'As soon as the whistle goes you start learning to play together. Help each other. Have confidence in each other. Turn yourselves into a team.'

It wasn't easy to have faith in John Carpenter. For the first ten minutes I thought he'd be murdered: he was marking too loose, jumping too early, tackling too late. But somehow nothing was getting past him. I suddenly realised he had his own methods and his own timing. A forward would burst clear of him and he'd lunge out a telescopic leg to hook the ball back. A high cross would seem to have stranded him, but he'd just get his head to it. Each time it looked like luck — but it always came off. When he knocked the ball out of the area he seemed to do it blindly, but time and again he found a team-mate. You could see the Manchester forwards getting frustrated at being held by this freak and seeing their best passes caught up at his feet. Alport, their big striker, threw a heavy shoulder-charge into him, but he simply absorbed it, without breaking step, and won the tackle.

I had plenty of opportunity to watch him, because Manchester were nearly always on the attack. With the rest of our back four beginning to settle down around Carpenter the defence looked pretty stubborn, but our makeshift midfield was nowhere. Ian Farthing had no protection, and was being hustled off the ball before he could get a pass away. Only Mick Long was showing for us, chasing everything, often beaten, but always coming back. Dooner and I were having a thin time. Our orders were to push up and look for the long pass — but nothing was coming through. Then just on half-time I flicked on a clearance from Brine, and Dooner broke through on a beefy run to force a corner. Farthing took it, Henshaw back-headed from the near post, and I hit an overhead volley the keeper only just clawed wide. It was the sharpest thing I'd done in weeks.

At half-time the atmosphere in the dressing room was high-charged. We'd kept them out, we'd hit back, we'd half-worked as a team. Cowley was pleased, but concentrated his attention on the problem of making more space for Ian Farthing.

We went out eagerly for the second half, and were a goal down in three minutes when the City left-back hit a dipping shot from twenty yards. Paget had no chance. With the Maine Road crowd coming to life the Blues pounded us after that. In the next quarter of an hour we could have folded, but didn't. Carpenter was still tangling up the middle, and Brine sorting things out all round him.

As the pressure began to ease, Farthing at last found some room to move, and I began to see he was a bit special. He was a scraggy-looking player, whose heading and tackling were nothing much, and who was completely right-footed. But he had the gift, commoner in lefties, of total precision in the one good leg. He'd swing it like a golf-club, chipping, lofting or driving. Already he was reading my game, and dropping the ball a shade short, so I could come off my marker. I was moving like a striker again, quick and sudden. With smarter support up front I could have pulled us level, but Dooner wasn't making the right runs, and no one was coming through from mid-field. When I did manage a one-two with Long I got in a shot the goalie only just touched over. Then Carpenter came loping out of nowhere to head the corner inches wide. By this time there were less than five minutes left, but I was certain we could score. City forced a corner in return, but someone hooked the ball out to Farthing, just clear of the box. I ran right, yelling for a pass, but Ian hit a huge diagonal drive into space down the left. Mick Long belted forty yards to catch it, kick ahead and sprint for the line. Ben Dooner and I went storming down the middle. As the centre swerved back Ben middled it with his nut, but the header looped high off the keeper's knee. I have a clear memory of the ball hanging motionless in mid-air as I sprang clear of the centre-back to volley it into the net.

It's hard to describe how fucking marvellous we all felt after that drawn game. For me it wasn't just that I'd scored. I'd played, in fragments, as I'd not played for a year. I'd remembered how I used to do it. I felt as I imagine you'd feel getting your first hard-on after an operation on your balls. The rest of the side were just as chuffed. Brine had come off as a skipper, Carpenter, in his own peculiar way, had come off as a stopper. Ben Dooner had had his moments, and Mick Long had done wonders as a stand-in midfielder. Collectively we'd held off a good side and fought back against the odds for a point. Cowley must have got something right. Footballers are superstitious buggers, because they know they need the help of fortune. On the strength of one point we were ready to believe that Cowley was a witch-doctor.

Cowley himself seemed satisfied, but not overjoyed. On the Monday he went over the whole game with us, pretty much ball by ball. His main message was that though the defence had done well the attack had struck only a spark or two because they'd had no service. Our middle three needed to carve out some room for Ian Farthing, so that he could strike his long passes to me or to Ben Dooner, or to anyone breaking from the back.

It was to strengthen the midfield that Cowley brought in Neil Herrick, who arrived on the Wednesday. Unlike Carpenter and myself Neil had been in demand, being recognized as a highly promising player. Cowley had only managed to get him to Manston by will-power and shrewd talking. You could tell Neil would do us some good before he'd even kicked a ball. He was slightly built, but quick, wiry, sharp, chatty. He must have spoken a thousand words to every one of Carpenter's — all I'd got out of Long John so far was that Pat Arnold had sent me his regards.

From the first minute of his first practice game Neil was screaming for the ball and calling the moves. Such cockiness would have been hard to take from most twenty-one-year-olds, but from Neil it seemed all right — partly because it came so naturally to him, and partly because he got stuck in so hard himself. Slight as he was, he'd take any knock and never stop moving. When he went down he was head over heels to his feet again. If a tackle missed he'd be straight back for a second bite. I'd never seen a busier player. In some aspects his game was raw, but he looked as though he'd learn fast. He was just the force our midfield needed, and he went immediately into the side, with Barrett dropping to sub.

Before the kick-off on the Saturday he was so seething with energy he couldn't keep still or keep quiet. For ten minutes he was hopping from foot to foot, rubbing his hands, and calling: 'We can do this lot! Let's go! Let's get out there!' Apart from Carpenter, who was sitting quiet again, all knees and elbows like a grasshopper, we were all tight-strung. A win at home after the draw at Maine Road would make survival look at any rate a remote possibility — but Manston hadn't had a win in ten matches. Cowley calmed us, but chiefly he talked to Ian Farthing. 'You'll have the space today,' he told him. 'You'll have men running for you. Show us your class.'

It was strange after the tension in the dressing-room to run down the tunnel into no more than a half-hearted cheer. I didn't know then, what I learnt later, that the Manston fans were a funny-tempered lot. Years of poor results at the club had made them cynical. As they'd not had too much to cheer they'd come to specialise in jeering. They were glad if Town won, but their real pleasure was in seeing the other side lose. Failing that, they'd found there was a sour enjoyment in things going wrong for their own club. If we'd lost at Maine Road they'd have booed us on to the pitch in style. As it was we'd wrong-footed them. They didn't have anything obvious to moan about, but they certainly weren't going to waste any enthusiasm. We kicked in in near silence. If there was going to be any cheering we'd have to earn it.

And so we bloody did, though it took us a bit of time. For a third of the game we were too jumpy, too hasty. We had most of the play, but couldn't work an opening. Promising moves would collapse. Dooner and I would go for the same space, Farthing would over-hit a long pass, Herrick would win the ball and waste it. We badly needed a goal to settle us down, but I couldn't see where it would come from. It came from nowhere, just on the half hour. I ran to meet a corner, but Farthing hit it long, and I was left stranded, ten feet wide of the near post. As I turned back the keeper punched clear, and Rees had a whack at goal from outside the box. His mis-hit shot came straight at me. Barely seeing the ball, I took it down with one foot and fired it in with the other. One up. No time for thought: my body had scored on its own. The reflexes were back in tune.

For the rest of that half we played well. Early in the second we began to play brilliantly. Somehow the strain was gone, the timing had come right: we'd picked up a rhythm, like dancers. With Herrick or Long chasing back there was always an extra man to take a pass, draw an opponent, and put Ian Farthing in the clear. They knocked out neat little triangles or squares: Carpenter to Brine to Farthing; Rees to Herrick to Farthing; Brine to Long to Herrick to Farthing. Where the forwards harried they'd be pulled this way and that, till Ian was released into space. And like a bowler who'd struck a length Ian was drifting and swerving the ball with total command, finding gaps or making them. More often than not the long passes came to me, because I could read them early and take a yard off my marker. By this stage of the game Herrick was playing off me like a dream. Deep as he dropped back, if I could hold up the ball a second or two he'd be coming through the middle to take a pass. Not to be outdone, Long would be sprinting left and Dooner charging right. There was always something on. Farthing fed us and fed us again, till the defence was run dizzy, and only a brilliant display by their goalie was holding us up. We scored two more, through Long and Dooner, and could have had six. It was only Town's third win since they'd been promoted, and by far the biggest. When the whistle went we were cheered off the pitch. Even Manston's grudging fans had been impressed.

It wasn't just that we'd won: we'd played half an hour of brilliant football. The sports writers just couldn't make sense of it. Jack Dalston's verdict in the *Gazette* was typical:

Town produced some scintillating football, so far removed from their recent performances as to seem almost miraculous. All the new boys'had a part to play. Neil Herrick won the hearts of the crowd with his fearless tackling and eager running. John Carpenter, ungainly as he looked, did a useful stopper's job at the heart of the defence, while at the other end Vincent Gilpin was as slick and deadly as in his heyday with City.

But stealing the show from all three was veteran campaigner Ian Farthing. Given more room and more responsibility he was unrecognizable as the hesitant performer of recent years. 'There isn't a better passer of the ball in English football,' claimed new manager Geoff Cowley after the game. On this showing it's hard to disagree with him.

About the general performance of the side Cowley is more cautious. 'It's a start — but we're still bottom of the division. We've shown what we can do. Now it's up to us to keep on doing it.'

Perhaps the caution is justified. A glance at the table will remind optimistic fans that their team still has a mountain to

climb. But yesterday's performance certainly offered a ray of
hope. A fortnight ago you wouldn't have risked an Irish penny
on Manston's chances of avoiding the drop. After two matches
under Cowley's leadership anything looks possible.

We ourselves couldn't understand how we'd done it. An
hour of respectable effort and suddenly, for no reason, we'd
been flowing. That half-hour clinched Cowley's authority
with all of us. He'd known what he wanted to do, he'd done it
against all advice, and it had worked — we'd felt it work. So
we believed in him, the way you believe in a faith healer
who's made you feel better.

We were to need a bit of belief, because we hardly hit
another patch of form like that all season. But even when we
were playing badly and under the cosh, we had the incentive
to hang on because we knew what was in us. A moment or two
of that quality could win or save us a game. More often than
not we were finding enough to get us at least a point. In
January, a week after being knocked out of the F.A. Cup, we
gained our first away win of the season, and climbed away
from the foot of the table.

Barring injury the team was always the one that had scored
that 3—0 win. Cowley couldn't add to his squad because he
had no money, so his chief concern was to develop what
talents we could offer him. That first press conference was
typical, because he used it not to say anything about himself,
but to boost one of the lads — in this case Ian Farthing. He'd
played in the same side as Ian years before, and had formed
the opinion that he could be a great player if only he believed
in himself. At Manston, right from the start, Geoff put it
about that Ian was an undiscovered genius, a superb play-
maker with a magic right foot. The fact was that in the ten
years or so since Cowley had known him Farthing had hidden
his abilities pretty carefully. He could use the ball well on his
day, but he was chiefly known as a coward and a moaner.
Cowley did all he knew to build up his ego off the field and to
give him protection and room to manoeuvre on it. Geoff
would wheedle him and plead with him: 'You're the only one
who can do it for us, Ian. It's down to you. Go out there and

win us the game.' Whining and complaining, Farthing would do what was asked of him, hitting long through balls like Beckenbauer.

In a less obvious way Steve Brine was also changed. For years he'd been a loyal, hard-working pro, in the shadow of flashier team-mates. As captain he was a new man, a brilliant organiser of the defence and a shrewd, driving leader. But the most remarkable transformation job Cowley did was probably on Ben Dooner. In the case of Ian and Briney Geoff had talent to work on. Ben was just a big-hearted trudger, and at twenty-eight could have had no expectation of becoming anything more. Cowley reconstructed him from scratch. He had the two of us training together a lot to develop our understanding, so I used to hear him working on Ben. 'You've been selling youself short for years,' he told him. 'There's more to you than you've ever used. That's got to change. We're going to reshape your body and your game. We're going to make you feared.' Ben took to that idea. He was a hefty lad, but the only fear he'd ever caused was that he might accidentally tread on your foot. Everything Geoff asked of him he eagerly did. He was put through a course of weight training, he was put on a special diet. He had sessions with an athletics coach to improve his jumping ability and speed off the mark. Fifty per cent of all this — maybe ninety — was just propaganda, but it did wonders for Ben. If his body wasn't reshaped, his mind was. It helped, of course, that he was given a new role. In the past he'd been a target man, and a poor one, big enough to aim at but too clumsy to kill the ball or lay it off. Now, if anything, I was to be a sort of target man for Ian Farthing, and Big Ben was to be a trouble-maker. By the end of the season Cowley had him careering through the centre like a runaway truck. He could look crude, but he could also look bloody formidable. He scored a few goals, he won us a few penalties, and above all he caused a bit of havoc.

Geoff showed no particular interest in any of his new signings. It was as though he'd expressed enough confidence in bringing them to Manston Park in the first place. He probably also reckoned that we could look after ourselves —

Herrick because he was young and cocky, Carpenter because nothing upset him, and Gilpin because he'd be all right as long as the goals kept coming — and they did keep coming. After that conversation in his car I don't think we had a confidential talk in years. In fact I came to be amazed that he'd told me as much as he had, because I never again heard him talk about his own personality and ambitions — at least, only once more. He was a quieter man than any other manager or coach I've worked with — literally quiet: he had a fair amount to say, but never raised his voice. Even those who'd never seen him play could tell he was a hard customer — but not from anything he said. It was all in his manner. The old competitiveness and violence had been converted to concentration. He hated to waste time or emotion or energy. The impression you had of him in training was an impression of watchfulness. Whenever you glanced up, somehow that great double eyebrow would catch your attention, and you could sense him staring from under it, weighing up every movement you made. No one could touch him for analysing a player — one of his own or an opponent. He could take your game to pieces, tell you how you moved, where you ran, what you saw, how you tackled, passed or took a pass. I liked that. I was a fine-tuned player, a touch player: I needed a coach who could spot the small things going wrong. By February I was playing as well as I'd ever done — perhaps better. Having seen how Dooner and some of the others had been developed, I used to wonder how much of the credit was mine and how much was Cowley's. But it didn't matter to me that much. Whatever I was doing had come out of myself. Why it was coming out now when it had been blocked so long I didn't fully know and didn't care — as long as it kept coming.

It so happened that in February we played four sides in the top eight. Scrapping, tussling and containing, and then hitting back in sharp fits and starts, we somehow grabbed a point a game. All the same, it was clearer to me by then that we had some serious limitations. Dooner was improving, but he only showed in spasms. Mallison was past it. Henshaw and Long had no class, though Long almost made up for it by sheer heart. When they were outplayed in midfield Herrick was kept too busy to look after Farthing. A couple of hard knocks, and Ian would hide for the next half-hour. But the great strength of the team was that even on our bad days we were never demoralized. Having fought that near to safety we were sure as hell going the rest of the way. Funnily enough we weren't that close, off the field. Rees, Farthing and Brine were all inclined to be loners in their different ways. Mallison was a good bit older than the rest of us, and Paget was taken up with a dry-cleaning business he'd started. As for Carpenter, though he didn't seem thick or unfriendly, you could never get to know him. If you started a conversation with Long John it would quickly wind down, like a ball bouncing lower and lower till it stops. I myself was what I'd always been — sociable in small doses. But on the field the squad had a lot of mutual respect. Each of us knew the others would play flat out. The only whiner was Ian Farthing, and he was allowed to get away with it because it did him good. We were such a stubborn, rubbery side that coming from behind was almost our speciality. The opposition would go one up and pile in for the second, rocking us right back on our heels. What with Mallison's lack of pace, Paget's lack of reach, and Carpenter's awkwardness we'd look ragged and uncertain — there for the taking. But somehow we'd hang on and hang on. Then a prod out of defence, a long ball from Ian Farthing, and we'd be whipping through their guard to equalize. When that happened away from home there was always the same reaction from the crowd — a sudden disgusted silence, as though they couldn't believe their bad luck. But luck hadn't done the job: it was planning and character.

All that spring I was having a good life off the park, scrappy and disconnected. I couldn't be held to anything. What I was enjoying was exactly what was supposed to have spoiled my early days at Oldfield — living out of a suitcase and only getting back to see Claire for the odd night. We actually got on better like that. At least, I did. In my spare time I was back to my old ways of prowling around, on foot or in the car, and feeling out the place. Although I was sleeping in a hotel I made myself at home in the town.

Round about Easter Harvey gave me a ring, having had a week's leave in London. He didn't want to talk over the phone, but arranged to visit the hotel. To tell the truth the move to Manston had put Harvey, Karen and Jonathan right out of my head. Now they'd re-entered it I was suddenly nervy.

At the first sight of me Pete was all teeth, beaming with joy.

'Back in the goals! Didn't I tell you? Marvellous! Fucking marvellous!'

He was genuinely delighted that I was scoring again, but he stayed with the subject so long he obviously didn't fancy what was coming next. I noticed him wriggling as he chattered, like a little kid dying for a pee. That made me more edgy myself. When I did mention Karen he started talking about her readily enough, but avoided my eye. Yes, he'd traced her easily, from the information I'd given. She and her mother were still at the same address. She wasn't married. She was still (for Christ's sake) working in the canteen at Ferris Clark's. She was in good health.

At last Harvey gave me a quick glance. 'Vin — you're not going to like what's coming. . .'

'Get on with it.'

'I got to talk with her. Like we said. She found out you sent me.'

He looked so uneasy I guessed the pay-off: Karen was with him, and waiting to see me.

'You great prat, Harv. How did you let it out?'

'When I asked about the kid. There isn't any kid.'

I felt like Dawes kicking a ball that wasn't there.

'D'you mean it's died?'

'No. It was never alive. There never was one. She made it up.'

I couldn't say anything. My face must have been pretty blank. Pete hurriedly went on again: 'I told her I'd see you. I told her I'd try to explain. What happened: she made it up in the first place to get you interested when you'd gone off to

129

Stanborough. You just offered her money, so she took it, out of revenge. Then she couldn't stop because she'd have to pay it back, and she'd spent some of it. But she knew you'd find out one day. She didn't know what to do. She's been worrying herself silly. Honest, Vin, she's bloody terrified . . .'

'Sod me!' I said. 'So she should be fucking terrified. It's fraud. I must have given her bloody thousands.'

'She'll pay it back, Vin. Give her a bit of time. She'll pay instalments.'

I stared at him, with my mind empty. Karen had done me completely. What with a few minutes here and a few minutes there I'd spent hours thinking of that kid, and the little fucker had never existed. I wasn't sorry to hear it — I wasn't exactly angry. I didn't know what I felt. Now you see him, now you don't. And he'd cost me thousands. Of course if I'd ever tried to see him the whole thing would have been blown: it was neat, really. I suddenly started laughing, a bit like I'd done that time with Pat Arnold. Sex could turn ridiculous quicker than anything else. Harvey watched me for a minute a bit hesitant, but then joined in with his jackass laugh, full of relief. I realised he'd been stiff with worry.

'What are you going to do?' he asked when we'd calmed down.

'Nothing. Bloody serves me right. She can keep the money. But she won't be getting any more. What's she done with it, for Christ's sake?'

'It's mostly in the bank. She was too scared to spend it. That's why she can start paying you back.'

'No — let her keep it. She can buy a car — or an electric-chair for her mum.'

'Will you write to her?'

'No thanks. You tell her.'

Harv went off quite happy, pleased to have good news for Karen, pleased to be doing a favour for a well-known foot-baller, and pleased that his old mate could take a generous line. I didn't feel so good myself. For the first time in years I really remembered Karen, and what it had been like to be with her — remembered her white face and her black hair. It was embarrassing to think of her writing that letter. Terrible. Like seeing someone's operation scar. It showed how bad she must have felt when I nipped off. I couldn't imagine Claire ever writing a letter like that — but then she wasn't a loser.

In my memory the last part of that season seems easy. I knew we'd stay up, and we did, by three clear points. By the end the newspapers were taking our achievements pretty much for granted: a miracle stops looking like one when it happens by degrees. Having scored thirteen goals — one more than Geoff asked me for — I regarded my own performance in the same way. My year of poor form seemed like an illness which I'd recovered from and need never get a second time. Once again I was a leading scorer and an England prospect. It felt normal.

The close season was crowded and lively. Claire joined me at Manston, and we moved into our third home in two years. Now that Town had dodged the drop and I was back in the news she was in good spirits. She was also pleased at having shown herself to be a shrewd operator in the area of buying and selling and decorating houses. We'd made some ridiculous profit, such as £15,000, on the sale of the Oldfield place. She came to our new residence, out near the Manston training ground, full of expensive ideas. Luckily this time she was willing to employ professionals, and didn't ask much from me apart from applause.

In June I took her off to Majorca. We were both feeling confident. A few months previously I wouldn't have fancied making a trip like this without a false name and a false moustache: now I was signing autographs and buying drinks, happy as a sparrow. Claire found the whole trip a turn-on — the aeroplane, the sunshine, the hotel, the beaches, people chatting us up. The only thing she couldn't come to terms with was the amount of time I spent swimming around with a snorkel, renewing my acquaintance with the fish. In other respects it was one of the best fortnights we ever had together. With the sun, and the rum and coke, and the social life all getting to her, Claire was as amorous as she'd ever managed to be.

The pay-off came on the last night of our stay, when she said to me in bed: 'Wouldn't it be nice to have a baby?'

Having just got rid of one I didn't fancy being lumbered again straight away. I said something about waiting a year or two. It was all I could do to sort myself out, never mind being responsible for someone else. Claire didn't pursue the subject, but the conversation gave me a pang of fear, because I knew she'd come back to it. Since our marriage she'd been wearing some device which fielded my sperm like Gordon Banks. She was a strong-willed girl in her way, and when she thought the time was ripe, out it would go with no further consultation. I'd been given an early warning.

On the way back through London we had a day or two at Beaufort, as a contrast to the Mediterranean. Nothing much had changed there: maybe Dad was a stage more sunk into himself. His cat had died, but he'd laid in another, and looked after it extra seriously, as though needing it to do a bit of living on his behalf.

On the first evening we were on our way to the pub when Mum said: 'I expect you've been wondering what we've been doing with the money you send us.'

I hadn't, actually — assuming that Dad must have insisted on putting it all into a Building Society, or something equally as boring.

'Come over here,' she said. 'We've got a surprise for you.'

She unlocked one of the garages that had been built behind the flats, and showed us a brand-new Mini.

'Very nice,' I said. 'But neither of you can drive.'

'Not yet,' said Mum. 'I've just started lessons. I'll soon be driving us around.'

It was typical of her to take it on, but I couldn't think of anywhere that Dad would want to go to.

Chapter *10*

When the players reported back in July, sun-tanned and cheery, we found Geoff Cowley looking exactly as he'd done in April — pale and serious. We felt as though he'd not set foot outside the stadium all summer in case he lost his concentration. We imagined him sitting at his desk, hour after hour, with no expression on his face, or else strolling slowly round and round the pitch, brooding over the coming season. That suited us. We'd worked hard to keep Manston in the First Division, carried out that miracle, and then buggered off for a well-earned rest. Now we were refreshed and ready for work, and looking to Geoff to turn us on again. The previous season we'd had a clear aim, survival, and we'd achieved it. Now it was up to Cowley to lay on a new challenge for us.

But he didn't. He got us down to training in a workmanlike way, as though keeping us fit was the only business of the club. Through practice games he taught us to accommodate a couple of new players. We won out pre-season friendlies with something to spare. But all this time Cowley seemed to be in low gear. He kept his thoughts to himself, and he gave us no firm lead. In fact he hardly said a word about the coming season. It was laughable, really, how disconcerted we were. Fifteen or sixteen grown men, all experienced players, waiting for a message from the medicine-man.

Then in the week before the League programme started he gave this puny interview to the local paper. Every comment he made was as pale as his face. What was he looking for in the new season? Well, the first aim was for Town to finish a bit higher in the League than last time. Had he set himself any targets? He was waiting to see what the team could do. Would it have a new look, what with the new signings? Well, Dick Starling was taking over at left-back because Mallison had been appointed player-coach to the reserves. Charley Mount should give us a bit more power in the engine-room. And we'd have Howard Bush available again on the wing. Would the changes make for exciting soccer? They should give us a few more options. Any chance of Manston winning a major trophy? Well, you had to remember that Town could only afford a small squad. A couple of injuries at the wrong time could destroy any hopes we had. But any predictions? Ask again at the end of December. Any message for the fans? Be patient, and judge the team by results.

It was terrible, colourless stuff. We were passing round the paper in the dressing-room, and every one of us was depressed, even old poker-face Carpenter. This was the time of year to make some boasts while you still could, if only to whip up morale and sell a few more season tickets. And this was the manager who'd dragged us to glory the previous spring, promising the fans the impossible and then bringing it off. We couldn't think what had got into him.

On the Friday, after he'd picked the team for the opening match, he got the whole squad together and at last told us what was in his mind. For a pre-season pep-talk it was pretty low-key. He hardly raised his voice, but spoke very intently, or intensely as though he was telling us a secret plan.

'Since I took over Manston we've played twenty-two League games. And we've taken twenty-five points. If we'd done that well the whole of last season we'd have finished seventh in the First Division. Seventh. Now we're starting again with a stronger squad and a clear pattern of play. We'll do better yet. On our day we can beat any side in the League, home or away. You know that from last season. Everyone should know it. But we're still not a fancied team. No one can fathom us. We don't get our due because we're first and foremost an awkward side. We take the opposition by surprise: they can't believe they won't do us. Now we want more of those surprises, week in and week out. We won't be looking for publicity, we'll be looking for results. You've already shown what you can do in a tight finish. If we're in touch with the leaders next March we've got it in us to win the League. On the quiet, out of nowhere, we can win the League. We start tomorrow.'

Basically, what Geoff had told the newspaper was sensible, while what he told us was crazy. Manston was a club with no money and comparatively few supporters. The squad was so small that if Dooner and I had been injured at the same time Cowley might have had to play the tea-lady at number 9. Even at full strength we could boast few well-known names. If you'd had to pick one side from our own team and pretty well any other First Division team, only about four of our players would have been in with a shout.

But we believed Cowley's speech to us because he'd shown us what he could do — or shown us what he could get us to do. He could make players, put together a team, squeeze out a result. What he'd told us stood to be true: if we could do just a little oftener what we'd done in the spring we'd be title contenders.

It was also true that the squad was stronger. Howard Bush, the little black winger, was recovered from his broken leg. At the back we had Dick Starling, a utility defender bought from Nottingham. And above all Cowley had somehow twisted enough cash out of the Board to buy Charley Mount, an experienced midfield player well-known as a hard man. Having played against him on several occasions I was glad we'd got him. He'd give us some needed weight and strength. Although only medium height he was squat-built and heavy, a non-stop worker and a numbing tackler.

The idea was that with Mount's power and Herrick's

running in the middle of the park we could afford to play three men up front instead of two. So Howard Bush would come into the side instead of Mick Long. But for an accident, that could have meant the end of Mickey's career at Manston, except as a sub. The accident happened to Dick Starling, who broke a toe in the opening game. On an inspiration Cowley tried Long at left-back, and he did well enough to keep his place all season. His tackling and positional play left something to be desired, but he was good coming forward, and he had great heart. He had passion. For the first time in his career he was in a team he thought could win something big, and he was ready to give anything to stay part of it. There were others in the squad in the same situation. Brine, Mount, Paget, Dooner, Rees — they'd all spent three-quarters of a full footballing career working their guts out in middling sides. With just a sniff of success in the air at last they were all playing as though they had three balls. If there was something to be won they were ready to bleed for it.

Charley Mount and 'Bramble' Bush also did something extra for the morale of the side, each in his different way. Bramble was a little mad zig-zag dribbler who could cut a crooked hole through any defence when he was in the mood. But although he was a good, well-meaning lad he was totally absent-minded. Not only would he forget to look up: he could pass to an opponent or run the ball over the goal-line through sheer lack of thought. It would never have surprised me to see him dribble clear off the pitch and up over the terracing. Similarly he'd run and tackle back when he remembered to, but he was just as likely to forget. So we had to shout at him the whole time, to pull him back or push him forward or tell him when to pass. In a strange way that was good for us, because it kept us thinking and communicating on the pitch more than ever before. If we stopped calling the moves Bramble would go to sleep.

Charley, of course, was very different, totally alert, totally committed. For all his reputation as a chopper I wouldn't have called him a dirty player. He was so low slung and heavy-muscled that meeting his tackle was like hitting a concrete bollard. Being hard to hurt himself he wasn't fully aware how much damage he could do. And being a natural fighter he looked to take on anyone who was putting it about. An accidental thing against him was that he was ugly. Basically he looked like a frog: his head seemed to slope directly out of his thick shoulders, and he had a frog's bulging eyes and long mouth. In the thick of a game, with the eyes staring and the lips clenched he looked like a frog gone mad. Referees would book him for his villainous appearance. But his force and determination did a lot for Manston. Physically we were a lightweight side. It was reassuring to have a strong man among us. With Mount beside him Farthing was ready to come out of hiding.

It wasn't surprising, therefore that we got good results from the start of the season, and that Ian was our star player. With Mount and Herrick to clear him a bit of room he came into his own as a play-maker. Half our good moves started from him. Time and again Carpenter would find him, with a flip of his big boot or a sideways nod. A stride or two and a quick look round, and Ian would be dropping the ball on my chest, or curling it forward for Bush or Dooner to run at. Cowley had him taking penalties, corners from both wings, and all free-kicks anywhere near the penalty-box. He could bend his shot round the defensive wall or loop it on to Dooner's head. Twice that season he scored direct from the corner-flag by swerving the ball up for the wind to drift it in. Geoff had got him to believe that he was some sort of magician, and he became what he believed.

The strange thing was that his success made him still more of a moaner. Instead of being grateful to find stardom at the age of thirty-one he was resentful that it hadn't come earlier. He kept reading about himself in the papers — where they picked up Cowley's hints and called him the best passer of a ball in England, or Britain, or Europe — till he came to be his own greatest fan. Since he had few interests outside football he found plenty of time to brood over his bad luck and blame other people for it. In fact he'd had no bad luck in the past — he was exceptionally fortunate now. Mount and others were covering for his lack of courage, and Cowley was working on his brain. He was in a privileged position. But all the time he gave off discontent like body-odour.

We tolerated his whining because in our own way we had a great spirit in the squad. I say 'in our own way' because we weren't getting any more sociable off the field. Howard Bush was a joker, and kept up our spirits, but he spent most of his time with Neil Herrick. Charley Mount was a mild character in his private life, enjoying a laugh and a beer, but he was another family man, happiest at home with the kids. What held us together wasn't friendship but a sort of secret contract: 'he'll do his bit of the job if I do mine.' City hadn't been a friendly club, either, but there we'd had a superiority complex: we'd always expected to win, and thought something had gone wrong if the result went against us. At Manston it was nothing like that. We felt permanently like the under-dog in a cup-tie, looking to nick a result against the odds, and knowing we'd only have a chance if we made maximum use of all the resources we'd got. Ian was allowed a bit of moaning because he was one of our much needed specialists. If he got it off his chest he'd be more efficient. Coming home from one of our stolen away wins we weren't overjoyed. What we felt was a kind of professional satisfaction, like a bunch of bank robbers who'd pulled off another shrewd heist.

All through the autumn we stayed with the leading group, never higher than fourth or lower than eighth. If we suffered a defeat we'd bounce back a week later. For all our limitations we were a well-balanced side. Mount and Herrick were a great well of energy in the middle. Brine kept us sharp at the back and I kept us sharp at the front. We compensated for each other in unusual ways. Paget was weak on high crosses, so Carpenter looked after them. Long did some of Brine's running, and Brine thought for both of them. Mount tackled for Farthing, I made space for Ben Dooner. We all overlapped like the slates of a roof. Another advantage we enjoyed was that we never got complacent. We couldn't because we weren't good enough.

By contrast we were regularly under-rated, and it was easy enough to see why. Anyone could tell how we should be taken. The goalie punched at crosses he should have been catching, one full-back lacked pace and Carpenter looked so clumsy. Everything at the other end stemmed from Ian Farthing, who was known to go to pieces if you stood someone on him. So team after team tackled us in the same way, pushing up on Ian, breaking down the flanks and thumping over long centres. It ought to have worked, but it rarely did. Brine covered for the full-backs, Carpenter got his head to the crosses, and Mount looked after Farthing. Then after we'd soaked up a fair spell of pressure we'd break and snatch a goal.

To make matters worse for the opposition, they usually suffered from frustration. Class forwards hated to be tied up by a long freak like Carpenter. Hard defenders didn't relish being sold by a sharp little sod like me, or a clockwork golliwog like Bramble. As they got mad, so we got on top. Our sour bloody supporters used to milk this effect all they could, jeering with joy when John threw out a leg to rob some international striker or Bushy left a full-back tackling air. They weren't great at getting behind their own team, but they had a great line in derision. It was hard for a visiting side to keep its nerve and its temper.

So the results kept coming. But still the strength of our challenge wasn't fully recognized. As it happened we had a couple of games in hand of the other leading clubs, making our points total better than it looked. And in any case Geoff Cowley kept his comments on our progress pretty cautious. Yes, he was pleased. Yes, we were doing surprisingly well so far. Of course things might look different in the spring. But meanwhile, yes, he was quite pleased. It was when he was talking about individual players that he let himself go, building us up with words. Brine and Carpenter were the best pair of central defenders in the League; Herrick was the busiest chaser; I was the deadliest striker. Actually it was true that I was in good form. The whole side had a great will to win: and if we went into the last quarter of an hour on level terms we always reckoned to grab a victory. As the opposition tired we fought that much harder and got more men forward. All ten outfield players would be pushing up, pushing up, looking to attack: there was this energy or force running right through the team. But two times out of three I was the one who set up the goal or stuck it away. I couldn't have done it without the pressure behind me, but I was the sharp tip of the side.

Claire was in good form, too. She was pleased with the way the house was coming on, and since the Majorca holiday she'd got a new relish for being a celebrity's wife. A couple of women's magazines had interviewed her and taken pictures of her standing in her newly designed kitchen. By now she was in the habit of working on herself as hard as she worked on the house, redecorating all visible surfaces. When we were going out for the evening she took so much trouble with her skin and hair and nails and clothes that the preparations seemed more important to her than the occasion itself. If she had her choice we'd typically go to a flash restaurant, where most of the time she'd be only half with me. Her eyes would be wandering to see if there was anyone else she knew, or anyone who was recognizing us, or anyone of general interest. Usually this bothered me very little because my thoughts were on sex. I'd be sitting there with a hard on, feeding it with steak and red wine. My brain was in neutral and my prick was king for the evening. Since I had to make some conversation for the sake of sociability I often talked nonsense. For instance, I'd natter on about the steak, and the life it had had when it was still part of a hearty young bull in the hills of Devonshire.

To tell the truth conversation wasn't all that different at home. When I wasn't interested in what Claire was saying I'd drift into a light-hearted piss-take of some sort. For example, one evening she'd got it into her head that we should buy a budgerigar: What did I think? I just opened my mouth and let my imagination ramble:

'A budgerigar? Good idea. Why not get a couple and have them breed a family? We can teach them to talk, so they can chat among themselves. Mind you, for real conversation they say a mina-bird's the thing to get — as long as you don't mind the droppings. They're great talkers and great crappers. Crap their own weight every three hours. Maybe a cockatoo's better. Or a couple of each. We could build out a little room next to the kitchen for an aviary. The birds could fly and talk and sing and crap, morning and night.'

Claire never knew how to reply to rubbish like this, other than by saying 'Don't tease me' or something of the sort, and it didn't count as being nasty. I found it another useful little way of clearing a bit of space around myself.

To understand my behaviour, then and later, you have to remember that once or twice a week I was swopping knocks and banging skulls with some rugged fucker, bigger and heavier than me, whose basic purpose was to shut me down by fair means or foul. Thanks to Cyril Islip I was a nasty handful, but I had to be all concentration to hold the edge physically and still play football. Quick as I was I took some thumps and gashes. I got through the second half of a match against Stoke City in a state of concussion, and came off remembering nothing — not even the result. As it happened I saw the highlights of the game next day on TV and found that I'd played pretty well. All done on automatic — made me wonder if I was some kind of robot. Before the season was over I had a glimpse of my own shin-bone, and had one testicle —the left — swell up like a coconut. But the worst for me was the evening when, feeling perfectly OK, I went up to the toilet and found myself pissing blood. I all but passed out — the only time I can recall that happening. Later the doctor told me what was wrong — something quite trivial — but to me it still seemed like a mix-up inside, as though the water supply had been accidentally connected to the gas. I suppose all these things took their toll. Physically and mentally I was over-strained, though I didn't show it. In fact I was flat out not to show it, which probably strained me more. But the total effect was that on a Saturday night I hadn't much to offer. I was good for nothing but eating, drinking and screwing. And the screwing wasn't up to First Division standard. Claire tossed herself about a bit, and managed a little squeal, but she seemed only to do it because she thought it was expected. After a hard Saturday I could have done with more appreciation.

The player I'd come to envy was John Carpenter, who still didn't seem to feel any nervous strain at all. As soon as he'd finished a game or a training session he was off into a world of his own. I remember I once paid him a surprise visit at his home, which was in a country village well away from the town, and arrived to find him on his back underneath an old car, with his great long legs sticking out from under the bonnet. All around him were components: he'd taken the whole engine to pieces. His gingery-haired wife took me off to get a cup of tea, and told me he'd got four vintage cars that he was always working on. Two of them he'd rebuilt completely. For me a car had always been just a magic box — I'd never cared to look under the bonnet. So Long John's expertise impressed me. Later when he'd washed his hands and come to join us he had these two big dogs with him, Airedales, that followed him and watched him wherever he went. Full-time fans. I began to understand how John was so calm. He did most of his living on a different level from the rest of us. When he was mixing with the lads in the squad he was friendly enough, but in a limited way, like, say, a Chinese visitor who's got enough English for casual conversation, but goes on thinking and feeling in Chinese. John was more at home with his animals and machines than he was with human beings.

I could have done with some hobbies myself, but I found it hard to settle to anything. I needed to have my curiosity tickled. Some books I quite enjoyed, but I was more of a dipper than a reader. If I had the story of a round-the-world sailing-trip I'd turn straight to the storms. I liked books about exploration or true adventure, and anything to do with natural wonders, such as spontaneous combustion or the yeti, or the day it rained frogs. Driving round the villages outside Manston I used to stop off to browse round antique shops. I fancied the idea of collecting something, but I didn't know anything about art, and Claire looked after the furnishings, so in the end I settled on pocket-knives. The collecting itself was quite interesting, but once you had the knives you couldn't do much with them but clean them and look at them.

In January, after playing at White Hart Lane, I met my old man and ground out a bit of conversation with him.

'How's it going, then, Dad?'

'Not too bad.'

'Is Mum all right?'

'She's fine.'

'What about Terry?'

'He's all right.'

'Any changes at the timber-yard?'

'No, they don't change much.'

I could sense he felt strained, but couldn't make out why. Then just as he was making to go, his big blue face turned agitated, and he said: 'One thing to tell you, Vince: your Mum's gone off. She's left home. She's gone off with this bloke.'

'What bloke?'

'Bradley is his name. Jimmy Bradley. He was her driving instructor.'

I had to stop myself from laughing. It was like some soft story in the Sunday papers. Presumably she'd only met this Bradley through buying the car, so he couldn't be the same bloke I'd seen nipping out of her bedroom window. Mum was a goer.

'Christ!' I said. 'Will she come back?'

'I dunno. She says not.'

Poor old sod, I thought. And then: that's why she went off — because he's a poor old sod.

'How are you making out, Dad? Are you cooking for yourself?'

'I boil up some eggs. Or bring home a pie.'

I couldn't think of much more to say, but gave him a big cheque in hopes to cheer him up.

A couple of days later Mum herself phoned.

'I hear you had a talk with your Dad?'

'Yeh.'

'Well, you know it all, then.'

'Only that you left home.'

'I'm sorry for your Dad, but I was so shut in there. I was bored.'

'Yeh. Well, I left home myself.'

'I don't know what he wanted me for, except to cook and clean up. That's no sort of life. I like to get about a bit.'

'You always did, Mum.'

'You'd like Jimmy,' she said. 'He's a joker.'

The whole situation left my mind blank. I didn't mention it to Claire, thinking that whatever she said about it would be wrong.

That March I played my first full international. The service I had was so different from what I'd got used to at Manston that I didn't really shine. I had a fair game, a useful game, but I didn't shine. I wasn't discouraged, but I knew I'd have to adapt that much better if I was to be an England regular. Several other Town players were also getting recognition. Farthing was too old to be capped, and Mount was kept out by a good crop of midfielders, but Neil Herrick was in the Under-23's, and Rees was back in the Welsh team. And already one or two people were beginning to say that Carpenter might make an England stopper, for all his awkwardness. But the big turn-up was when some official or other discovered that Dooner's grandmother had kept an Irish terrier, and he was capped for Eire.

The sports writers had been looking for Town to come unstuck that spring, when our style was rumbled or we ran out of luck. But we stayed in contention, always able to pull something out of the bag. Even if Dooner and I were shut out the goals would come. Neil Herrick scored several, usually nipping forward on the one-two. Charley Mount powered a couple from outside the box. Going forward we tended to be a left-sided team, so Rees often found some clear space on the other wing. Long John Carpenter was always a danger, loping in late to meet Ian Farthing's corners. Apart from Briney, who looked after the shop when the other lads moved forward, all the outfield players got on the score-sheet. The surprise packet, in a way, was Mick Long. His performances that season were something I couldn't explain: he was a poor footballer who regularly played well. As a full-back he should have been a liability. He had no positional sense, his control was weak and his tackling was clumsy. But he made himself useful by sheer grit and graft, and several times he actually turned a game we could well have lost. Under the very hardest pressure he was liable to come up with something extraordinary, storming through the opposition in a solo run, turning up on the right wing, or swerving in an impossible shot from thirty-five yards. His abilities were mediocre, but he had these moments of inspiration.

With eight matches left to go we were fourth in the table, only three points behind the leaders, but still no one was giving us a chance. We didn't have the experience, or the tradition, or a big enough squad. What wasn't appreciated was the spirit we had in the team now we'd come so far. We were like a channel swimmer within a mile of the French coast: fucked as we were it would take a lot to stop us. And at the back of us all the time, was Geoff Cowley. He'd not only put the side together, he held it together. At this crucial period of the season his determination and concentration kept us going, flowing through the squad like electricity.

I've often been asked the secret of his success, but have no clear answer. But it comes back to the difference between the violent bugger who worked me over at Millwood and the steel-haired manager who never raised his voice. He'd learned to contain all his stresses and turn then into energy. I've sat beside him on the bench at a tight game and seen the tension stiffen and shake his body so powerfully that you could tell how the bile and the acid must be churning up inside, burning his guts and killing his hair-roots. But at the final whistle, win or lose, he'd get up without a word.

For that last fifth of the season he had to ease us forward match by match, each one like a cup-tie. Injuries were starting to tell, because our reserve strength was so frail. Dick Starling had to play three different positions in consecutive games. Henshaw came into midfield. When Bramble was injured Mick Long was pushed forward and old man Mallison was recalled at left-back. Several of us who played regularly were carrying bad knocks. But we'd hang on, game after game, chasing, smothering, bluffing, whipping in a counter-attack when the chance came. In my mind I kept going back to those six games at Stanborough. If a poor side under a pissy manager could pull that off, then Town had to have a chance under Cowley. Repeatedly the character of the squad pulled us through. Brine would keep the marking tight and get us organized against the set-pieces, Mount would come pounding out of defence shaking his fist to drive us on, Herrick would be everywhere, winning the ball, flicking it forward, screaming for the return. Up front, although slowed down by a knee injury, I stayed sharp enough to grab the half-chances. We inched forward: a 1—0 win, a 1—1 draw, two more 1—0 wins, a 2—1 win when we'd been a goal down. We lost 0—2 at Molyneux but won our next home game by the same score. In the circumstances it was a great run, but it cost us, physically. We went into our final match of the season, at Villa Park, needing a draw to take the title. Herrick and Dooner were out with injuries, Mount was playing with stiches in his head, Rees and Farthing were heavily strapped, and I could only reach three-quarter pace. We couldn't manage anything much in the way of attack, but Carpenter and Brine defended like heroes, and Paget made three great saves. With half an hour to go I skidded in a cross from Howard Bush, and we all thought we were there, but Villa equalized two minutes later. For the rest of the game they pounded us non-stop, and we pulled ten men back. Alone upfield I limped to and fro, waving for passes that never came. The defenders were just belting the ball off the pitch at every opportunity, and so I could do nothing but watch and suffer. When the whistle went, with the score still 1-1, I was so drained that I just flopped down into the mud, too knackered even to feel happy.

Chapter 11

I'd never been the player to win the heart of a crowd. They'd cheer on the battlers, Mount and Herrick, and Ben Dooner on his good days. They'd applaud Howard Bush when his dribbling came off, and boo him when it didn't. There was a cheer for Ian Farthing's long passes or for Carpenter's last-second tackling. But I myself never gave the fans much to see. My best work was in quick turns and single touches. My goals were numerous, but not spectacular, mostly coming from close range. But somehow in the autumn following our championship season I became what you could call a star. Playing for England had helped: I'd won two more caps and scored my first international goal in the summer tour of Eastern Europe. But television probably had more to do with it. There'd been a little number about me one Saturday lunchtime — 'Today the spotlight falls on Vince Gilpin' — using the words 'quick' and 'deadly' every ten seconds. Then I'd scored the September Goal of the Month: a long ball from Farthing, a header from Ben, a volley from me. I came to be interviewed pretty regularly after a televised game, being able to string a few words and wisecracks together. Thanks to the publicity the Manston fans gradually warmed to me a little. When I scored or went near, the old sing-song would echo round: 'Vin Gil Pin! Vin Gil Pin!'

Being better known, I was regularly approached in shops or bars or restaurants. I never minded saying a word or two and whipping off my vicious autograph. Actually I was interested how the signature always came out the same, as though my hand was a machine. Once at the sea-side I wrote it in huge letters on the sand with a length of driftwood and then looked down at it from a cliff and found it to be no different from usual. Now Town were champions there was plenty of public relations work to be done, and I did more than my share, visiting schools and hospitals and fêtes. But I still valued my privacy. I liked to be able to disappear. Once again I was helped by the ordinariness of my face. If I combed my hair differently, or grew a little weedy moustache, or stuck on a pair of sun-glasses, hardly anyone would spot me.

This mattered, because I was right back in my old routine of prowling the town. What with mid-week matches, some of them miles away in Carlisle or Turkey, the P.R. visits, and regular treatment from the physio, I'd got into a useful routine of not spending too much time at home. I had many small interests, but rarely pursued any of them longer than half an hour at a time. Without being anything of a drinker I dropped into every pub in town. I'd go to the public library and dip into a book or two, though rarely borrowing any. But most of the time I was just browsing the streets: not just the main ones, but side-streets, suburbs, back-alleys, tow-paths. I really inhabited that town. I could have mapped the place.

A lot of exploring was done indoors. One Wednesday I walked into a church and sat through half an hour of service. There were only five other people there, all over sixty. It could have been a voodoo ceremony for all it meant to me, but I put a fiver in a box at the door by way of good manners. Sometimes in a big department store I'd talk about buying a hi-fi or a three piece suite for no particular purpose. More often I'd drop into a dark little sweet-shop for a Mars bar. A proportion of the people I talked to guessed who I was. Altogether I made quite a few acquaintances, as I'd done at Stanborough, without being too sure what I was about. Perhaps I wanted to be recognized as the star they couldn't recognize.

My absences caused very little discontent at home. Claire had picked up the idea that in my profession I might be called away at any time, like a doctor or a soldier. If I came in late I just had to say 'Extra training' or 'Heat treatment'. In any case she had numerous activities of her own by this time, even apart from the house and garden, including riding lessons, modern dance classes, and having her mother or an aunt or some school-friend over for the day.

One of these visitors had quite an influence on me. This girl — I'll call her Jill — was staying for the week-end. On the Sunday afternoon she saw me score a goal on the Big Match, and then crack a joke or two in an interview. An hour later I had to drive her to the station, and all the way there I could sense her glancing at me. We were talking about the footballer's life, one of the few subjects I knew much about. When we pulled up in the station car park she said:

'Doesn't Claire get jealous?' Her voice sounded a bit unnatural.

'Why should she?'

'You star players must be able to get any girl you want.'

'Do you reckon?'

'Yes.'

The look that went with the word was enough to make me re-start the car, and drive us out to Merton Woods, which were dark and leafless, this being December. We finished in time for her to catch the next train.

Over the next few days I thought about this episode. Never before had Jill shown any interest in me or in football. She didn't seem bothered about meeting me again. For her this had been a one-off. Something had worked on her pretty directly, and the only possibility seemed to have been the television programme. Perhaps she thought that every man who'd appeared on the box had a luminous dick. I remember Pat Arnold saying that there were thousands of women up and down the land with a hair trigger needing just a touch. My talking picture on the screen had done the trick for Jill. Truth to tell I hadn't greatly relished our car-fuck at the time of doing it, what with the gear-lever and the awkward angles, but later I got a good deal of pleasure out of it. There'd been the surprise, the excitement, the compliment. I fancied more of all that, and was soon getting it.

The great thing about Jill was the way she'd left town as soon as her knickers were back on. The perfect lover. Unlike Pat Arnold I wanted no risk or hassle. I was looking for security and privacy, but I didn't fancy hookers. At that stage my ideal bang would have gone through three stages.

Stage One: *She*: 'Aren't you Vincent Gilpin?'

Self: 'I am actually.'

She: 'You're my favourite footballer.'

Self: 'Thank you.'

She: 'I don't know how to say this, exactly, but would you come and screw me immediately, in the privacy of my own flat?'

Self: 'If it would help.'

Stage Two: *She*: 'Oh, that was fantastic! Oh, I've never felt anything like it! How do you do it?'

Self: 'I just played my normal game.'

Stage Three (ten minutes later):

She: 'The awful thing is, I'm emigrating to Australia tomorrow, so I'll never see you again.'

Self: 'That's life.'

It never worked like that, of course — in fact my little grind with Jill was as close as I got to my ideal. And underneath I was soon hankering for a bit of continuity, as with my greengrocer's wife, for a change from variety. By the end of the season I was getting a taste of both. The personalities concerned included two shop assistants, a bar-maid, a traffic warden and a girl in a travel agency. After all I began to remind myself of Pat Arnold. In a way the screwing was a logical result of all my wandering around. Wherever I went exploring I came to have half an eye to the chance of getting my end away.

Altogether my life seemed to have taken on a kind of natural balance. There were three parts to it: football, poking around and home. The last part was the weak one of the three. The total number of hours I spent awake at home wasn't that large any more, and though I talked to Claire a fair amount I was saying less than ever. She'd changed a lot, and so had I. I suppose it often happens: you marry one person and find youself living with another. When I allowed for what she wasn't interested in and what I didn't want to tell her, there wasn't that much left over to talk about.

Mum dropped me a couple of letters and phoned a few times full of chat. She nattered on about her new bloke as though I knew him or cared about him. 'Jimmy's been working long hours lately,' she'd say, or 'Jimmy's trying a new hair-style.' I hadn't seen his old hair-style — for all I knew he could have been bald. She'd also say: 'Your Dad's all right. I was in at the week-end to cook him a meal. He's coping quite well.'

That season after we'd won the championship was a strenuous one for Manston. We were like a runner who'd won his first marathon and was entered for a second. We knew we could do it, but we also knew what bloody hard labour it was going to be. In fact it turned out to be more like a double marathon. Naturally, as we were champions, every team we played was out to gun us down. Without striking peak form we'd somehow managed to stay alive in both the European Cup and the League Cup. The fixtures were piling up. By now we had experience enough to pace ourselves, regularly doing no more that just enough. The results were very respectable, but we'd lost some of the old enjoyment. My own form continued good. That second championship medal had meant a lot more to me than the first. City could possibly have taken the title without me, but Manston never could: I'd been a key man. Knowing that helped to heighten my game. So did playing abroad, whether for Manston or for England. I'd trot on to a pitch a thousand miles from home and find some swarthy big bugger from Tashkent or Istanbul jostling at my back wherever I turned. But I'd know I could take him; I'd know I could get a goal off him. And more often than not I did.

There was only one cloud: I still hadn't quite clinched the England place. I'd played effectively, I'd scored — but I'd

151

not yet left my mark on a game. More than anything I wanted to be *the* England striker, an automatic name on the team-sheet. I looked to put on an international performance or two that would make that sure. I had to prove that I could do it on my own, without Cowley, without Ian Farthing.

In January Town were lying third in the League and went smoothly through to the fifth round of the F.A. Cup. The last week-end of the month Dad was making one of his routine phone-calls, and seeming, as usual, to run out of things to say, when he suddenly cleared his throat like a gun going off and asked if he could come and stay for a few days. Naturally I said he could, and we did our best for him. Claire showed him over the house and fed him some decent meals. I took him to a mid-week match and a pub or two. But all the time he was subdued. You couldn't tell what was going on behind the face. All his reactions were half a pace slow: even walking down the street he seemed to hang back half a yard. It was like leading an elephant on a string. I was expecting him to mention Mum, but he never did. Once or twice I gave him a lead-in to make it easier for him, but nothing came of it. I couldn't work out what had brought him.

The bright spot of his stay came unexpectedly. After training one morning I took him to a pub nearby, and in walked John Carpenter and his wife, Sally. Over a lager or two John and my old man moved into quite a lively conversation. I'd hardly ever heard either of them say so much at one sitting, and I couldn't understand it. The talk was nothing special — mostly about the recent news in the papers, such as a big bank-raid and the sinking of an oil-tanker. If I'd said to my Dad what Carpenter was saying, or said to Carpenter what my Dad was saying, I'd never have got these long answers. Somehow the two of them hit it off — Christ knows why. I wasn't the only one to notice the oddity of it: Sally Carpenter was having a little grin to see her husband so chatty. She wasn't a great talker herself, but what she did say was smart, and when she wasn't speaking you could tell she was up with the play, if not ahead of it, from the alertness of her eyes.

'Do you see your dad much?' I asked her.

'He was cremated last October.'

'I'm sorry,' I said, embarrassed.

'You needn't be. He was dead at the time.'

She smiled to show there was no needle. I guessed she must talk all round old Carp at home, like my mother had talked round my old man. Long John still puzzled me. He puzzled everyone. At least I'd come to understand him better as a footballer. It wasn't that he had no timing — in fact his timing was excellent. He just worked off a different clock from anyone else's. I could only guess that his social personality was unusual in a similar way. He hadn't struck the normal balance between what goes on in your head and what you get to communicate. The players had come to see this strangeness as a kind of strength. He was our totem pole.

The day after that meeting Dad said at breakfast: 'Well, I'll be taking off today.'

'You haven't stayed any time.'

'I've got a few things to do,' he said, which wasn't true.

I thought he might come out with something on the way to the station, but he didn't.

'You're all right, Dad, are you?' I asked him, after buying him a ticket.

'Yes. Oh yes, son. I'm all right.'

He went slowly off down the platform, like a patient newly out of hospital.

Gradually, through February, as the results kept coming, you could feel the tension tightening at the club. Tim Sheridan was the first to put the situation clearly in print. After we'd drawn the away leg of the League Cup semi-final he wrote:

Geoff Cowley can and will deny it, but those close to him know that he's beginning to dream the impossible dream. He thinks Town have it in them to achieve an incredible quartet of trophies: League championship, for the second year running, League Cup, F.A. Cup and European Cup.

A tall order? As tall as Mount Everest. But Everest was climbed in the end.

Tim's article had some truth in it. Getting as far as we had had been a long hard slog, pretty much like struggling up a mountain. And now we'd fought our way high enough to feel a bit dizzy if we looked round. Geoff was staying typically cautious, but I knew him well enough to read in his face what I felt in my own mind: we could do it. The previous season, having gone so far, we'd nicked match after match when it counted. Why shouldn't we do it again? Our weird mixture of rejects and bargain-buys would have an even chance against any club side on earth. And just round the corner was a success that would never be beaten and probably never equalled.

The atmosphere was even getting to our supporters. It was true they never lifted us like Liverpool or Newcastle fans: success was still new to the club. They came and watched us like they'd watch a high-wire act, as ready to jeer a fall as cheer an achievement — but at least they were coming. The day of the return leg of our League Cup semi-final the Chairman announced plans for the building of a massive new stand, and said that Manston was going to be one of the great clubs of Europe.

We celebrated by losing 1—2. After going a goal down in three minutes we fought back to equalize before half-time. We were into a familiar situation from which we'd won a score of times. We knew the last quarter-hour would see us home. But twenty minutes from time their right-back scored with a wild swing from thirty yards, and from that moment they all retreated to crowd us out till the final whistle. Even back in the dressing-room we could hardly believe it. Cowley told us, which was true, that we'd played as well as we'd done all season, but that didn't help. After weeks of walking on water we'd suddenly got our feet wet.

Characteristically Cowley picked us up again straight away. There was plenty left for us to do. When we went off to play the second leg of our European Cup quarter-final we were 1—0 up from the home tie and already into the semi-finals of the F.A. Cup. And we were still clinging on to third

154

place in the League. Tim Sheridan's write-up of the match can tell the story:

Yes, that dream CAN come true. Last night's drawn game leaves Manston still on course for the impossible treble. After a twelfth-minute header from Bellini had cancelled out their first-leg advantage Brine and his men hung on grimly against all-out attacking pressure and the non-stop hostility of a baying, whistling crowd. In a fiercely competitive, sometimes brutal, game Mount, Long and Dooner were all booked, along with three of their Italian opponents. Town forced a couple of corners early in the second half, and Mount pounded a thirty yarder that glanced off the cross-bar. Otherwise it was one-way traffic. Mount, Herrick and Brine fought tirelessly in an over-taxed defence, and Carpenter worked wonders, stifling attack after attack with his leggy tackles. Stumpy goalkeeper Paget can never have played better: twice he foiled Bellini with world-class saves. With the ninety minutes all but up the aggregate score was still level at 1—1. Manston were plainly tiring fast, and looked ripe for the taking in extra time.

But as the referee was looking at his watch the British champions staged yet another of their last-ditch rallies, striking back with a goal of classical simplicity that broke the Italians' hearts. Ian Farthing, cruelly harried early on, and anonymous for most of the game, hit a curling diagonal pass deep into the opposition half. Gilpin killed the ball and turned on it in a single movement that left his marker flat on his back. Calmly he drew the keeper and squared a short pass that left the goal wide open for the exultant Ben Dooner. Manston had won in the ninetieth minute.

Between matches now we were like soldiers back from the trenches, needing a complete change. The squad was re-peatedly praised for its character, but you wouldn't have seen much evidence of it off the park. Several of the lads, notably Herrick, Bush and Long, devoted much of their energy to screwing anything that didn't scream. Rees and Ben Dooner were betting men, who watched the gee-gees at every opportunity. Ian Farthing was another betting man, though his preferred animal was the greyhound. I'd have a lager with Steve Brine or Charley Mount, and occasionally an afternoon at the races with Ben, but I wasn't that close to them. It struck me that for a successful and sociable character I had few real friends. It was so long since I'd heard from Harvey that I thought he must have been posted abroad again. Once or twice I was even tempted to give Brian Ruddock a ring, to get away from myself. But I didn't. My social life more or less disappeared into my sexual life.

One old mate who did put in an appearance was Pat Arnold, in town on a scouting trip. He'd stopped playing the previous year, and by now seemed quite a bit older than me: I was a footballer and he was an ex-footballer. But he still looked handsome and daring, especially when his white teeth flashed in a grin. After ten minutes of soccer gossip he got on to his favourite subject.

'The thing I don't understand about sex,' he said, 'is why the moment of pleasure can't be pro*longed*. It's all over in focken' *seconds*. Why shouldn't you come for a full five minutes, to make it worth your while?'

I agreed with him. I'd long thought it was a hell of a hassle you had to go through to extract the juice you could spread on a single cream cracker.

'Still,' he said, 'the point is we like it well enough to go on performing. The human race is kept in existence. That's all Mother Nature cares about.'

'Have you been adding to the human race, then?'

'Not lately. But Mother Nature doesn't know that. Luckily she's not too bright.'

Later, over a drink, he remarked: 'That's a hell of a strange soccer team you're in. How do you get those results with those players?'

'Hard to say. On paper we're not too brilliant. But on grass we take a bit of beating.'

'How much of that is down to John Carpenter?'

'A lot.'

'I played in front of him at Belstone, and I'd seen nothing like him. Nobody could pass him, but he never looked like a player. The man's body is out of pro*portion*. You'd think he'd been stretched on a focken' *rack*. But he's one hell of a stopper.'

'He's the best.'

'You think he's that good?' Pat gave his sudden handsome, cocky grin. 'I'll tell you something interesting about him. I fucked his wife.'

'You fucked Sally?' I was taken aback. 'How did that one come about?'

'Big John was in hospital with mumps, so I paid him a visit like a good coach should. And there was his wife in need of a lift home. And one thing led to another.'

'Did she enjoy it?'

'Ach — now you're getting subtle.'

It was a sort of compliment to Carpenter that I should be impressed by Pat screwing his wife, and that Pat had known I would be.

'Did he ever find out?'

'Not from me.'

'Must be quite a responsibility being a coach. Do you fuck all the players' wives, or only the first team's?'

'Three wives in three years,' said Pat. 'Team spirit comes first.'

The night before the F.A. Cup semi-final my mother rang up to wish me luck. As she no more gave a toss for soccer as such than Claire did I was waiting for the real purpose of the call, but it was a long time coming. At last she said:

'Your dad came to stay, then?'

'Yeh.'

'So he told you the news?' She sounded nervous.

'No. What news?'

'Jimmy and I have split up.'

I didn't know what to say. I tried: 'Have you moved back to Beaufort, then?'

'No,' she said. 'No.' Her voice had slowed right down.

'Where are you living, then?'

The phone seemed dead for a moment. Then she said: 'I've moved in with a friend.'

'What's his name?' I asked, kidding.

'Andy Gillard.'

'Sod me!' I said, without meaning to. Breaking loose is

one thing, old scrubber is different again. 'Who's Andy Gillard?'

'He's very nice. A widower. I met him at work.'

'What happened to this Jimmy, then? Did you go off him?'

She laughed a bit crazily. 'I expect I would have done. But he went off me first.'

'And Dad knows all this?'

'Oh yes. I thought he was going to tell you.'

When she'd rung off I thought again: 'Sod me!' I was glad to be 150 miles away. Dad must have come up to break the news to me, and then not been able to . Perhaps he'd felt ashamed.

When my Uncle Peter died, after a long old age, he went in two quick stages. First he had a stroke that put him in hospital, and then, a day or two later, he popped off. Manston's big ambitions went the same way. We took the field for our semi-final in good heart, though Brine, Farthing and Dooner were all out with injuries. Mount played alongside Carpenter in the centre of the defence, and for forty minutes we had the better of the play. But then we went one down to a penalty after their striker had dived head first over Mount's fair tackle. We still weren't too bothered: we'd broken back against many a better side. In the second half we roasted them. Bush, Herrick and Mount all had shots saved. Three times I was inches wide. Young Mostyn, in his first F.A. Cup-tie, had a header cleared off the line. With Mount, who was skipper for the day, powering us forward we forced corner after corner, but we hadn't got Ian Farthing's right boot to make the most of them. A quarter of an hour from the end, when Carpenter had moved up to meet a free-kick, they broke away, three against two, to score a second goal. And that was that.

I felt so low all the next day, which happened to be my twenty-seventh birthday, that I could hardly speak a sentence. There was a surprise present from Claire. Because of the hours I'd spent peering down into the Mediterranean when we were in Majorca she'd bought me an illuminated, bubbling aquarium, full of little shining fish. I couldn't help but laugh at it, which hurt her feelings.

As the second leg of the European Cup semi-final was on the following Wednesday, Cowley had just three days to get us into some sort of shape, mental and physical. The press had been whipping up the tension — 'Manston's dream becomes a nightmare' and so on — and in any case the odds were against us because we only had a 2—2 draw in the home leg to take with us to Spain. With away goals counting double a 0—0 or 1—1 draw would be enough to put our opponents in the final. Our only consolation was that Brine would be fit to play, though with his thigh heavily strapped. We didn't feel great.

But in his talk before the game Geoff warmed us back to life. 'It'll be a hard game,' he said, 'a cruel game. But it's made for us. It's made for our style. We've been getting ready for this game for two years. Back home we took the game to them and gave away two silly goals. Out here it's going to be different. Two-two's going to puzzle them. They'll be in two minds. They won't know whether to come forward and try to clinch it, or just hang on to what they've got. That's made for us. Just hold them, hold them. Damp the game down. Let the tension get to them. One strike, and we're there. Go out there and kill the game, till the crowd get moody. If we hold out for an hour we'll take the tie. One strike, and we're through.'

What he was saying was fairly obvious, really. You can't say anything too clever about a football match — and if you could the players wouldn't understand you. Geoff got to us through his manner, his concentration, his intentness. We caught the mood, and remembered what we were capable of.

Within five minutes of the start I'd begun to feel confident. It was shaping up as Geoff predicted. The other side were holding back, waiting for us to charge at them, so they could get us on the break. But we played safe ourselves, spoiling, smothering, content with possession. In half an hour there wasn't a clear chance at either end. The game had gone off the boil, and so had the crowd. There was nothing for them to cheer. At half-time Cowley was quivering.

'Great,' he said. 'You've got one foot in the final. Just hold it as you've been doing and watch for the break. One strike will do the business.'

That meant me. If one of us was to make a strike against the odds, it had to be me. It was my job, and I relished it. Before I went out for the second half I re-laced my boots like a sniper checking his gun.

The crowd woke up again as we kicked off, and at last the Spaniards began to come at us. Rees had to concede a corner. A shot flew inches wide. Paget saved a header and then pushed a shot round the post for another corner. The pressure was on, and the stadium shook with the noise. As our defence smothered and scrambled you could sense the Spaniards sensing a goal. That was good. They didn't know how we could bend and bend without breaking. Up near the centre-circle I was prowling and tingling, tensed for the strike. At last a clearance came soaring out of the floodlights. With my marker on top of me I dabbed it back to Herrick and broke for goal. Neil hit the ball left for Bush to chase as I went down the middle, screaming for the cross. It came low and I hit it first time. The goalie parried and I hit it again. The shot struck a post and I hit it a third time. It was in.

The Spaniards only needed one, but they had barely a quarter-hour to go, and we were masters at sitting on a lead. Herrick and Mount were destroying everything in sight. Neil chased and harried, tackled, passed and ran as though he was defending single-handed. Charley stayed near the penalty arc, but again and again attacks broke against him. Anything that did get past, Long John Carpenter swallowed up. We weren't troubled.

With Cowley signalling five minutes to go someone fired a savage shot, but Mount stuck his head into it and the ball rocketed over the touch line. Their full-back took a huge throw. Half a dozen heads strained for it, but it cleared them all. Brine yelled Paget off his line to grab it, but as Ray plunged in out shot Carpenter's long leg and stuck the ball past him. It was John's first own goal for Manston. The stadium went up like a powder keg.

We tried to come back. Mount and Herrick drove us upfield again, but we had nothing in the tank. Bush could hardly raise a trot, and my legs were like stone. Somehow we pounded into them, but without a thought in our heads. It was just heart and good habits that had us stringing a few passes together. Their defence were tired, too, and kicking anywhere. Carpenter came charging up, swerving past two defenders and having a shot blocked. Then he was sprawling across to the wing, forcing a corner with a huge sliding tackle. I'd never seen him so frantic. Neil Herrick swung at Long's cross and got us another corner, with the whole crowd whistling for full-time. This time Mick hit a deep one, and Carpenter got to it with a colossal leap to head it back across goal. I volleyed the dropping ball left foot from chest high and caught it perfectly. It shot down from the bar and was hacked off the line as the whistle screamed. We'd lost 1—1.

Later, as we sat in the plane roaring through the dark, I was still dazed with disbelief. We'd done everything right, I'd snatched us our win — it seemed impossible we could have blown it. Across the aisle Steve Brine was sitting with fixed eyes, shell-shocked, and next to him Charley Mount was sunk down in his seat, his frog face pure misery. In the dressing-room Neil Herrick had cried and cried, but now he was perking up again. He recovered as quickly as a kid. In the row behind me Ian Farthing was moaning to anyone who'd listen that the result would have been different if he'd been playing. He could have been right, but he was a tit.

Next to me sat Long John. After the game he'd said 'Sorry, lads — sorry' and not spoken another word. Now he was sitting very upright and very still, his eyes shut in behind his glasses. I thought again that his head was much too small for him — it would have looked more at home on my body than on his. Steady and silent as he always was, I knew that own goal must be burning him up. Sooner or later he'd need to spill out some words about the game, and his mistake, and our lousy luck. He'd have to — it was human nature.

At last he turned to me and said: 'How's your dad keeping?'

'Fine. Yeh, fine.'

'Lives in London, doesn't he?'

'Yeh.'

'Sally's mother lives in London. She's on her own now. We're thinking of having her to live with us.'

'Won't she miss London?' I asked, just for something to say. 'Friends and so on.'

'You're right, Vince,' he said, seriously. 'I've been trying to balance it up.'

'I thought you were going over the game.'

He looked at me, quite surprised. 'No,' he said. 'No point. It's over. We lost. Thanks to me, we lost. Nothing to think about.'

He absolutely meant it. I closed my smarting eyes and could feel little aches and strains all over my body. John Carpenter had upset me. Here was a season's effort, a lifetime chance, blown by one mistake. We'd run our marathon and been pipped on the tape. It was his fault. Yet by the time he was on the plane he'd already cleared his mind of the game and moved his thoughts on. Life must be so easy for someone who could only get upset that far. If I took football that lightly I'd be totally useless — I wouldn't be able to drive myself hard enough, I wouldn't have the edge. Carpenter didn't think like a normal human being any more than he moved like one. His mind could absorb a disappointment like his body could absorb a shoulder charge. The plane roared us on, side by side. Lying back, two-thirds asleep, I was wondering whether John's temperament made him happier than Pat Arnold, or happier than me. Perhaps he couldn't feel much about anything.

Theoretically we still had a chance in the League. But we were done. Even Geoff Cowley knew we were done. By a last reflex we managed a draw on the Saturday, but after that we slithered. We finished the season in sixth place, not even qualifying for the U.E.F.A. Cup. After all the dreams of quadruple or treble honours we'd come up clutching nothing.

What poisoned my thinking for weeks and months was the

thought that we *could* have done it. We could have won all three cups and the League with it. There'd been nothing in fate to stop us. We'd just needed an ounce more effort, an ounce more luck, an ounce more will-power.

Chapter 12

That was the year which changed my life and shaped all I've done since. At the time those losing cup-ties seemed like the end of something, but they were only a stage in a process. The stub-end of that season became my first bad time since joining Manston Town. We'd lost direction, and the whole club was out of sorts. Paget and Farthing started to talk about retirement. Howard Bush was transfer-listed after an incident in a night club. There were repeated rumours in the press that this or that player might be lured away to Liverpool or Manchester — Herrick, Gilpin and Carpenter being the names usually mentioned. Long John's blunder in Spain had done him nothing but good: it made reporters realise how rarely he slipped up. I doubted that he or Neil wanted to move any more than I did myself, but you couldn't be certain. If those two left, it wouldn't be the same club. Everyone was edgy. It was a relief to hear the final whistle of the season's final game.

My body was back to reasonable fitness for the England tour of South America, but inside it my mind was a flat battery. I had a poor game in Chile, but grabbed a goal, and a fair game in Peru, where I failed to score. I hadn't actually tarnished my international reputation, but you couldn't say I'd enhanced it.

The summer break I'd been looking forward to felt like a long hangover. Claire and I tried Majorca again, but it was a bad year for that bit of the Mediterranean. Half the days were cloudy, and the beaches were poxed-up with rabbit's turds of black oil. Even the swimming wasn't what it had been, because there were jelly-fish about. After I'd been close-marked a couple of times I didn't feel at ease in the sea.

Back on land I had Claire to contend with. She was in good spirits and enjoying the holiday — in fact enjoying it more than I was. I realised how much she'd changed since our previous visit. She was handsomer, better dressed, bolder. People noticed her, and she enjoyed being noticed. If I hadn't been a well-known footballer she would have had the advantage of me. As a foreman from Ferris Clark I wouldn't have got a glance out of her. She was only an inch shorter than I was, and had no great taste for my style or my sense of humour. However, none of that need have mattered much. The tricky thing was that something about the temperature or the atmosphere of the place had revived her desire to get pregnant. I saw her looking at the little kids on the beach. Three evenings in a row she raised the subject, throwing me right back on the defensive.

'Give me one more season,' I said to her. 'If only Town had won something this year I'd feel different. I need another success behind me. Just give me one more season.'

It didn't sound that persuasive even to me, but it was the best I could do. Maybe there was even a bit of truth in it. In the end I did succeed in bringing her round — or at any rate, she stopped arguing. I'd won myself some breathing space, but I could sense she wasn't pleased.

After the flatness of the summer I was looking forward to training again, but the first day back at the club was even better that I'd hoped. All the doubts and feuds had melted away over the close season. Howard had made his peace with Cowley and come off the list. No one had retired, no one had left. On the contrary, Geoff had managed to sign Martin Connaught, supposedly the best young full-back in the country, from Sheffield. Here was someone else persuaded we had a future.

165

There was something strange about those early training sessions — something I couldn't put my finger on. Then it suddenly came to me: the lads were light-hearted. The previous season we'd fought grimly from match to match, guarding what we'd got, playing the percentages, as we struggled for this or that trophy. Now, for the first time in over a year, we had no responsibilities. We weren't champions, we weren't playing in Europe. We could relax a little.

Cowley himself caught the mood — or maybe he'd created it. In practice games he kept trying to ease us into a freer pattern of play.

'Let's loosen up our game,' he said. 'Let's please the fans.'

If Manston fans could be pleased, this was the season to do the job. Already in July the North stand was being demolished, to be replaced by one twice the size. For a year the ground would be at three-quarter capacity, but then we'd have thousands more tickets to sell. We'd need to play soccer the public would relish.

In practice the team was moving well. I could feel my own optimism beginning to flow again, but it was optimism for the club rather than for myself. I was in good fettle, but I'd never been able to turn on my real game until serious competition started. Naturally I was in hopes to recover my best form, but I had no reason to look for miracles. At twenty-seven I couldn't expect to take myself by surprise.

But I did. We won our first four matches 3—1, 3—0, 5—0 and 4—1, and I scored in all of them. The whole side was singing: everything Geoff had planned and worked for had come off at once. Brine, Connaught and Carpenter had locked up the penalty box, Herrick and Mount were running midfield. Up front Bramble was back on his corkscrew dribbles while Dooner was bucking and rearing in the centre. All this would have seen us doing well — but we were brilliant. The extra ingredients came from Ian Farthing and me. Ian was in peak form again, chipping, swinging, swerving, dropping his passes to every thin point of defence. And at the receiving end of that service Vince Gilpin was playing out of his skin.

166

I couldn't believe the transformation at the time, and I've never been able to explain it since. Perhaps it was the pay-off for years of hard graft and concentration, but plenty of players give all they've got and earn no such reward. In any case it had nothing to do with improvement in the normal sense. It wasn't a development, it was a change — a change of being. I could feel it inside myself. Even to describe it is impossible: I can only offer comparisons. A jet plane starts roaring along the runway. Faster and faster it goes, shaking and straining, but it's nothing more than a big motor-coach with wings until it's suddenly airborne. Switch on an electric kettle and the water heats up and heats up, but you see nothing of what's going on till boiling point is reached, and the spout steams. That's how it was with me. Seven hard years of League soccer, and suddenly I was airborne, I was bubbling. I was a new player. Every aspect of my game was different, but the root of all the changes was that I was quicker — my mind was quicker and therefore my body was quicker. The gain was so clear-cut it felt like something chemical, as though I'd been speeded up by hormones in my food, or in those jelly-fish stings. I was reading the moves before they were made. I'd be clear of a tackle before it was complete. Opponents I'd respected in the past would seem to be coming at me in slow motion. Sometimes it felt like playing against kids. I could switch direction or lay off a pass without so much as physical contact. Wherever I moved I had time and space.

I wouldn't claim that I always felt as good as I've described, or played as well. If I had done I'd have been netting three or four goals a game, and Town would have been unbeatable. I couldn't hit this new level of form in every match, or for the whole of any one match. But I could feel it always there to be reached. It was available. It was a fact.

Manston were playing with a confidence that was worth a goal start. We expected to win, and we won. In our first ten League games we dropped only a single point. When I was turned on it took two men to hold me, and that left gaps for others. Bush and Dooner were feeding off my form. But the whole team was moving so freely that goals could come from anywhere. In one 6—0 win Carpenter, Herrick, Farthing and Connaught all scored. We were so tight and determined, so varied and sharp, that we could take any opposition to pieces in the end. One team took the lead against us in the first three minutes, and held it by flat-out effort for another eighty. Then we scored four.

The weather was glorious that autumn. Week after week of sunshine kept the ground hard and the ball light. Manston's training ground is in parkland on the edge of town, surrounded by tall trees. That year they stayed fresh and leafy well into November, when they were stripped by high winds. Even after that, one particular tree remained green for so long that I thought for a time that its leaves might cheat Nature and hang on for another year's life. All those weeks my form matched the weather. In November I was picked for my first World Cup qualifying match, and had the chance to see whether I could do for England what I'd been doing for Manston. Neil Herrick was on the subs' bench for the first time, while behind me John Carpenter was making his international debut. Not only did John defend well, he did a double duty by hitting me several long balls in the Ian Farthing class. From one of them I put us ahead, just before half-time. I'd never felt more quick and precise. In the second half I made another goal and scored a third to give us a 3—0 win. It had been far and away my best international performance. 'Vince Gilpin has finally arrived as England's striker,' said the papers the next day. 'Gilpin's Glory' was one headline.

That was the great period of my whole soccer career. The balance between effort and results was completely changed: I was getting maximum achievement with minimum pain. Off the field it was a similar story. Everything I wanted was coming to me without a struggle. For instance, I was screwing tirelessly, all over the place, but with a good luck or natural judgement that kept me clear of complications. I'd greatly increased my range of contacts. If the cops had ever been after me I reckon there were five or six women who'd have been willing to hide me out. That was the inner circle — and for each of them there were a couple of semi-regulars. But the real change in the Gilpin sex-life was a matter of quality rather than quantity. I don't mean that my partners had become better-looking or extra skilful — they hadn't. It was just that for some reason I was getting sharper physical pleasure on my own account. As with the football, everything worked that autumn. Any old fuck seemed marvellous.

But then all the time I was in a high mood that went beyond my exploits with boot or prick. Those who haven't experienced such a mood, or at least had a glimpse of it, will hardly be able to tell what I'm talking about. Look at it this way. Day to day living is just a series of activities, one after another, most of them very familiar. You get up, you have breakfast, you go to work, you come home. So much time up, so much time in bed. Half an hour of chat, half an hour of screwing; ten minutes for a tea-break, two for a pee. You dig the garden, drive your car, read the paper, watch TV. That's how life goes. That's what it *is*. It's what we're stuck with. I suppose most people, most days, quite like some of the bits, and dislike others. If you suffer from a depression I suppose all of them must seem tasteless. For me it was the opposite — everything sparkled. I was like a goldfish swimming in champagne. That autumn a stroll, a meal, a drive, a chat could be a treat to me, like an ice-cream to a kid. And the football and the fucking went right off the dial.

Proof of my mood was how often I laughed. Almost everything seemed funny. All my life I've loved laughing, but that was the only period of my professional career when it came naturally to laugh on the soccer field. One such incident became famous — a Goal of the Month shown again and again on the box. I was chasing in a bouncing ball from the right wing, flicked it up over the centre-back's head as he came to tackle me, and nipped round him to nod it past the keeper as it dropped. The goal was so neat, so perfect, that I just burst out laughing. The camera caught me full face, braying like Pete Harvey. It was the same with sex: any time I was on the job I was liable to start giggling. Whether it was sheer pleasure or a sense of the ridiculous I can't say, but quite often I was chuckling as I came. In one case I was taken so hard that I laughed myself out of the girl concerned, rolled clean off the bed, and giggled away into agonies on the carpet. The girl was really offended. I had to explain that I wasn't laughing at *her*. And that was the truth: I didn't know what I was laughing at.

In any case I wouldn't have wanted to hurt her feelings. I was well disposed towards everybody that autumn. For instance, I did everything I could to make Claire happy in the areas that chiefly interested her. Anything she wanted she could have. A conservatory? By all means. A car of her own? Buy it tomorrow. I also pleased her with unexpected gifts that she wouldn't have thought of — a sun-dial for the garden, or a barometer or a ship in a bottle. Buying presents for people became a minor hobby of mine. On my Dad's birthday I had him sent a barrel of bitter, a bunch of roses, a pair of binoculars, two dozen tins of cat-food and a year's subscription to *Playboy*. He had to like something out of that lot.

My soccer form, and Manston's with it, was continuing to be uncanny. After losing our first match of the season, on an off-day, we won the next four in a row, all by a three-goal margin. Even the miserable old Manston fans had to warm to performances like that. By now they were turning up in reasonable numbers and acquiring new habits, such as cheering. The effect was a bit lop-sided, now that the North stand had completely gone and that side of the ground was given over to the builders. When the crowd were really roaring it felt as though you were deaf in one ear. By now I'd become the main focus of applause. If there was a lull in the game a great ghostly cry would start up, and echo round the stadium: 'Vin Gil Pin! Vin Gil Pin!' to the familiar tune of 'Three Blind Mice'. Sung slow and steady it sounded like a hymn. It gave me a great lift, not so much on a personal level, but because it showed we'd got the town moving, we'd got it singing.

For all I was playing so much better than ever before, I several times had the feeling the experience was familiar. At some stage in the past I'd known what it was to become a different person. Finally it came to me that what was in my mind was that year at Ferris Clark when my body had suddenly matured. But then, of course, there'd been a visible cause for the change in form — extra height, stronger legs and so on. This time there was no cause you could see or explain. The extra power had come from nowhere, and might go as suddenly as it had appeared.

That fear was never in the front of my mind, but it often niggled at the back. For the first time in my career I developed a little streak of superstition. I got the idea that to keep my form I must keep on the move, like a top that never stops spinning. I never thought this out — it didn't make any sense — but I behaved as though it was true. From the time I got up to the time I went to bed I saw to it that every moment of my day was full. There was travelling and playing, training and treatment, public appearances, charity visits, advertising work, social life, eating and drinking, sex. I never stopped. Nor did I ever get really tired, partly because I was sleeping well, but chiefly because the activity seemed to feed me new energy, as though I was a self-winding watch.

As it happened this policy also stood me in good stead as far as privacy was concerned. If Claire, or any other woman, tried to find out what I'd been doing on any particular day she soon got lost in the detail. Make your whole life a maze and you're never stuck for a hiding place. But this wasn't the main consideration. I'd always been restless by temperament, and now I'd come to feel as though this constant action was necessary to keep my body taut and my nerves quick. Ben Dooner was still living on the diet Cowley had set him. This was my version of a diet. It also suited my sexual style. A meal and a drink, a few laughs, a quick fuck, and then out — that had long been my ideal, and now I was achieving it more often than not. Women prefer you to hang about a bit after you've done the business, so I'd make a gesture in that direction, but not much more. I might as well have been kissing the milkman or the cat. Sometimes I made daft excuses to cut these proceedings altogether. On one occasion the phone happened to ring just as I finished screwing this secretary in her own flat. I went straight to the phone with my dick flapping. 'What?' I said, ignoring the voice at the other end. 'Are you sure? OK, I'll come right away.' I hung up and started hauling my clothes on fast. 'Sorry,' I said. 'Emergency. Got to dash.' I was out of the flat before she remembered that no one could have known I was there. Still, that was an unusual case: most of my regulars knew the score and didn't complain. In a way they chose themselves by accepting what was on offer. If the deal had ever been put into words the minus side would have looked pretty terrible: limited time together, irregular meetings, no future, and nothing too personal in the conversation. On the other hand I was famous, friendly, liked a laugh, and was in good physical shape. And I was generous: after all, I was already running my marriage on the basis that what I couldn't give in fidelity I'd make up in presents.

This varied sexual activity gave me a lot of pleasure and a lot of confidence. Indirectly it did something for my physical fitness. I'd always been a hard trainer, but now I felt an extra little pressure to push myself, as though fucking would soften my muscles and I'd need to re-harden them. Charley Mount, another hard trainer, had a similar motive. When he'd sunk a pint or two over the odds he'd punish his thick block of a body as though he was wringing the beer out of his pores. You could say it was guilt driving us — but everyone needs a driver of some sort.

After seventeen games Manston were several points clear at the top of the table. It was unheard of. The soccer writers were saying that the title race was as good as over — and this was still late November. I'd already scored twenty goals, only two short of my best-ever total for a whole League season.

In our eighteenth match, which was played at home, I equalled that total before half-time, scoring first with the left foot and then with the right. We were cruising to an easy win, but I stayed sharp, looking for the hat-trick. Twenty minutes from the end I'd drifted into space on the left, having lost my marker, when Herrick hit me a low pass. As I moved to meet

172

it the ball took a deflection, making me check and swing my body round. And for no apparent reason my left shin broke, with a crack they could hear on the terracing.

All day Sunday I hardly spoke, though I squeezed out a grin and a thumbs-up sign for the TV cameras. The doctor who'd put my leg in plaster reckoned I'd be out for a couple of months at the absolute minimum. All my previous years in League soccer I'd never missed more than three consecutive weeks through injury. I was numbed.

But worst of all was the way the injury had come about. It was nobody's fault, and I'd been under no pressure. My body had just broken down of its own accord. The doctor tried to explain what had happened, but I took nothing in. If one leg could suddenly crack, why not the other? Why shouldn't I fall apart completely? I huddled into myself like a bird that's lost its beak.

In the days that followed I rallied a little but remained demoralized. It wasn't just that I couldn't play soccer, my whole pattern of living was destroyed. I was conditioned to work up energy and work up energy like a dynamo and then burn it all out on the park. Now I had no outlet. The power built up and had nowhere to go. I could have punched the wall like Brian Ruddock, out of sheer frustration. On top of all that I had my special worry: the magic form I'd been in could be lost for good. When I was fit again I might be no more the very good pro, the outstanding club-man, that I'd been in previous seasons. My little spell of inspiration might be over.

All I could do was wait and see — and the waiting seemed endless. Since the start of the season my non-stop activity had speeded the time up till the days flew past in a blur. Now I was parked in a chair, too depressed to want to think, each minute dragged. Cowley would drop in on me, and many of the lads would stop by, but I hardly welcomed visits: I'd rather have hidden in a cave till I was fit to compete again. There were letters and get-well cards. I answered a few a day to get my arm and brain moving, but they did nothing for me.

Claire must have had a hard time, too. After the years of things going well for her she was quite unprepared for bad luck. Like me, she didn't know what to do or say. To complicate matters she was out of the habit of spending more than two or three successive hours with me, except asleep or on holiday. Suddenly here I was, parked in the house with her, day after day, glum as a slug, or fuming with strange moods. I'll admit I must have been piss-poor company, silent for long stretches and then coming out with nonsense or fantasy that could easily turn sour. She didn't know how to take me. I remember one such conversation when we'd been watching a TV film of a nightingale — this plain little bird singing its heart out on a twig.

'That's lovely,' said Claire. 'That's beautiful.'

I didn't disagree, and at that moment I was reasonably cheerful, but I said: 'Suppose it was a pig making that noise.'

'What do you mean?'

'It's all chance isn't it? Why should it be a feathery bird? It could have been pigs that made that sort of noise. We'd have had pig-song instead of bird-song. The birds could be grunting and snorting up in the branches, and the pigs chirping away in the sty.'

'Vincent, you do talk a lot of rubbish.'

'No I don't. It's a serious question. Would you like that noise just as much if it came from a fat, filthy, stinking pig?'

With my tone I was adding 'you stupid bitch'. My voice was shaking with rage that had bubbled up out of nowhere. No wonder Claire was taken aback — I was surprising myself.

But all those weeks I was home she had nothing to offer. As she didn't know what would raise my spirits she behaved as though life was normal. In a way I was pleased by her uselessness, because it gave me something else to be sullen about. I sat scowling at her fancy wallpapers.

Manston drew their first match without me, but then lost the next. The week after they drew again, but Herrick had to come off with a calf injury. He was out for ten days, and meanwhile Town lost again. Des Roberts wrote:

174

'A month ago you couldn't have got a price on Manston for the League championship. Geoff Cowley's men had lapped the field. But since the tragic loss of Vin Gilpin, marksman extraordinary, that huge lead has been largely whittled away. Town's rhythm has gone, and so has their confidence. After the heady successes of the autumn it's beginning to look like another heartbreak season for the club that Cowley built.'

I watched the team on TV, or read about them in the papers, with my dud leg itching inside its shell. The days were still crawling past, but they'd taken on a bit of shape. In the morning I'd browse through the sports pages and then tackle some fan-mail. At least my signature still looked mean. Another activity was watching the tropical fish Claire had given me. If you stared long enough you could feel you were peering out of a submarine. The fish looked comfortable enough, for all they were far from home and had sod-all to do. Living till they died was their full-time interest. Some afternoons I got out to the nearby park and sat on a bench among the old people and the young mothers with babies. I either liked it there because it was peaceful or hated it because it was lifeless, I wasn't sure which.

A diversion came one morning when Harvey phoned me out of the blue. He asked after my leg, and so on, but obviously had something else on his mind, and gradually worked towards it. He'd left the army, was back in London, and had got a job as a lorry-driver. The following week he'd be passing through Manston: could he drop in on me? He needed a word with me in private. I fixed a time when Claire would be out, feeling pretty sure from his manner that he was in need of money.

He turned up looking very serious and polite, as though he was going to be interviewed for a job. Again his first topic of conversation was my broken leg, and his eyes kept going back to the bare foot at the end of it that had scored so many goals. I'd never seen him embarrassed as he was that morning. He talked only with an effort, and when once or twice he let his laugh out the noise seemed to embarrass him more. His face still had the old sideways tilt, and as he turned it further aside to avoid my eye he looked to be trying to twist it right round to the back like an owl. I was wondering whether to offer him the money before he asked, to put him out of his misery.

At last he said: 'Look, Vin, I've got to tell you something.'

'Yeh?'

'The one thing is — you musn't take it wrong.'

'Go on then.'

'Remember I saw Karen for you . . . ?'

Immediately I knew why he'd come. 'Are you going to tell me she had a kid after all?'

Poor old Harv looked utterly taken aback. 'No, Vin. Nothing like that. I came to tell you that me and Karen had got married.'

'Have you, then?'

Not knowing what more to say I started to laugh, as I'd done the last time I'd seen him. It was a forced laugh at first, but it gradually took me over, because Harvey joined in to cover his own embarrassment. It amused me that we were both laughing for nothing. The louder I chuckled, the louder Harvey chuckled. There was a whole variety of things we could have been laughing about, given the situation. I couldn't know what was tickling Harv and he couldn't know what was tickling me. That was part of the joke. Various memories were jostling in my mind. As we finally sobered up I had to wipe the tears off my cheeks.

'Congratulations,' I said. 'Good health, mate. But why were you so fucking serious? And why didn't you ask me to the wedding?'

Harvey was serious again. 'It was the money,' he said. 'She conned you out of all that money. Then I get the advantage of it . . .'

He really thought that I might think he'd deliberately set out to do me. He was too innocent to know that he was incapable of doing anybody. It took me ten minutes to talk him round. When his face had completely cleared he said: 'Well look — can I bring in Karen? She's outside in the lorry.'

When she came back with him it took a further quarter of an hour and a couple of drinks to work through *her*

176

embarrassment, to say nothing of mine. She kept very quiet, but Harv and I worked overtime to carry things along, laughing and shouting. It was pretty terrible, really. Neither Karen nor I knew whether to do any apologising, so I talked fast enough to prevent the question arising.

After the second drink we went out together for a meal, and the situation eased. Without bursting into long speeches Karen relaxed a little. She looked as I'd remembered her — a white face behind black hair — but she was more confident, and smiled more. Harvey must have cheered her up. It came out in the conversation that not only had she stayed on at Ferris Clark — she had her new husband there with her. Harv's new job was with the Transport section, and he regularly saw my old mates Bill Duckworth and Bob Amos. After all his travels he was back where I'd started. Karen was perfectly friendly in her manner, but in a routine style, as though she was keeping her personality behind glass. Only when we were saying good-bye did she suddenly catch my eye and give me a real smile, a direct smile, that recognised what we'd once had between us, and took me back to those afternoons and evenings in the London parks.

When they'd gone I was for some reason depressed. Even my big laugh with Harvey had left a bad taste behind. What was there to laugh about? Over the meal he and Karen had looked very happy together. In fact they even seemed to feel a little bit guilty that between them they'd cut me out. But there was Karèn marrying a lorry driver, after nearly hooking an international footballer. And there was my old friend Pete Harvey picking up one of my cast-offs. I felt sorry for both of them, and even more so because they didn't know enough to feel sorry for themselves.

Manston managed a win and another draw before the year was out, but they were nothing like the team they had been. The papers put the collapse down to my absence, and I liked to think that they were right — but there was more to it than that. As Geoff Cowley pointed out in a TV interview, the balance had been lost. I'd hobbled along to the home matches and seen the signs. Without me to play off, Ben

Dooner couldn't time his runs. Noel Mostyn, who'd taken my place, was useful in the air, and a sprinter, but he had no knack of reading a pass or finding space. Ian Farthing was having to hold the ball while he looked for a target, and was therefore getting caught in possession. Mount and Herrick were tending to push to the right to help him out, with the result that Bushy was getting no sort of service and kept drifting out of the game. The side was still hard to beat because the defence was tough and well-organized, but up front nothing was happening.

The two individuals who were getting the worst of it had to be Farthing and Dooner. Poor old Ben had only ever made something of himself by sheer labour — dieting, training hard, working every minute of every game. If he didn't get the right prompting and try his best he was nothing. Now he was getting no prompting at all, and was trying too hard — so he was nothing again. He'd chase balls there was no hope of catching, jump too soon at a centre, blast a shot twenty foot wide. The crowd had speedily returned to its old habits as the results went wrong, and had developed a special jeer for him. In his frustration he'd put himself about desperately in the box, and then get booked. He hadn't scored in ten games, and was looking haunted. If anything Ian Farthing was even worse off. The weather had finally broken, and the heavy grounds soon drained his strength. He was moving like an old man, slow and bony. When he was chopped he took a long time to get to his feet. Once again he was whining about minor injuries and bottling out altogether if the going got rough. The poor bugger had gone from brilliant to clapped out with no intermediate stage, as though he'd had the football equivalent of a stroke. If it hadn't been for his dead-ball kicking he'd surely have been dropped — it was that bad. From the first, Ian had been a vital part of the Cowley machine, and as he wore out the machine ran down.

Naturally I'd been counting the days till the plaster came off, but when it was finally removed I was fucking aghast. The muscles had wasted so badly I didn't recognise my own limb. When I got home from the hospital I took off my trousers and stood in front of the bathroom mirror, amazed. There was a weedy leg side by side with a footballer's leg. They didn't make a pair. A few weeks out of soccer and I was shrivelling away. I'd heard of running fast to stay in the same place — I had to run flat out to stay the same size. I was so lop-sided that if I'd tried to walk with my eyes closed I'd have gone round in circles.

But the doctor was happy with the way the bone had knitted up, and said it was just a matter of rebuilding the muscles. 'You'll have to work at it,' he said, which suited me. After the weeks of nothing I was ready to work myself dizzy: I craved for the activity. My body hadn't put on much weight, but my mind had. The physio, Eddie Gunn, drew up a programme of exercises, and I sweated through it day after day. There were various routines with weights and pulleys. I had to bend and stretch, push and pull, lift and lower. Very gradually the muscles came out of hiding. I toiled over that sodding leg as though I was going to enter it for a prize. To strengthen it further I spent hours just running up and down the terracing, like a spectator who'd got shut in and gone mad. Nearby the new stand was going up. The builders and I were working away side by side in our different ways. I have a powerful memory of those weeks of extra training. It was a difficult, tiring, boring period which I basically enjoyed.

As soon as I could walk freely I was back on the prowl, dropping into shops and cafés I'd not visited for weeks.

'You fit again, Vin?'

'On the way.'

'Hurry it along, son. We need you back.'

As long as I'd been laid up I hadn't so much as phoned any of the women I'd been seeing in the autumn. I'd felt so cut off from all that life that it could have been my dick that was in plaster. Now I had to go the rounds, renewing the old relationships — reintroducing myself, so to speak. I was like some old dog scampering round piddling on fences and bushes to mark out his territory. It was all a bit ridiculous. Not that that bothered me: it's all right knowing when you're ridiculous as long as it doesn't stop you doing what you want.

I fucked my way through February and into March, working off the frustrations of the winter. The only ill-effect that I was aware of was a sort of underlying anxiety about my soccer prospects. Here I was screwing away like an international footballer: pretty soon I'd have to start playing like one.

During this period Manston were still steadily slipping. Thanks to Carpenter and Brine they rarely lost by more than the odd goal, but they were seldom winning and seldom scoring. In February they were knocked out of the F.A. Cup and overtaken at the top of the League. Cowley took to hovering round me when I was working away on the leg.

'How's it coming, Vin? Keep working. Keep working. I want you back out there. You're the man to lead us back.'

Again and again he'd say things like that, egging me on. It wasn't the words that counted, it was the manner, concentrated, intent. I could feel his will-power feeding into my own.

I've said nothing about the pain of the broken leg, because there's not much in it. You can't describe pain any more than pleasure. But it had been pretty bad — bad enough to make me nervy about kicking a ball again. Here was the mended left leg looking all right and feeling all right, but I didn't fancy swinging it full force into a shot. In practice sessions I was moving freely, but always favouring the right foot. At last Cowley kept me back for some special shooting practice against Ray Paget.

'I'll keep knocking the ball in,' he said, 'and I want you to hit it right foot every time. Every time. But when I shout "Left!", let that left foot go with all you've got.'

I started off very jittery, waiting for the shout. One, two, three, four passes, but not a word. I hit them all right foot, as he'd said. The call surely had to come any time now — but it didn't. Pass after pass, and no matter what the bounce I was hitting them in rhythm, hitting them right foot every time. It happened so often I was half hypnotized, moving and shooting automatically. When he did yell 'Left!' the word was so sudden and sharp it seemed to jump me out of a trance.

Geoff's pass sat up perfectly, and I belted it so hard with my left foot that I all but cut Ray Paget in two. I was back in working order.

If all went well I stood to get in nine or ten League matches. My first serious try-out was a mid-week game in the Central League. 'Ease your way into it,' Geoff had told me, and I took his advice, attempting nothing fancy for the first forty-five minutes. But in the second half I opened up a little, shielding the ball, turning fast, taking on defenders. We had a 2—0 win, and I clipped in the second goal. Without doing anything spectacular I'd played well, and finished full of confidence. There was no trace of the injury — in fact I had more of a twinge in the other leg.

Next day there were the local headlines I would have hoped for: 'Gilpin's Back — and Still Scoring'. But I'd woken up to find my right ankle stiff and swollen. I couldn't believe it. When the physio told me to rest it for at least five days, I could have cried. What I did do was to drive to the flat of a waitress I knew, and fuck her with hardly a word.

The fact was I was bloody desperate. This was the crucial period. If I could get in a few games for Manston, and knock in a goal or two, they might still just nick the League title, and I could get back into the England side for the World Cup qualifying matches in May. And after my great start to the season I wanted games enough to look for top form again — my new standard of top form — while I could still remember what it felt like. Everything had seemed to depend on the leg healing and me working myself back to fitness. All that had gone according to plan, and now here was some other bit of my body packing up. It was a fucking nightmare.

This new set-back didn't do my home-life any favours either. Claire said 'What a shame!' when she heard about it, but that was all she could manage. I just slumped into a chair for hours on end, staring at the TV or the fish tank, hardly speaking or even thinking. Since I was disgusted with myself I took it for granted that Claire would also feel disgusted with me. She did begin to look a bit tense that week, but she hadn't got the words to put her anxieties into, and

I couldn't much care about them, having bigger ones of my own.

The ankle settled, and I had another Central League run, this time without complications. The headlines broke out again: 'Gilpin Poised for Come-back'. But two days later I had to limp out of a practice game with back trouble. I was in despair. My left leg was recovered, my right ankle was recovered, and here I was, hobbling again. Where would it ever stop? And why should it? I seemed to be going the same way as the Manston team — a stress in one place would bring on a stress in another.

'For fuck's sake,' I said to the physio, as he worked on me yet again, 'what is happening to me?'

'How old are you?' asked Eddie, though he knew.

'Twenty-seven. Twenty-eight next month.'

'Twenty-eight next month. Well, that's your calendar age. I tell you, Vince, there's parts of your body already fifty-eight. You've pushed yourself hard and you're paying the price. For years you've been throwing your body about like a rally-cross car — spinning it, accelerating, swerving, colliding. Something has to give in the end. If you were a car I could get you some replacement parts — new wheels, new brake linings, new suspension. As a human being you have to make do with what you've got.'

He was giving me a massage as he said all this, and luckily his hands did more for me than his tongue. Over the next few days he gradually loosened me up again and took the pressure off the nerve, but meanwhile the season was passing me by.

Ever since breaking the leg I'd cut myself off from the squad. I couldn't feel part of it when I was contributing nothing. When I resumed full training I felt a bit like a gate-crasher. But I was close enough to the lads to sniff how the morale was suffering. Ben was forlorn, Ian was endlessly on the moan, Bushy was getting wayward again. But for me the root of the problem was Martin Connaught. There was no doubt about his talent: he was a good defensive player, and he could pass the ball with both feet. He'd been in excellent form all season. But it never seemed to me that he committed himself to the club. He'd joined it to taste some success, and if the success didn't come fast he'd be looking elsewhere. For ability he was way ahead of Mick Long, whose place he'd taken, but he hadn't Mick's passion. If Connaught was playing well and the team was losing, he'd just blame the others: if they were doing as good a job as he was the score would look different. Mick would have tried something, taken a chance, desperate to pull it off for the lads, even at the expense of making a prat of himself. Connaught was for number one: he wanted to travel first-class. He was a band-wagon player, who'd have been happier at City. As Manston lost form his enthusiasm cooled.

But for all the problems Cowley kept bringing the side up to scratch. We clung to our place in the top three. By now the dominant figure by far was John Carpenter. Since his success with England it had gradually dawned on people what an extraordinary performer he was, and they were looking at him with new eyes. His play seemed to grow to meet the new expectations. Not only did he look capable of tangling up any strike force on his own, he was regularly getting forward to make trouble at the other end. Since I'd dropped out he'd scored five goals and made several more, mostly following dead-ball kicks. He was no more talkative than he'd ever been, but like Cowley he gave out a determination that spurred on everyone else. He kept alive the title possibility that I was expected to clinch.

But I couldn't make it. Those were miserable days. Basically I was back to rights, but again and again a little snag would have me limping back to the treatment room. There'd be swelling in my ankle or a twinge in my back. I still hadn't given up the race to get back — but suddenly Cowley pulled me out of it. He called me to his office and told me to take a week or two right away from soccer.

'But that'll bring me to the end of the season.'

'So be it. You've been straining after fitness, Vin, and I've been driving you. We should just let it come.'

When I told Claire I was going to stay a few days with my Dad she was happy enough not to come. I didn't stay with

183

him, but I did pay him a visit — a surprise visit. When he opened the door to me he looked dismayed, but it took him an hour to get the reason out. The timber-yard had closed down, and for months he'd been out of work. Having no hobbies or friends to speak of he passed his time pottering about as Uncle Peter had once done. All that was left of his old life was the cat, the trips to the swimming bath, and reading the *Daily Mirror* inch by inch. In the afternoons, if it was fine, he'd take a stroll in the park. He was back in the world I'd recently been visiting, of mothers, babies, invalids and pensioners.

I went to the pub with him and took him out for a meal. Probably he was pleased, but it felt like giving mouth to mouth treatment to a dead man. He mentioned that Mum was still dropping into Beaufort from time to time, and I asked how she was. He had to think about that one: 'Mixed. I'd say mixed.' I didn't ask him to explain.

It crossed my mind to pay Mum a visit, but I didn't fancy running into her bloke. I did drop in on Harvey and his bride, but only for a quick drink. My only other London treat was a last squint at the old timber-yard — or rather, at the place where it had been. They were flattening the whole area to build more Council flats. Maybe one day they'd flatten Beaufort to make way for a timber-yard.

What I chiefly did with the break was to visit Alan Ruddock, in Dorset. I'd phoned him on an impulse while I was laid up, and he'd invited me. In the years since I'd seen him he'd lost some hair and gained some flesh, but otherwise he looked well. He and his wife, Eve, were very cheerful, very easy-going. After the months of pressure to get fit, the change did me some good. I took it as time off from normal life. They had two sons, aged nine and six, who treated me as some sort of hero, and my only exercise was a little kick-around with them. Alan himself still took an interest in football, and asked me a lot of questions, but he never mentioned his own career. His active involvement in the game consisted in coaching his elder son, Billy, and watching him play in some local league.

'Not bad for nine, is he?'

'Bloody sight better than I was at that age,' I said.

It was true, but it didn't seem to me to signify. However smart the kid was now, it was long odds against him being as good as his father had been. And if he took after his dad in ability he might also inherit his dodgy knees.

To all appearances Alan had made himself a good little all-round life. He wasn't that well off by the standards I'd got used to, but his work as a builder was bringing in a fair wage. His own house was in smooth shape, because he'd done a lot of work on it and obviously knew his job. If he'd had my income to go with his talents he'd have made an ideal husband for Claire. Eve was nice, and so were the kids, and the four of them seemed to get on well as a family. They liked the area they lived in. There was rolling green scenery in all directions, and the sea was only two miles off. For me it was all too quiet, but the Ruddocks seemed contented to be caught up in the activities of the village. When we went to the pub they knew every person there.

On the Sunday Alan took me fishing in a nearby river, but for more than an hour we never got a bite.

'It's a pleasure to hook one,' he said, 'but I'm not too bothered. I like just sitting here.'

'You could do that without the fishing rod.'

'Wouldn't be the same. If you're going to sit and do nothing, you've got to have a purpose.'

For the first time since I'd arrived we started talking about the season we'd had together at Coombe Forest. Alan recalled the day he did his knee in, and I said what a different life he'd have had if he'd gone into League football.

'D'you reckon?' said Alan, as though he was surprised. 'I can't see it myself. Most of what you do is the same for everyone. You've got to eat and sleep and work. Then you've got entertainment and family life. Nine-tenths of it is the same for everyone.'

'But that's what counts, isn't it? The odd tenth. That's what you look forward to.'

'The other nine'll do me.'

Actually he caught a couple of pike in the end, with teeth

like needles, and we ate them that same night. But I was bothered by the thought of Alan having all the strength and skills I remembered and putting them to no purpose. My old man could have carried out that bit of fishing. How could Alan take it so easy? Why wasn't he more restless? Something in him must have gone to sleep. The thought of it made me uncomfortable. Here he had this quiet way of life, and it seemed to fit him like an old shoe. I couldn't decide whether my stay was calming me down or driving me nuts. After five days I was fairly relieved to be setting out for the Midlands again.

I took a roundabout route home, and when I was having a snack at a café near Bath a lad came over for an autograph. He was smart to recognise me, because since breaking my leg I'd got behind a little beard again. A red-haired woman at a nearby table caught what was said and turned to me when the boy went out.

'Are you really Vince Gilpin?'

'I used to be.'

'What happened?'

'I broke my leg.'

'Will you be able to play again?'

'Next season.'

She tried a little smile. 'It doesn't look as though it's bothering you at the moment.'

'No. Apart from soccer I can do anything.'

That many words plus one glance and we were obviously in business. Town had a rearranged League match that night that I'd been meaning to watch, but they'd do no worse without me. Claire was expecting me, but I could sort that out with a phone-call, which I proceeded to do.

So this girl, whose name was Julie, spent the night with me at a motel. I say 'girl' — she could have been thirty. As far as I recollect we didn't have a bad time, though she was very intense when we'd finished, giving me long hard kisses on the body as though she was trying to suck out a thorn. I was out of the habit of actually sleeping with anyone other than Claire, but the bed was wide, and anyway, once you're unconscious there's no problem.

186

In the morning, naturally, there she still was. I bought a paper to look at over breakfast and found that the back page was all Manston. Not only had they lost the night before, but Charley Mount had been sent off. This put him one up on Howard Bush, who hadn't even played. After another row with Geoff Cowley over late-night drinking he was on the transfer-list again. And Ian Farthing was apparently lined up to go to the States when the season ended.

It seemed strange that all this should have been going on while I'd been humping a red-haired pick-up in Gloucestershire. Julie pretended to be sympathetic when she saw the headlines, and started grabbing at me again, but I was suffering from severe loss of interest, and soon left. On the drive home I was very depressed. I remember thinking that for five months I'd been drawing handsome money for doing nothing — at least nothing that did anyone any good. A footballer who doesn't play football has cancelled himself out.

Things *had* taken a turn for the worse at the club. Only a lingering hope of the championship had kept the squad together for the past few weeks, and now that hope had all but gone. Bushy had blown his top because Geoff had signed a young left-winger named Fenn, obviously as a replacement. Ian had decided his own time was up. Tempers were strained. Even Neil Herrick wasn't smiling.

Ironically, none of the other contenders had quite been able to kill off Town's title chances. We still stood to sneak it if we won our last three games — and we took the first two 1—0, with Herrick and Carpenter getting the vital goals. If we'd got two points from our last match, away from home, we'd have been virtually sure of the championship. My old club City were level with us on points, but our goal average was so far ahead of theirs that any sort of victory on our part would oblige them to win about 14—0 to nudge ahead.

I went to Town's final match knowing inside that we wouldn't win it — and we didn't. We went one down in the first half, and though Carpenter loped through to equalize ten minutes from time we never looked like winning. I nipped off without speaking to anyone. It seemed I'd squeezed the last drop of piss out of that stinking half-season.

Three days later, to everyone's disbelief, City dropped a home point to the bottom team in the division and handed us the title. We'd won the championship without a single cheer. I'd played enough matches before breaking my leg to qualify for a medal — which I'd earned by any standards, since I was still by far the club's leading scorer. I was pleased, of course, but only in a dim way. It was like winning a posthumous V.C.

Chapter 13

All that spring the reporters sniffed round in case my career was dead. In self defence I kept quiet or talked rubbish. It wasn't till early August, when I was back in full training, that I felt confident enough to open up a little. Jonathan Woolley got an interview out of me for one of the heavy Sunday papers:

COMPENSATING CIRCUMSTANCES

Nine months ago Vince Gilpin of Manston Town was playing and scoring with dazzling fluency for both club and country. Somehow, at twenty-seven, he had hit a rich new vein of form and finally established himself, beyond all doubt, as a striker of international ability. But then injury intervened, at first in the form of a broken leg. Gilpin was laid up for weeks. Progress reports, however, were reassuring. It was confidently predicted that he would return to First Division action in time to play a significant part in Town's fight for the championship. Through March and April there were repeated promises of a come-back, but each was frustrated by further injury — a damaged ankle, a strained back. Gilpin had still not returned to League football when the season ended.

It is hardly surprising, therefore, that doubts have been expressed about his international future. Even if he regains a regular place in the Manston side, will he not have lost something of the quickness and alert self-confidence on which his game was based? With England well on course for a place in next year's World Cup Finals the question assumes a certain national importance. For once in a way we have it in us not merely to qualify but to put in a serious challenge for the trophy itself. The England defence has taken on a reassuringly resilient look since harnessing the eccentric talents of John Carpenter. We have notable midfield strengths in the tackling of Lomax and the shrewd running of Gary Pargeter. But to win matches England will badly need the goal-snatching abilities that Vince Gilpin demonstrated so abundantly last autumn. This week I visited Manston to hear Gilpin's own assessment of his prospects.

Having interviewed him on a number of previous occasions I wondered how forthcoming he would choose to be. Many a professional footballer discards his playing personality with his jock-strap, but Vince Gilpin the private citizen has a good deal in common with Vince Gilpin the goal-scorer, 'Quick', 'unpredictable' and 'evasive' are adjectives appropriate to either. Gilpin will chat freely and genially to reporters; but he has a knack of side-stepping or even up-ending questions he doesn't care for. There was a notorious example a year or two back, when a television interviewer asked him how it felt to score his first goal for England, and got the reply: 'It's hard to put into words. How does it feel to be asking me?'

When I began our conversation by recalling that episode he harked back to a time when his team were due to play Brighton in the F.A. Cup:

'This press-photographer came to the training ground with a sea gull — a stuffed sea gull. He wanted a picture of me shaking my fist at it. A sea gull representing Brighton — get it? There was some caption like: "Vince hopes to stuff a whole team of seagulls on Saturday". Well, it's rubbish, isn't it? If you're treated like a little kid or a performing dog you don't feel like giving serious answers. At least I don't. You'll have to win my confidence, won't you.'

Gilpin's elusiveness extends even to his appearance. With a well-cut suit hiding his whipcord muscularity, and a sun-bleached beard covering the bottom half of his face he looks a slight, innocuous figure, unlikely to catch the autograph hunter's eye. As a confidence-winning gesture I told him I liked his (brown and orange) tie.

'So does my wife. But then she chose it. She chooses my clothes, but I choose my hair. What do you think of this beard?'

I said I wasn't crazy about it.

'Nor am I. I'll have it off when the season starts.'

Did that mean he would be fit to play?

'Why not? Physically I'm back to normal. I've stopped breaking down and swelling up. I'll be out there.'

Was he hoping to make England's next qualifying game in October?

'Well I'm hoping. But we'll have to see how it goes. I'm league-match fit, but it may take a month or two to get international-match fit. Geoff Cowley keeps telling me not to rush it. He reckons sharpening your game is like sharpening a knife — try too hard and you take the edge off instead of putting it on.'

Why all the stopping and starting in the spring?

'Same thing in a way. I was trying to get back too soon. The physio said I was over-compensating. I'd be favouring one leg because it wasn't quite back to rights, and I'd end up straining the other one. I should have taken more time. Now I've had the summer.'

So no more need for compensation? My question produced an unexpected Gilpin swerve:

'You always need compensation in soccer. If there was a team of midgets, they'd have to compensate by keeping the ball on the floor. Take me. Suppose the perfect striker should have about twenty different skills or strengths. Well, I've only got about fourteen of them. So I have to compensate for the ones I don't have. The best players are the best compensators. But it's hard work.'

Did he think he could recapture his extraordinary form of last autumn?

'Why not? I have to, don't I? It has to be in there somewhere — I've just got to find a way of getting it out. Luckily there's Geoff Cowley behind me — he can get anything out of anybody.'

Won't the changes in the Manston side make the comeback harder?

'Yes. But if you're a good professional you adjust quick enough.'

What of Manston's chances of keeping the title?

'Have a fiver on us. The reporters are writing us off, but they always do at this time of year. They always say it's a transitional season for us, or we're over the hill. Don't listen to that. The core of the team stays the same — Briney, Mount, Herrick, John Carpenter. Any side with John Carpenter in it is going to take some beating. No one can make head or tail of him. He commutes in from Mars every morning. And anyway, Geoff Cowley will have something up his sleeve. He always does.'

Chatting with Vince Gilpin is an agreeable but slightly disconcerting experience. For all his engaging frankness he likes to keep something in hand. There is a restlessness in his manner that suggests a lurking wish to move on. After a time I noticed his eyes beginning to wander as though the conversation wasn't fully absorbing his attention. Characteristically he noticed me noticing this trait, and apologised for it:

'Just a habit. Probably comes from soccer. Some players have this all-round vision — take in the whole game at a glance. I'm not like that. I have to keep looking about to work out what's going on.'

He seemed to me a young man who knows very well what's going on. It was reassuring, therefore, to find him fit, energetic, confident — apparently even perky. But was I mistaken in sensing the faintest hint of underlying wariness? Gilpin is realist enough to know that serious self-assessment can only begin when he is brought face to face with First Division, and later with international, opposition. Over the next few months he faces the lonely prospect of finding out what he still has in him. For England's sake, as well as his own, I hope it proves to be nothing less than he is looking for.

Chapter 14

To pace myself back to full fitness I'd gone in for pre-season training a week before the other lads. The new stand was finished and gaping. Cowley said to me: 'If you'd hit the net half a dozen times less often, that wouldn't be there. Now you can help me fill it.' I was more than willing, provided my body was back to normal. The early signs were good. In five days of working-out I had no special problems and seemed to be moving as easily as ever.

But the return of the other lads didn't give me the extra lift I'd been counting on. For all the sun-tans and the good cheer there was something a little bit wrong. There'd been changes, of course. Bush had gone to Bristol, and Farthing to Vancouver. Peter Fenn, the winger signed in April, had still to settle in, and there was a brand-new midfield player — Stuart Selby, from Newcastle. But none of this need have altered the atmosphere. Everyone struck me as older. Rees had a few grey hairs and Brine had a lot; Dooner was overweight and guilty about it. Even Neil Herrick looked less like a school-boy. I felt as though I'd been away three or four years. Several of the squad must have been reckoning that their time was almost up: all the papers had been saying that having nicked the title Cowley would have to rebuild. Poor old Ben was in the worst plight. Now I was back he was the one likely to make way for me. Noel Mostyn, the other front runner, was a limited player, but young and improving — two qualities Ben lacked. The last hope for big Doon was that our old partnership might spark up again. 'Come on Vin,' he kept saying, 'let's get back in business' — obviously fearing we never would. Having let his big body go during the summer he was buckling to and driving himself through miseries, sweating, groaning and vomiting. When we got down to serious training Carpenter and Brine, Connaught and Herrick and Charley Mount looked as hard and competent as ever, but as a squad we somehow didn't have the air of title holders. Even Geoff Cowley was frowning more, as though he had private worries.

It had been easier to relax the previous summer, because we'd simply been picking up our familiar style. Now we had to move towards a new one. With Farthing and Bush gone, and Dooner turned back into a pumpkin, we were obviously going to find it harder to make and take chances. Cowley's solution was to push more men forward. He was willing to trust our back four to absorb the counter-attacks, or at least to hold them up till help arrived. Two of the midfield players were to press forward all the time behind the front three, giving us plenty of movement, plenty of options. We were all supposed to chase and interchange, moving the ball fast and harrying the defence till the openings came. This called for quick thinking and good close control. In our early practice games there were problems. Ben Dooner was much too ponderous, and Fenn, who had the necessary skill, was essentially a touchline runner, unused to switching positions. The rest of us didn't shape up too badly — but I did miss those pinpoint passes from Ian Farthing. And I worried about the risk of becoming one chaser among several.

Basically, though, Jonathan Woolley had got it right: I was perky — glad to be playing again, glad to be back in charge of my own life. Any worries I had about team changes or new tactics were minor ones. Up to a point I wasn't even that fussed about my own immediate form. Cowley was repeatedly telling me not to rush things. If necessary I could take half the season to get my game going again. I had a lot to prove, but I knew I could do it because I'd done it before. Here I was, at the peak of my career, playing for the League champions and competing for a World Cup place. I felt very definite.

Luckily I was free to concentrate, because all the background things were in order. My private life was nicely set up here and there round the town. The house was by now totally complete and redecorated, even by Claire's standards, and very comfortable it was. Claire herself was looking good and dressing well and more confident than she'd ever been. You could have taken her for a Company secretary. I was proud of her in the way I was proud of the house, though I suppose I didn't have a deep enough interest in either.

Having got his new squad together Geoff Cowley, in his typical fashion, went round and round it, like a perfectionist putting up a tent, adjusting a peg here and a rope there. Dooner was put back on his diet, Fenn was given special training sessions to force him to cut inside, and Selby was found new digs because he was homesick. In various interviews Geoff claimed, among other things, that Connaught would be the next England left-back, that Paget was good enough to play till he was forty, that Selby could be the surprise player of the coming season, and that I'd be back to my best form by Christmas. It was the old recipe for getting a footballer to surpass himself — a bit of pressure and a bit of praise — but from Geoff's mouth it always seemed to work. Selby was a characteristic Cowley signing — a Second Division player, experienced for his age, but hardly noticeable outside his own club till Geoff moved for him. At first I couldn't see much to him. He had sound basic skills, but didn't look as though he could leave his mark on a First Division game. Now that Farthing was gone we badly needed a play-maker, but Selby wasn't the type. Geoff's idea seemed to be that we could make up the loss by quick, patterned passing, but in practice the patterns were a bit slow in coming. Like me, the squad need a few games to work up some form. I wondered whether Cowley himself was having doubts, because he was frowning more than I'd ever seen him.

I stopped wondering what was on his mind because just as the season was getting under way there was something on my own. It started from a letter I received among the fan-mail that summer:

Dear Vincent,

You won't recognise the writing, but you know me very well! Remember a night in Bath last April? *I* certainly do!

You'll be pleased (I hope) to hear that I am now living in Manston. See address (and phone number!) at top of page. I'll be hoping to hear from you.

Love,
Julie

It was that girl from the motel. I'd hardly given her a second thought, but now she'd turned up it seemed a pity to waste her. I gave her a ring, and followed up with a quick visit. All the signs were that she'd be a handy addition to my little squad. She liked a laugh, a drink and a bang, and she knew how I was situated.

Then one morning I was walking to the training ground, which was less than a mile from the house, when I ran into her by chance.

'What are you doing in these parts?' I asked. I'd not seen her for a week or more.

'I'm going to the Greenway Garden Centre.'

'That's right near our training ground.'

'Is it?'

'Shouldn't you be working?' She'd told me she had an office job at Streeter's, in the centre of town.

'I've got the day off.'

As it happened I was ripe to see her, and fixed a meeting for that same afternoon.

The following week it happened again — chance meeting near the training ground. I took advantage as before, but was getting suspicious, and decided to keep a look-out. Three days later there she was in wait. I just managed to nip down a side street before she could see me. As far as I was concerned the message was clear: cut off communications. I took to

196

driving to the ground, though I'd enjoyed the walk, and didn't call her again. No woman was going to get on my back. A week or ten days passed with no problems — and then the phone-in started. It was gradual. Three or four times Claire had answered the phone and had the caller ring off without a word. One evening I picked up the receiver myself, said our number, and heard Julie's voice say 'Hallo, Vincent.' I rang off like a shot, but within seconds the phone was ringing again, 'Vincent, it's me —' I cut her short and left the phone off the hook. How she'd got my number I didn't know. It wasn't in the book, and I'd taken care not to give it to her. For the time being I more or less gave up answering the phone, but Claire took several more blank calls.

Manston drew their first three games of the season, 1—1 in each case. I scored a goal of sorts, and was close to the centre of the action, but without doing anything very brilliant. Our new style of dab it and run kept me active but didn't create the situations that suited me best. Dooner had started the season alongside me, but he'd lost a yard of pace, and was always labouring. Fenn had his moments on the wing, but only a few of them. As Geoff had prophesied, Stuart Selby was the surprise. Without doing anything spectacular on the ball he had the knack of turning up where he was needed — cutting out a pass, nipping on to a throw-in, or ghosting in to meet a centre.

For our fourth match Mostyn took over from Dooner, and we won 3—0, playing ten or fifteen minutes of brilliant football. Mostyn, Selby and I all scored, and the papers said that the old Geoff Cowley magic was at work again. But a week later we went down 0—2, hardly stringing three passes together all afternoon.

So it went on. For every two steps forward we took one back. For a few minutes in most games, a bit longer in some, we hit a rhythm going forward and ran the other side dizzy. But when the passing and running slipped out of sync we'd be all over the place. Luckily the defence was as steady as ever, with John Carpenter blocking up the middle like a tree. Whether his game had matured, or whether you looked at him differently now he was an international it's hard to say, but you hardly noticed the freakishness of his style any more. He simply took over one third of the field. Thanks largely to him the muddle and inconsistency weren't fatal. Manston didn't get into the top three that autumn, but we stayed with the pack. If we could get our act fully together by the new year we'd be quite nicely placed.

What worried me sometimes was that the spirit of the side wasn't quite what it had been. We were more subdued. Selby was a quiet lad, Ben Dooner had lost heart, and Martin Connaught only cared about his own performance. Ray Paget was preoccupied with his dry-cleaning business. John Carpenter had moved into town over the summer, taking a bigger house where there was a granny-annexe for his mother-in-law. But outside training we saw no more of him than we'd ever done: he'd be off walking his dogs or re-building his cars. On away journeys, especially, we missed loud-mouthed Bushy shouting us into life. Except when Mick Long made the side Herrick had to rattle around on his own on these journeys, having no one to cackle with. It dulled him down a little. On the park, too, I was beginning to notice a change in him. Over the previous couple of seasons he'd improved pretty well every aspect of his game — but he wasn't quite the force he had been when he was just a crazy, non-stop chaser. It had suited him to be young. But when we were down in a match it was still Neil, Briney and Charley Mount who rallied us and flogged us forward.

The new style made it hard for me to judge my progress. I'd be laying off quick passes and nipping into space, but if the return didn't come there wasn't much I could do about it. I did some neat things with Herrick and Selby, or more rarely with Mostyn or Fenn, but too often I had a promising move killed by some other bugger's weak first touch. This was frustrating, and could have led to bad feeling, but it didn't. I had it constantly in my skull that it was the long haul that counted. The previous season I'd started at top speed and then broken down. This year I'd take it steady. I'd almost have been worried if I was playing too well — though it would have been nice to be certain I still had it in me. Meanwhile I was scoring pretty regularly, if not as often as I could have wished. The team needed a few more goals all round to pull the crowds in. After half a dozen home games there were still hundreds of seats in the new stand untouched by human bum.

In late September the ankle gave me some trouble again, and I had to play a couple of games with a pain-killing injection. One of them was on a stormy Wednesday night when our short passes kept sticking in the mud, and we were put out of the League Cup on our own ground. But I'd recovered by the week-end, and we pulled off a good away win to lift us into the top five and make us think we were getting things right.

The morning after that match, the Sunday, Claire and I slept late. When I did eventually get up and pull back the curtain I found myself staring straight at Julie, who was standing by our front gate. She saw I'd seen her before I could let the curtain drop. I didn't know what she might be up to or what I could do. Any moment she could have knocked on the door asking for me or pretending to be a Jehovah's Witness. But nothing happened. When I squinted out again ten minutes later, she'd gone. The only immediate follow-up was another of her silent phone-calls around midday.

The shrewd bitch had hit on just the trick to get me edgy. I couldn't stand to be cramped and shadowed. Some men could have tackled her directly, called her bluff or scared her off — but that wasn't my nature. I was still the dodger, the shifter, the disappearing man. Now I'd been tracked to my own front door I was sweating.

Later that week a note was pushed through the letter box with just my name on the envelope. Luckily I was the one to pick it up. It said:

Vince — what's wrong? Don't you want me any more? I moved to this town to be nearer to you, but now you seem so far away. Why are you avoiding me? I've been missing you so much.

You can't just walk away from me now. Not after those times we've had. I won't give you up because I can't.

I love you,
Julie

Claire came in while I was reading the note, and I was so flustered I all but ate it.

By an instinct I already guessed that this wasn't going to be just an inconvenience but real trouble. What I could never have guessed was the shape the trouble would take. Within two days of receiving Julie's note I happened to be giving Sally Carpenter a lift home after she'd come back with Claire from a keep-fit class. Out of the blue she said: 'I was walking along behind you the other week, and you kept stopping, and slipping into doorways . . .'

'Are you sure it was me?'

'Yes. You were dodging that girl, weren't you?'

'What girl?'

'The one with the red hair who's been hanging round your street.'

I pulled into the kerb and switched off the engine.

'What do you know about her?'

'Nothing. I saw you dodging her, and later I've seen her near your front garden. That's all.'

'Have you said anything to Claire?'

'Of course not. Why should I make trouble?'

'So why mention her to me?'

'Curiosity, I suppose. And I thought you might need some help.'

Being a man who never gave his secrets away I was badly wrong-footed. But her freckled face looked so sensible that I found myself saying: 'If I tell you about it, will you keep it quiet?'

'Of course.'

I hesitated. 'You won't even tell John?'

'We don't have that sort of conversation.'

So I told her the story, tidying it up a little. The street we were parked in was quiet, just the odd car whizzing by. Sally listened carefully and then said: 'It's really getting to you, isn't it?'

200

'It seems to be.'

'Have you never had such problems before? I've heard it's not unknown for footballers to screw around.'

She had a little grin there, and so did I, knowing more than she thought.

'I've heard that, too,' I said. 'But after a one-night stand you don't look to have the girl on your back forever. What can I do? She'll be down the chimney next.'

'Seriously — what's the worst she can do?'

I'd already thought that out. 'Tell Claire, talk to one of the papers, or try and kill herself.'

'Would she do that?'

'Doubt it. Might swallow a few aspirins for the drama. *Then* go to the papers.'

'You couldn't buy her off?'

'She's not after money. Be easier if she was.'

Sally was frowning over the problem like a lawyer or a doctor.

'There's nothing for it,' she said. 'You must have it out with her.'

'I can't. It's not in me.'

We talked a bit longer before I drove her home, but neither of us had any bright ideas. It was only later that I realised that two things had come out of the conversation. One was that I'd enjoyed Sally having that little glimpse of my private life. It made me feel quite close to her — closer than I'd felt to Claire in that way for quite some time. The other was that indirectly I'd been reminded where I could go for help. That night I called Pat Arnold.

According to Pat the game-plan he put to me was an old one, but it was new to me. I put it into effect the following Friday evening, filling it out with a few little tactics of my own. It worked like a charm. The next day I had my best game for nearly a year. Although I was on the pain-killing injection again I scored a goal with each foot. In fact the whole side fizzed at last, running, calling, switching, weaving patterns. We hit five and could have had eight. At the final whistle the half-capacity crowd cheered us off the pitch. They weren't to know any more than we were how the club would be knocked sideways over the next couple of weeks.

Lurking in my mind all that week-end was a desire to tell Sally Carpenter how I'd sorted things out. For the first time I'd understood Pat Arnold's pleasure in confiding in someone. Also I had a curiosity to see how she'd react to the story I had to tell. She might not care for it — in fact I wasn't too sure I cared for it myself. But she knew what I'd been up against, and she had a past of her own. It would be interesting how she reacted. After all, she'd started the conversation in the first place. At last I risked calling her, and found her quite agreeable to meet me in a coffee-bar in a quiet part of town. I still remember my mood as I drove there — a bit excited, but chiefly thinking that whatever happened it would be a mixed experience, slightly strange, like eating chocolate under water. What was I doing, talking about my sex-life with John Carpenter's wife?

'All right, then,' I said to her when we'd settled. 'I solved the red-haired problem. I'm a free man.'

'Lucky for some. What did you do?'

As we were headed straight for the dodgy bit, I slowed down. 'Something none too charming, to tell the truth.'

'What?'

'It wasn't my own idea. I got it off an old mate of mine.' (And yours, I thought.)

'Go on.'

'You may not like this . . .'

'Well, you brought me here to tell me. Get on with it.'

'All right. I called her up, and laid on a nice evening — flowers, champagne, chat. Then I broke it to her after the meal.'

'Broke what to her?'

'I said sorry I'd been avoiding her — I hadn't known what else to do. I still didn't like to tell her, but I had to. The truth was, I'd found I'd got V.D.'

'Yuk!' Sally made a disgusted face, but at least she didn't get up and walk out.

'I told you it was a bit rough.'

'A bit rough? It's a bit sick.'

'What else could I do?'

'Now she'll go for a check-up herself.'

'But it'll be clear. I haven't got it, so she won't have it.'

'She's really in luck, isn't she? How did she take it?'

I shuffled a bit. 'Well obviously she didn't like it . . . but she saw I was trying to play fair by her.'

'You are a sod.' Sally was looking at me as though I really was rotten with the pox.

'I knew you wouldn't like it. I told you you wouldn't.'

'Well who would? Apart from your friend.'

'What else could I do? It worked, didn't it? It got her off my back. No one got hurt. I gave her a nice good-bye present.'

Sally opened her mouth as though to curse me, but suddenly laughed instead.

'No one could take you for an England striker. You look about twelve years old.'

For a second I was mad, but then I caught her eye and suddenly relaxed. We were quite close again, quite intimate. She was inside my guard, and I liked it. Now she was jeering at me her white teeth looked very good against her freckles and blue eyes.

She said: 'You must lead a daft life.'

'Maybe. You seemed quite interested in it the other day.'

'Perhaps. Perhaps I was.'

'Why?'

Her blue eyes were on me all the time. 'Boredom, it must have been. I don't have enough to occupy my mind.'

I'd wondered before about her home life. She'd said about John: 'We don't have that sort of conversation.' What sort could they have, when he was silent so often? Maybe the silences got her down. Maybe that was where Pat Arnold had come in.

'You need a hobby,' I said.

'Perhaps I do,' she answered in a neutral voice, and finished up her coffee. 'Can you give me a lift back?'

In the car we said very little, but there was an atmosphere. I could hear her breathing slightly quick, and my own face was hot. The Carpenters' house was set well back behind a hedge. I pulled into their driveway and stopped in front of an empty garage.

'Thank you,' said Sally, making no move to get out.

'Is John off in one of his cars, then?' I was a bit dry in the mouth.

'He's taken my mother to the pictures.'

'To the pictures?'

Quite slowly I put my left arm round her shoulders and pulled her towards me and tried kissing her. For a moment she didn't respond at all, but then she suddenly clutched my head and ground her mouth into mine so hard that she cut my lip. That did it. I wrenched her round, grabbed at her breasts and then shoved my hand up into her clothes, snarling in my throat. For a moment or two she whimpered and strained, but then suddenly jerked away, pushed me off, and stumbled out of the car. She called out something like 'No more' or 'Not here', and ran to the house. By the time I'd got after her she'd slammed the front door behind her. I rang the bell long and loud, and then knocked till the door shook, but she didn't answer.

On the drive home I tried to sort myself out. Partly I was still hot with sex, and thinking I'd get another chance at her later. Partly I was scared I'd blown the whole thing by moving too fast. Partly I felt a bit sick about it all. I wasn't like Pat Arnold — I'd never moved in on a friend's wife before. Then again, to be honest, I was a shade nervous. Though none of the lads knew Carpenter well, nobody mucked him around. There was something formidable in his personality, and physically he was all muscle and bone. You never saw him hurt. If he knew what I'd been about he might do anything from sod-all to trying to kill me.

Next morning in training I had an eye on him, but noticed nothing unusual. Afterwards I nipped home fast, thinking there might be a call or a visit from Sally. All I had for my trouble was a restless afternoon. The phone did ring about tea-time, but it was Geoff Cowley, who for once in a way had missed the morning training session.

'Vince, I need to see you.'

'Can it wait till tomorrow?'

'No, it has to be now. Get over right away. I'm in my office.'

Before I'd put the receiver down I knew what Geoff wanted to see me about. There was only one thing this urgent that he couldn't talk about over the phone. He'd heard I'd made a grab at Sally Carpenter. For some reason she must have split it straight to him. It was crazy. 'Nothing happened,' I kept telling myself, all the way to the ground. That was the line — and it was true. All the same I was feeling bad.

Geoff was actually waiting for me in the main entrance, looking tight-faced and tired. With the grey hair and the big grey eyebrow and the weariness he could have been sixty. It was impossible to believe that he'd once played against me, and kicked me with both feet. Hardly speaking, he led me out through the players' tunnel on to the pitch, and then along the halfway-line to the centre spot. It was getting dark, and the new stand loomed over us, pitch-black. An empty soccer stadium at night is always depressing, like a closed church or a ghost village.

'What's this all about?' I asked, trying to sound easy.

Geoff didn't answer at once — just stood with his hands in his raincoat pockets, staring round through the gloom at the deserted stands and terraces.

'You were the first player I signed for Town,' he said. 'Nearly four years ago.'

I waited.

'I wanted you to hear it from me before it got out on television. I'm leaving.'

Being geared to something so different I barely made sense of his words.

'Leaving? Why? Where are you going?'

'I'm going where you've been. I'm going to be manager of City.'

'City?' I couldn't think, but I was speaking. 'Why? What for?'

'It's hard to explain, Vin.' He'd lowered his voice,

as though there were people all round us, instead of emptiness.

'But we're champions!' Suddenly the thoughts were tumbling into words. 'We're League Champions, Geoff. You built this side out of nothing. You built that bloody great stand. You're just putting a new team together. How can you walk out on us? It can't be just the fucking money.'

'No,' he said. 'It's not the money.'

We stood there on the empty field.

'You don't sound overjoyed,' I said at last.

'No,' he answered. 'It's not like that.'

'Well what *is* it like?'

'You know City . . . It's a club with the whole town behind it. You get a real crowd there — not like this Manston lot. There's money there. I can buy the players I like.'

'May not suit you, Geoff,' I said, meaning it. 'You like doing things the hard way, coming from behind, making a team out of bits and pieces. What you going to do when you can buy anyone you want?'

Geoff dug his heel into the turf, thinking. 'You're right, Vin,' he said. 'It may not suit me. That's why I'm going — to find out. See if I can handle a big club.'

At the thought of him starting again on his own I suddenly felt sorrier for him than for us poor buggers he was leaving in the shit.

'You can handle any size of club, Geoff,' I said, and shook hands. 'City'll murder everyone but Manston. Good luck, mate.' Later it struck me as ridiculous that I'd been trying to cheer him up for landing one of the two or three top jobs in soccer.

'Thanks, Vin. Let's see you back in the England squad.'

'All right then. Who'll take your place here?'

'No idea. Up to the directors. Look, I have to go. I'm having a word with John Carpenter and Steve Brine. You're the ones who did it for me. You three and Ian Farthing.'

'You're the one who got it out of us.'

We walked off the park together, to no applause.

Geoff's going put the club in turmoil, especially when the idea got around that he'd have stayed if the directors had seriously tried to persuade him. Apparently there were two reasons why they'd been willing to see him go. One was the new stand, that had never yet been more than half filled. The other was that he'd run the club so quietly that the directors had felt neglected. They weren't satisfied with owning a succesful store — they wanted to stand in the window and wave at the customers. Furlonger, the Chairman, put out a statement: 'Geoffrey's record here speaks for itself. We gave him his chance and he took it with both hands. We wish him well at City. But there are other managers and other methods. We'll hope to make as good an appointment this time as we did the last time — and maybe brighten the club's image in so doing.'

The younger players weren't so bothered, because they hadn't seen the difference Cowley had made to the club. Brine and Paget and the rest of the old hands were very low. We'd sit around after training swapping guesses about the new manager. Some preferred one man, some another. John Carpenter only said: 'It's Geoff Cowley's team. Who else could make it work?'

I didn't have too much to say myself, but I was probably more sapped than anyone. It was in my nature to like working and playing against the odds, making something out of a no-hope side. We'd had a little team of us at Manston who'd dragged the club up into Europe by its boot-laces, and transformed our own game in the process. But always it had been Geoff who'd planned and led the charge. Where would we be without him? Where would I be?

The only thing that could make me forget that question was thinking about Sally Carpenter. Every day I was waiting for some sort of signal, but there was nothing. Once or twice she'd even been to the house to see Claire, but always at times when I was bound to be away. I tried phoning her when I knew John would be out, but got no reply, unless from her mother who'd have me speedily ringing off. Several times I drove or strolled past the house, looking out for her, but with no result. 'Christ!' I thought, 'I must give this over. I'm getting like Julie.' As much as anything now I just wanted to know what was going on in Sally's head. Was she angry or guilty or what? She could have turned right off me, or she might be dying for it, and only need a word from me to turn the scales. But I could never get hold of her to find out.

With Cowley gone Mallison took over as caretaker for a couple of matches, both of which we drew. The following Monday afternoon I was in for treatment of the ankle, which had been troubling me again, when a message came through for me to go to the Board Room. Furlonger himself was there to usher me in like an uncle.

'Hallo there, Vince. As you were in the stadium we wanted you to be the first of the players to meet our new manager. A new manager, but for you an old friend.'

The directors stood round grinning with joy as I shook the hand of John Judd. I was grinning myself, with amazement and horror.

'Good to see you, Vincent,' said Judd. 'You've come quite a long way since I first signed you.'

'I'd say you both had,' said Furlonger, which set the directors laughing.

I drove home feeling stunned. Fate had pushed the button and Manston would go down like a fucking lift. No one had mentioned Judd's name in connection with the managership. He'd got away from Stanborough just before the drop, had a couple of seasons with a moderate Second Division outfit, and then gone to America, where he'd somehow produced great results. But that was Toyland soccer: it should never have got him the Manston job. The other candidates who'd been mentioned as possibles had all been streets ahead of Judd. I could only think that the directors had fallen for a talker.

Over the next few days Judd did a lot of talking — to television, radio, newspapers, and even the players. The same sentences kept coming up, though he varied the order:

'Geoff Cowley's done a fine job here — let's get that

straight. He built up a strong squad and he's got the silver-ware to show for it. That's not an easy act to follow. In all fairness it has to be said that the present team is in a transitional phase. I think Geoff would tell you that himself. My job, as I see it, is to build on what I find here, so I'll start by taking a good look at what we've got. What I already know is that we have an ambitious Board, and a go-ahead Chairman in Arthur Furlonger. We also have a great bunch of supporters; and I'll be applying some of the lessons I learnt in American soccer to keep them entertained before and during our home matches. We've taught America a lot about soccer, but they have something to teach us about presentation.'

He could go on like this indefinitely, cutting it off by the foot or by the yard. Naturally the other lads kept asking me what he was like, but I told them to wait and listen. Of course, it was possible he'd changed since his Stanborough days, as I had myself, but I couldn't see much trace of it. Here was our new side taking shape, and here was I trying to work and con and needle myself back to top form, and all out efforts were now to be judged by this prat. It was disgusting. In our first match under his leadership it so happened that we all played moderately and gained a moderate result — a 1—1 draw.

'Not too bad, lads,' said Judd, as though we'd be desperate for his verdict. 'There's a bit of work to be done — but all in all it wasn't too bad.'

Late the following week John Carpenter didn't turn up for training one morning. It was put about that he had flu, but I was immediately suspicious. On the ten o' clock news that night it was announced that he'd been transferred to Albion for an undisclosed fee. Claire was with me when the item came on, and she said I'd turned white. She was a bit shocked herself, but she hadn't the smallest idea how things were falling apart for me. I didn't know whether John was going because he thought Judd was a prick, or because of something Sally had said about me. Either way it wasn't likely I'd ever see Sally again. And the loss to the club would be disastrous.

Carp came in the next morning to say good-bye, looking no

more emotional than usual. After wishing us luck he'd have been on his way without another word. It wasn't natural. Someone had to take the moment on.

'For fuck's sake, John,' I said, 'What's happening? Why are you going?'

'Mainly family reasons,' he said, but with no edge.

'But it's a bit sudden . . .'

'Albion's offer was a bit sudden. . .'

'Judd must have accepted it sharpish.'

'Yeh. So did I.'

There he stood, tall and distant as he'd always been. He'd have looked just the same if he was off to Australia, or going out to be shot.

'But John,' I said, 'Albion are nothing. . . !'

'Nor were Manston when we first came here. OK lads — see you on the park.'

And he was gone.

The newpapers reckoned that Carpenter had forced Judd's hand, and they were probably right. John's contract expired at the end of the season, so he could have moved for nothing then. As it was, Manston picked up a fat fee for him. To appease the fans for the loss of a local hero Judd bought a new midfield man from Glasgow, Gordon Philp. Every crowd loves a Scottish ball-player. To make room for him Charley Mount had to drop back alongside Brine. As I've said before, I'm no great judge of a side, but I could see at once that these moves were wrong. Charley was a good player anywhere, but his lack of height could be a liability in the centre of the defence, especially as Paget was doubtful on crosses. Philp had clever feet, but he liked to slow the game down. He was all wrong for the quick-passing style we'd been working on. Judd had ballsed things up at a stroke. Though to be fair to him, the loss of Carpenter would have wrenched us apart whatever he'd done. We'd all lived off John's strength. Other players had their talents and their limits — you knew what they could and couldn't do. John was a monster, a marvel, a freak. You couldn't shake him or tire him. Without him we were just another bunch of players. Overnight our confidence went, and a team that loses confidence is just like a punctured football: you can't see what's gone, but the bounce goes with it. The results started slipping straight away.

I remember after the match that put us out of Europe, sitting in front of the fish-tank in despair. It wasn't just that we'd lost. Cowley and Carpenter had pulled us all together, and now we were coming to bits. For that season we'd squeeze by. We wouldn't be relegated, or come near it — we'd just be ordinary. Later things could get worse. Connaught would go, and maybe Herrick and Fenn. With several of the other lads getting on a bit, we'd be on a downward slope. That night I'd run my studs off. I'd hardly made a serious mistake, but I'd done nothing right. How could I ever find form with this lot? The previous week at Wembley England had just squeaked their way into the World Cup Finals. They'd played like pillocks, but I'd stayed on the bench all night. I could already have kicked my last ball for England. The thing might be to get out, like John Carpenter. But where to? A year before, any club in the country would have snapped me up, but here I was, twelve months older and half as sharp. Of course, the ankle had been nagging me — that could be part of the trouble. And the side as a whole were playing rubbish. But never mind the excuses. I'd told myself for months that this was the make-or-break season — and time was running out. If necessary I'd have to prove myself on one and three-quarter legs. I remembered the day-dream I'd had as a kid about a mistake in my birth-certificate. If only I was 26 instead of 28. Still, as I'd been a late starter I might be a late finisher. Perhaps I'd play till 37 and hit my peak at 32. Some did. My ankle told me I wasn't likely to be one of them. I thought of Bill Byers, strapping himself together for each game, and felt tired.

For the second time that season I asked for advice, calling up Geoff Cowley the same night. He was having problems of his own at City, but as I could have expected he listened carefully to my moaning, and eased extra details out of me with shrewd questions. Then he said: 'Vin, you've got no choice. Move now, and it'll be all distractions: new team, new manager, new house. You'll have blown the season before you know it. Don't waste your energy. As for the England game, it was perfect for you. We reached the finals, but those who played did themselves no good at all. You were fortunate to be out of it. Hit some sort of form in the next few months and you'll walk into the national side. So stay with Manston, and make your own luck.'

I'd needed to hear that message from someone other than myself. If I was to be an international striker again it would have to be with Manston. The season stretched ahead of me like a steeplechase.

Over the weeks that followed I was playing at the utter limit of what I could do, physically and mentally — playing as I'd done against Cowley himself, at Millwood. Each game left me shell-shocked. With the team still at odds I could find no fluency, but by sheer will-power I was scoring and making enough goals to keep us in mid-table. It can't be said that the effort made me better company. I could muster enough good-humour for training sessions and my private social rounds, but there was bloody little left over for competitive matches or home life. On the field, whether because I'd slowed down or was getting a clumsier service, I was caught more often and more painfully. In self-protection my own play got nastier. I was booked several times, and each time I'd done some damage. At home I was silent for long periods, or else singing tunelessly as I had done in a previous dark spell. Claire was very self-contained by this time, and didn't seem too fussed by my moods as long as she could put a reason to them. If I didn't speak for a couple of hours she'd say: 'Is your ankle bad?' Other times she'd uselessly try to cheer me up, saying things like 'At least you scored the goal', as though I was a sulking kid — which to all appearances I must have seemed. She seemed happy enough, but there wasn't much warmth between us. We still had sex, but only in the way you have a cup of tea.

Much of the time I was on the job elsewhere, getting inside a fair few women, half a dozen of which you could have called regulars. Compared with what the likes of Connaught and

212

Herrick were getting — starlets and so forth — I have to admit that my little squad didn't sparkle. If you'd put them in a row and asked people what they had in common, no one could have guessed. At least I bloody hope not. They weren't horrible, but several of them were homely. Somehow that seemed to suit me.

'Work hard, play hard' the saying used to go. I'd never worked so hard at football or played so hard at sex. The two things seemed to go together. It got so that when I was taking a shower after training I was already restless for a fuck. It wasn't a satisfactory way of life, because there was never a resting point. Just after you've come sex stops seeming important. Unfortunately, so does everything else. Every day I had my blank hours. At these times I tended to go wandering in places that suited the mood — poor dirty old districts where the street-name plates were rusting because the houses hadn't long to go, and the streets themselves could soon disappear.

I had acquaintances everywhere. If any of the lads was in need of a plasterer, or a tattooist, or a TV repair-man, I was the person they asked. I'd natter to anyone in these out-of-the-way places. Most of them seemed to have monotonous lives, and a chat with a known footballer gave them a lift, which in turn gave me a lift.

Manston had gradually abandoned Cowley's attacking strategy without settling for anything else in particular. Brine, Mount and Herrick kept us competitive, Connaught and Selby showed touches of class, and Fenn was brilliant on his day —which came about once a month. Philip was still settling in. Dooner had staged a mini-comeback, to the extent that he and Noel Mostyn were now alternating in the side, neither achieving much. Judd had appointed a middling-competent coach named Mill and detached himself from day-to-day training. The idea was that he'd concentrate on tactics and crowd-entertainment. He was more successful in the second of these activities, having already laid on a team of drum-majorettes, a display by police dog-handlers, and an electronic score-board with cartoon-figures and jokes to take your mind off the football.

What the team badly needed was a good Cup run. We got off to a fair start with a 2—1 win, admittedly to Third Division opponents. I reached home in good spirits, having scored the winning goal, and was surprised to find Claire also quite frisky. We went out for a meal with friends, and she was chattering, laughing and waving her arms about. In bed that night she bucked and squeaked, livelier then she'd done for years. Afterwards, very contented, she said: 'I've got a surprise for you, Vincent. We weren't just making love, we might have been making a baby. I've had that I.U.D. taken out.'

'Don't worry,' I told her. 'I had a vasectomy this morning.'

'You're horrible!' she said, laughing.

There was no point in fighting it — we were in for a baby. I didn't know by now whether I minded or not. It should have been a bonus that Claire was so turned on by the hope of pregnancy, but that wasn't how I took it. I liked sex for itself, not for the sake of something else.

Manston's fourth-round Cup-tie seemed to drag on forever. We drew at home and then drew away — two tough, mauling games, battled out bruise for bruise. In the second replay there were six men booked. After ninety minutes of all-in football, with blood showing on both sides, there was no score. We were all so burned out that in extra time player after player was going down with cramp. With five minutes left Selby jabbed a pass at me in the area, and I somehow turned and turned again, through two tackles, and snapped the ball wide of the keeper. That was it.

That night I watched the goal on TV, first at real-life speed and then slowed down. It didn't look possible. When the pass was struck I had my back to goal. There was a defender on me, and a second covering him. I seemed to feint right and swivel left, feint left and side-step right and then hit the ball, all in a single process. 'What other striker in British football could have scored that goal?' asked the commentator. 'If there were any lingering doubts about Gilpin's return to form that moment of magic must surely have put paid to them.' I thought: 'I'm getting there. I can do it again. I did it tonight.' But my ankle felt like hell the next morning.

Any football club feeds off hope. Already we were one up on Cowley, because City had gone out in the Third round to United, the League leaders. Albion were still in the Cup, but when we played a League match on their own ground, with Mostyn in my place while I rested the ankle, we won 2—0. Noel Mostyn took everything in the air against Grogan, and scored both goals. Even though Carpenter himself wasn't playing — he had flu — we felt we'd laid another ghost. By now Selby was looking good, and Philp and Fenn were starting to play. In the Fifth round we cruised through an away tie against a good Second Division side, with Herrick, Mostyn and I scoring a goal apiece. Our piss-poor reward was a Sixth-round match against United on their ground, where they'd not lost all season.

Dad phoned me on the night of the draw to ask questions there was no interesting answer to, such as 'You're away to United, then?' or 'That's a tough one, isn't.it?' He sounded very like his late Uncle Peter, except that there was a little bit of liveliness in his voice that I couldn't account for. The explanation came when he said 'Now hang on, Vin, I've got a surprise for you,' and my Mother took over from him.

'Hallo, love. How are things?'

'Hallo, Mum. Is that you speaking or is it a recording?'

She laughed nervily. 'No, it's me, Vincent. In the flesh. I'm back home again.'

Several questions sprang to my mind, such as 'Why?', 'How long for?', and 'Where's your bloke, then?' But none of them seemed right. The best I could do was: 'Well, that's very nice.'

'I thought it was time I settled down.' She gave another laugh. 'At my age.'

I realised they both expected me to be pleased or even delighted at this reunion, but I wasn't feeling anything much. As usual when in doubt, I tried for a joke:

'Go on, Mum. You're in your prime. Who knows what you'll be up to next?'

'No, I'm sobering down. We must all be sobering down. Len's getting married in the summer.'

'About time. What about a second honeymoon for you and Dad?'

'Second honeymoon?' She was laughing again. 'We didn't even have a first one. We couldn't afford it.'

That put me on the safe ground of presents, and gave me something to say. Before we rang off I'd promised to send them a cheque for a trip to Spain that Easter. Christ knows whether they really fancied the idea, but they put on a show of excitement, and at least they'd get some conversation out of it.

Claire heard my end of the call and guessed what had been happening.

'That's good news,' she said.

'Right,' I said — and so it ought to have been. But to me it was already turning into bad news. My Mother had been laughing on the edge of crying. I sent the cheque next morning, and a card with a joke on it; but what I was feeling was that my old man had long given up and that finally Mum was giving up too. She'd had her last little fling, but now she was done. The two of them would potter round the flat with nothing much to do or talk about, and help each other if one of them was ill. And there was Len getting married, and Pete Harvey already married, and Ruddock with his kids. And soon, perhaps, me with mine. Things harden round you like a plaster-cast.

To cheer me up I had Wembley to aim for, but to get there Manston had to win at Alton Fields, where no bugger gave us a chance. With the League almost sewn up United looked all set for the double. On the day of the match I felt low. I'd slept badly, and woke up with the hot, doped feeling of flu coming on. In the coach I got into a row with Connaught, accusing him of playing for Connaught United. He was really mad for once, and so was I. I'd have taken a poke at him if Charley Mount hadn't hauled me off. I was full of poison that day, ready to work off my grudges on anyone. By the time I'd changed for the match I was tight as a wire.

216

It was the last great game we played as a team, and fittingly enough Judd had nothing to do with it. His strategy was that we should pull nine men back and pray for a replay, with no higher attacking aim than a snatched goal on the break. That was fair enough, really: we were ready to give all we had, but we were a frightened side. A draw was the limit of our hopes. But once we were out on the pitch, for some reason our fear changed into recklessness. You could sense the different feeling in the squad. Chief cause was the wind. There was a gusty half-gale tossing the ball about like a balloon. A high cross would suddenly jerk higher; a through-pass would whisk away from you. You couldn't wait for the ball to arrive — you had to claim it, or you'd be left flat-footed. If you had the skill and the nerve you could flight your passes into the wind or against it. This was going to be a crazy game. As it happened three or four of us got a good early touch that gave us confidence. Fenn skipped past his marker and hoisted a high centre that left the keeper clutching air as it swirled back and up. I pulled the centre-back out of the middle and laid the ball back for Selby to biff a thirty-yarder that swerved, dipped and then thudded up from the bar. United tore back at us, and Paget had to throw himself at someone's feet and then parry a close-range shot. But we'd caught a belief that we could land a knock-out punch if we opened up the game. Mount boomed in another big swerver that the goalie only caught at the second attempt. Herrick dashed through on his own to shoot just wide. What with the wind, and the wild bounce, and the pace of the game we were half drunk out there. The roar of the crowd flapped on and off as the air thrashed and shifted.

Neither team slacked. The play swung from end to end at breakneck pace, with mistakes everywhere. A goal had to come, and it arrived after forty minutes. Fenn broke clear again, raced for the goal-line and struck a huge, high cross clean over the defence. Selby headed the ball back into the centre and I swung it into the net.

At half-time poor old Juddie was beside himself, not knowing whether to rejoice because we were one up or scream at us for totally ignoring his instructions.

'Tighten up!' he kept saying. 'Don't lose the aggression, but play it safer. Tighten up!'

We all nodded and then went out and played exactly as we'd done before. We had no choice — the wind whipped up the pace. But after about twenty minutes of pretty even knockabout the game gradually did begin to go the way Judd had wanted. Driven on by their crowd United were getting more and more of the ball and pushing us back. Everything was happening in and around our penalty area, but Mount and Brine were tackling to kill. We'd cover up for minutes at a time, and suddenly snap back. Mostyn had a header kicked off the line. I flicked in Philp's cross, but the goalie saved with his leg. United had the bark, but we had the bite.

But in the last quarter of an hour we began to sag. Mount's big chest was heaving. Philp and Fenn had run themselves out, and even Herrick was slowing. We were squeezed right back conceding corner after corner. If United had scored you'd have said it had to come. But there's no fate in football — you get what you pay for. Five minutes from time Mount blocked a shot in the six-yard box and Brine walloped a clearance way downfield. I volleyed it wide for Selby to chase, and set off after him. Selby went straight for goal, but the keeper rushed him and the ball broke right. At full tilt, with a man at my heels I reached it on the very goal-line and scooped it up and back for the wind to drift it softly into the net.

In the dressing-room we felt as though we'd all but won the Cup. Word came that Carpenter's lot were through on a disputed penalty. With the other two survivors both from the Second Division the prospects had to be good. We became favourites overnight, and the odds shortened still further when the semi-final draw kept us apart from Albion.

It's hard to describe the mood I was in at this time. Things were more or less working, but I couldn't tell how. Since Cowley had gone the team hadn't been right, but we were only one match from Wembley. Whether I was the player I had been I simply didn't know. I felt the same, but with the system gone from the side, and my ankle nagging at me, it was impossible to be sure. I never seemed to get a clear run. But I had my moments. The goals were coming, and coming when they were needed. The media reckoned I'd be back to lead England in the World Cup. I tried to tell myself that I'd come to terms with what I could do, allowing for the doubtful ankle. It was pointless to run for ninety minutes like Neil Herrick. I had to take a leaf from Bill Byer's book and keep a bit in hand for the crucial chance. Under pressure, under the maximum pressure, I could still find that extra half-yard. I was still a match-winner. But there was something desperate in it all. I could never relax. It was concentrate, concentrate all the time. The only proof I still had the killer punch was when I landed it.

The semi-final was grim — a lousy game scrapped out in the middle third of the field, with the whistle going twice a minute. I took some kicks and gave a few, and was one of five men booked. The only goal came near the end. After a corner had been half-cleared Philp hit a savage shot straight into Dooner's bum, and I whipped the rebound through a two-foot gap. It was a ridiculous way to get to a Cup Final, but much of life is ridiculous. At least Dooner's bum had its finest hour. And I took the chance well — I saw it and struck before anyone stirred.

Naturally John Judd, the whispering boaster, was now in his element, saying his piece again and again to any reporter who'd listen: 'I'm still feeling my way at Manston. This is a bonus. I'm certainly not claiming to rival Geoff Cowley yet, but I've done one thing he didn't manage — led the club to Wembley.' Judd had done nothing. I was the one who'd got us to Wembley, and to underline the point I'd scored in every round. Poor old second-rank Manston had done it again, this time without Cowley and without Carpenter and without Ian Farthing. I was the one who'd taken us through.

About a week after the semi-final Claire told me she was pregnant. Although I'd been prepared for the news it still depressed me. I had enough responsibilities already. Right through April I was troubled by the strange idea of this future baby gradually swelling like an apple inside Claire's belly.

Most of the other lads had kids already, and as far as I could see took the whole business in their stride. The strange thing was that I should find it strange. Claire was happy and calm out on her own, as though she didn't need me now. For years I'd provided the necessary money and now I'd provided the necessary seed. She could do the rest herself. My reaction was to make Claire sit back with her feet up at every opportunity, while I went off screwing. My little squad of women were on red alert. If I wasn't fit for Wembley it wouldn't be for lack of fucking.

Speaking of which, I had a phone-call from Pat Arnold a few days before the Cup Final. He was in the area to see a mid-week match, and met me after it at a pub. Naturally he asked about his pox-trick, and I told him the story, though without mentioning Sally. He nodded as he took it all in, but I noticed he was holding himself somewhat stiffly and deduced that he'd already sunk a few malts. He'd been talent-spotting, and I asked if he was still looking to become a manager.

'Hell, no,' he said. 'It's not *in* me to be a focken' manager. I couldn't fancy the responsibility. I'm a good number two.'

'You don't sound too crazy about it.'

'Why in hell should I? Playing was the thing. You can stuff the rest.'

His blue eyes were a bit blood-shot. Altogether he looked strained and out of sorts.

'Why not get out of the game?' I suggested. 'Try something different.'

'Christ, son, I'm too old to start real life now. Who'd employ me? At least I've a focken' ca*reer*. I'm a professional ex-footballer.'

He swallowed some scotch as though it was nasty medicine.

'How's your prick?' I asked, thinking to cheer him up.

'None too brilliant, actually.' He looked glummer than ever.

'You been out of luck?'

'That's right. In the quality, that's right. Not the quality of the women themselves, but in the quality of the actual fuck —

the actual sensation. It's gone *taste*less on me.' Pat twisted his mouth. 'I'm talking about when you *come*. That's the point of it all, for God's sake. That's what you're working *up* to. Take away the thrill of it and the whole focken' skirmish is a waste of time.'

'What's going wrong then?'

Pat leaned forward. 'I'm talking about something physical. Something *technical*. It's the actual spurt — the *spasm*.' He liked that word. 'The *spasm*. I've no real sensation in it any more. It's less pleasure than a good pee. No sensation. Have you had that experience?'

'Not yet.'

'I'm telling you, son, you won't like it.'

'It's probably just temporary . . .'

'I focken' hope so. But maybe it's my body wearing out. Have you thought what goes on down there when you're on the job? Have you thought of it? You're thrusting away, right? You're creating a friction. Then eventually the spurt — the *spasm*. I take it there's a *valve* mechanism of some description — a valve to let out the sperm. The friction prickles the nerves until the nerves open the valve. Out you spurt. And somehow the valve must be wired to the brain to transmit the *sensation* — what they call the *orgasm*. Well with me the valve system seems OK, but there has to be some kind of fault in the wiring. There's only a very weak signal reaching the brain. It's like drinking scotch and tasting water.'

His speech had cheered him up a little, though it hadn't done much for me.

'Have you thought of laying off for a spell?' I asked.

'I've thought of it. I haven't tried it yet.' He gave his first real laugh of the evening, but it tailed off, and he finished his drink. 'Sex is like football,' he said. 'Everything you do with your feet or your prick has to start and finish in the brain.' He paused as though he was looking to continue this line of reasoning, but then gave up.

Next morning the side was announced for Wembley. Thanks to his performance against Albion in the League

Mostyn was picked alongside me. Poor old Ben Dooner wasn't even sub. — Mick Long got the nod, as a utility man. It wasn't a great team — it wasn't like the Manston team of a couple of years back — but it looked good enough to win at Wembley. I just couldn't help wishing that it hadn't been Carpenter's lot we had to beat.

Chapter 15

A soccer match can't be described, because if you're inside it you don't know what it looks like, and if you're outside it you don't know what it feels like. But for the last eight minutes of the Cup Final I had the nearest thing I've known to a double view. I was inside and outside the match at the same time.

For some reason I was switched off by having scored. As the hugging stopped I felt very separated. I'd done my job and wanted the game over to prove it. The mood made me see external things again. There was the whole stadium round me foaming with life. The Albion fans were raising a last cry for a fight-back, while the Manston supporters were stamping and cheering us home. With a hundred thousand voices roaring up a storm the weather seemed to respond. Clouds had closed over the stadium, darkening the air, and a cold breeze was swirling round.

As the game re-started it was obvious that Albion were finished. Seymour and Dunn, up front, and the young midfield players had been running on hope, and now they were out of fuel. Mount, Brine and Connaught began knocking the ball to and fro at the back, with no one raising a sprint to harry them.

There was a stoppage when Onions went down with cramp, and I took a glance at John Carpenter. Now he was beaten I'd stopped thinking of him as an opponent. There he stood, six inches taller than me and a couple of years older, his narrow face red and sweating, his fists clenched, his long body tense with determination, the last man left alive in his team. I was suddenly sorry that he was facing defeat and that I'd been the one to put the knife in. For years we'd won and lost together, and his spirit had strengthened mine. But he'd broken away, he'd broken away of his own choice. One of us had to go down today, and it was going to be him.

As the trainer left the pitch and the game moved again I felt myself physically and mentally very tired. I was almost run out, and my ankle hurt like hell, but my mind was wearier than my body. I could still chase and turn for these last few minutes if my mind would send out the signals, but for some reason it wasn't doing so — at least, not of its own accord. It had to be kicked into action by a conscious effort.

Now there was rain falling, whipped into our faces by the wind. Normally I loved playing in the wet, but today the chill of it cooled me too far. The other lads were fighting on, spent as they were, while I stood in the centre circle with stiffening muscles. I hadn't had a kick since scoring. Grogan stood with me while Carpenter went plunging upfield to drive on his stumbling forwards. But there wasn't much he could do. Brine and the others tackled and spoiled and forced men wide. Onions was wiped out and there was nothing reaching the strikers. If someone had dug out the right pass I could have dropped Grogan and had a clear run on goal through the rain. I should have shouted for the long ball.

But Carpenter's upfield prowling had me worried, just a little. Such a hard man, such a strange man. I'd seen him turn many a match. And no one was picking him up. I trotted back into my own half to keep in touch with him, and just as I did so the ball was hit high to the spot I'd moved from, and Grogan was left free to control it and drive a pass out to the left.

There was a flurry of mis-kicks on the wet turf and somehow Onions got clear to hit a centre. Paget went for it but hadn't the height to catch it. He punched it well clear and the ball ran on to Carpenter, forty yards out. John shaped for a huge shot but suddenly lurched right into a great swerve and was headed for the area with no one ahead of him. I drove myself after him and thought I had him, but as always his stride was deceiving. As I did get close a flailing arm was keeping me off. I slid into the tackle full tilt along the wet grass, skidded a yard or more, but never touched the ball. Down we both went, and as we sprawled Jack Jefford was whistling for a penalty.

What followed I only lived once, of course, but I've seen it a hundred times since on video. I no longer know what I'm remembering and what I've invented. But if you look at the film you'll see that I took no part in the protests that followed Jefford's decision. Brine, Rees and especially Mount were jostling round the ref claiming that the trip, if it was a trip, was outside the area, and pleading with him to consult the linesman — which he refused to do. My mind was blank. I knew I should have been feeling terrible, but there was nothing coming through. It was like one of those dreams where you need to move fast to save someone's life, but your body won't stir — only in this case it was my mind that didn't stir. I watched Carpenter himself slosh the penalty home with the side of his boot, heard the crowd roar and knew the match was as good as lost, all without feeling a thing.

It was pure chance I was standing nearby when Charley Mount turned on the ref again, his frog face swollen with rage. I didn't even catch what Charley said, but I did hear Jefford shout 'That's it! Off!' and see him point dramatically towards the bench. Still I felt nothing — I was on automatic. All that could have driven me was some idea of what I would have been feeling if I'd been feeling anything. On that basis, and with the sharp reflexes of an England striker, I punched Jefford in the stomach and then in the face and kicked him twice as he fell to the ground. I'd have done worse if John Carpenter hadn't wrapped his long arms round me and wrenched me quite gently away.

Chapter 16

I've no clear recollection of the weeks that followed the Cup Final. Why should I want one? After Jefford had sent me off I could hardly speak or even think, any more than if I'd taken a kick in the head. Judd and Mount and the others talked to me, but their words weren't getting through. I had just enough of the dodger's instinct alive in me to have myself smuggled out of the stadium through a side exit. The Ruddocks drove me down to Dorset and the reporters were left clutching air.

That night Alan fed me a few drinks and kept me away from the TV It wasn't till breakfast the next morning, when he brought in all the Sunday papers, that I got the full measure of my situation. 'Appalling attack . . . crowd violence flared . . . forty arrests . . . Referee soldiered on after treatment . . . nine-man Manston beaten 3-1 in extra time . . . referee in post-match hospital check-up . . . two cracked ribs and a badly gashed mouth . . .' The comments were fierce: 'What Vincent Gilpin did was a disgrace to his club and a disgrace to the game of association football' — John Judd. 'Whatever the F.A. decide Gilpin will never kick another ball for Manston as long as I remain Chairman' — Arthur Furlonger. 'The lad's thrown away his future' — England manager. I was an instant write-off.

There was to be plenty of comment over the next few days, F.A. officials, club managers, newspaper writers, M.P.'s, bishops all had their say. Here was an issue that had people falling over themselves to stand up and be counted. Each one had a favourite aspect. I'd done the ref in a Cup Final, showpiece of our national game, watched by millions of viewers at home and abroad. I'd hit him not once but twice, and then kicked him and finally had to be dragged away. It was my action that sparked off the violence in the crowd. To all appearances I'd made the attack in cold blood. And as Jefford had booked me a few weeks earlier there could have been a revenge motive. To cap it all I'd expressed no regret. In fact I'd still issued no public statement.

A few people said a word on my behalf. 'It was my fault for starting it' — Charley Mount. 'I don't know what got into Vin — it was utterly unlike him' — Steve Brine. 'Vince puts himself under terrific pressure at the best of times, and he's had a very difficult season' — Geoff Cowley. And John Carpenter made one of his rare statements to a reporter: 'It's a tragedy for Vince. If only I'd grabbed him a moment sooner. But you shouldn't judge anybody by one action. You have to take the average of his career.'

The days I was with the Ruddocks Alan did no more than try and keep me occupied. I helped him put up a garden shed. We went fishing again. We took his kids swimming, though the sea was like ice. One evening he took me unrecognised into a village pub, where I got pig-drunk for the first time in my life. I recollect being powerfully sick, and then lying curled up in a corner of the toilet with my cheek on the cold floor. The little patch in front of my eyes became very familiar, very intimate — some dirty-white wall, some copper piping, and a cork-tile curling up at the corner. Pissed as I was I got out a pen and wrote my autograph, 'Vince Gilpin', an inch above the floor, where no one would ever see it.

When I went back home I continued saying nothing, to the frustration of many people, including John Judd, Arthur Furlonger, my solicitor, Claire and the P.F.A. rep and a couple of hundred journalists. Time and again I've been asked the reason for that silence, but there's no clear answer. I was silent by instinct. With every prat and wanker in Britain sounding off about me, I didn't fancy adding to the gabble. 'Can't he at least apologise?' was the chief complaint. Of course I should have done. But Jefford hadn't suffered that much. All right, he'd carried on after injury, but that was no more than I'd done fifty times. His reward was national fame and his own personal story, such as it was, in one of the papers. 'I won't prosecute,' says generous Jack. 'Vincent Gilpin will suffer enough without that.' I'd made Jefford unique — a popular referee.

In any case I've always believed that a man who provides some juicy news for the reporters and public deserves thanks. A spy or a murderer is sent to prison, and rightly so, but he gives a lot of people a lot of pleasure. If no one went too far life would get colourless. After the Cup Final I was villain of the month — contender for villain of the year. If I'd apologised I'd have ruined my reputation and spoiled everyone's enjoyment.

I knew what had to come, and I was bracing myself to face it. There were extenuating circumstances of various sorts, but they were peanuts. If I'd put up the best possible defence, sent flowers to Jack Jefford and generally licked shit I might have whittled down the sentence to what? A five-year ban? Even a late developer couldn't fancy a League come-back at thirty-four. On the morning of the hearing one of the papers said: 'This gravest of offences demands the gravest of penalties'. I quite liked that: it gave the matter some dignity. For the same sort of reason I even got a strange relish from the headline in the same paper the following day: 'Disqualified for Life'.

If I'm asked now, two and a half years later, how I feel about my attack on Jefford I still have a mixed response. Strangely enough, what brought home to me how ugly it had been was my brother Len telling me how much he'd enjoyed it. Mum and Dad had been aghast, but he'd been delighted to see the boot go into a referee. If that slob could get a charge from what I'd done, it had to be disgusting. But that obvious view didn't come naturally to me, because the episode had never felt like something I did: it was something that happened to me as much as it happened to Jefford. There was no rage, no excitement — I'd lost all the feelings I normally worked from. I was taken over.

Sometimes when I look at the video I think the whole thing was chiefly bad luck. Onions crosses, Paget punches, Carpenter lunges for goal. A quicker tackle or a different bounce could have changed my career. Other times I think that if I hadn't cracked then I'd have cracked later — maybe in a World Cup match. I could never have guarded against it, any more than I imagine an epileptic could guard against his first fit.

As a footballer I'd had something to do and somewhere to be. That state of affairs was instantly cancelled. There were offers for me to be an outlaw player overseas, but I wasn't interested. I'd finished with soccer. But Claire and I could no longer afford the house we were living in, and in any case had no business in the town. I needed a job fast, and had mates inside and outside soccer who might have found me one, but I've never been able to ask a favour. Since my only skills were in my feet the prospects didn't look brilliant. In these gloomy circumstances Claire did very well. She'd told the reporters that she'd stick by me, and proceeded to do so, more or less without question or complaints, even though I'd become bitter company. Having a baby inside her body seemed to make her very steady and practical. It was because she asked around that one of her uncles came up with a job for me, working back-stage of a big do-it-yourself store in the north midlands.

We moved to be near the job, and had been in our new house — our fourth, and much the smallest — three months before the baby made its début. It was a girl, named Mary after Claire's mother. I was quite interested in it, but fairly detached. Perhaps Mary will turn out to be a good athlete and tennis-player like my mother. And maybe one day she'll give birth to a footballer. Human beings are like those Russian dolls — one inside another inside another.

I still have the job, and seem to do it reasonably well. It's tedious, but brings in enough to support three. What I can't do is express myself or shine in any way. I live at the level of everyone else. I often wonder what happens to the energy and concentration I used to put into football. Maybe I don't produce them any more, like a mother stops producing milk. Or maybe they're turning sour somewhere inside me. I try to keep reasonably fit, though for no particular purpose. I walk a lot, and go swimming regularly, but never kick a ball.

I've made few new friends and don't come across the old ones apart from the Ruddocks. Pete and Karen Harvey were so heart-broken by what happened at Wembley that they always speak to me now as though I was someone they were visiting in hospital. Anyway Karen's now had a baby — a real one — that absorbs most of their attention. Soccer contacts I avoid, but I've been downcast by what's happened to Manston. I had no opinion of Judd as manager, and it was obvious that the club would suffer as some players retired and others moved on. But I never thought to see Town relegated. Mount still does a job for them, but he's in the veteran stage now. Neil Herrick's younger, but he can't run forever like he used to. Fenn, Philp and Mostyn have come to nothing much. Connaught got out.

Nobody understood about me and Manston — I barely understood it myself. Why was I so sold on a mediocre club with half-hearted supporters? After the Cup Final many reporters had made the same point: I'd had a good game, I'd scored, I was set to play for England in the World Cup — why go beserk because the F.A. Cup was slipping away? Probably because I cared about Manston. Yes, it was a pissy club. But me and Cowley and Carpenter — and a few others, but chiefly the three of us — had made something of it. We'd made it famous. We'd rolled it up to the top of the hill like a bloody great rock. Then Cowley had gone and Carpenter had gone, and I was left shoving on my own. But still I was doing all right till Jefford blew his whistle. Now the club's rolled to the foot of the Second Division, new stand and all.

Cowley's kept City in contention for honours, but he's won

nothing yet, and my hunch is that he's lost the edge he once had. I knew the club wouldn't suit him. John Carpenter is still playing for England. You could say he was the toughest of the three of us — but then again he's not fully human.

Claire behaved well not only to me but also to my parents, who've been to stay a number of times. The baby seemed to give them all something to talk about. Dad's still no chatterbox, but he seems to get a lot of pleasure from Mary sitting on him, or crawling on him. Perhaps he's better suited to be a grandfather than a father. Mum's hair has gone grey, which has presumably clicked the lock on her romantic life.

It suited Claire to become a mother, in the sense that she just got on with it to the best of her ability, and with great enjoyment. She wasn't trying to imitate or impress anyone else. There was little sign that she missed the pleasures of being a League footballer's wife. She's well fitted to normal life. I have a lot of respect for her. Unfortunately, however, motherhood affected her sexual style. The chief part of what pleasure she got in bed seemed to lie in doing me a favour. She'd feed the baby or fuck me — using different bits of her body to keep the two of us pacified.

It was this, more than anything, that gradually drove me out. I left quietly, without a quarrel, about a year after Mary was born. Claire hardly seemed bothered: she'd become complete without me. We're still on good terms, and I visit her a couple of times a week to stay in touch with the baby. But it's been a relief, more than anything, to see that she's been taking up with another bloke lately.

I live in a very small flat, shut in on myself like a tortoise. The life I lead is very level, very quiet. I don't even see many women. These days I have less optimism that they might be interested in me, and less heart for the wisecracks that used to get the game going.

I keep asking myself how I'm feeling, as you would after a serious illness or accident. In general I don't feel too bad, which I take to be an unhealthy sign. It's as if I'd had a pain-killing injection for my whole body: it makes life easier, but cuts down on the pleasure as well. To stay alive I have to remember that what I'm missing is what matters most to me, or used to when my feelings were sharp. I need to compete. I need to want to compete.

Last week I read that Stanborough is bankrupt and may have to close. It's not surprising. You could say it's been closing for years, and the goals I scored just postponed things. If human beings abandon that stadium there are plenty of forces waiting to take over. In a few months the pitch would be knee-deep in weeds and there'd be creepers climbing up the stand. Birds would nest on the roof and crap on the seats below. The paint would peel, the wood would rot and the corrugated iron would rust. Even the terraces wouldn't last long. Plants and insects could take the concrete apart in no time, not on purpose, but just as a side-effect of eating and growing, fighting and fucking and moving around. You have to fight back, or you're lost. If I was at Stanborough, even now, match-fit and not disqualified for life, I could still save the club. I have it in me.

When I brought down John Carpenter at Wembley I never made contact with the ball. So my last touch in first-class soccer was a goal. A good way to go. I have a photograph that catches the very moment I scored. I'm in space, with both feet off the ground. Carpenter's down and the goalie's beaten. The ball's frozen in mid-flight, so that you can read the maker's name on it as it crosses the line.